The Halsey Brothers Series

Marshal in Petticoats
Outlaw in Petticoats
Miner in Petticoats
Doctor in Petticoats
Logger in Petticoats

DOCTOR IN PETTICOATS

The Halsey Brothers Series

by

Paty Jager

Windtree Press
Beaverton, Oregon

DOCTOR IN PETTICOATS

Contact Information: info@windtreepress.com
Cover Art by Karen Ronan
Windtree Press
Visit us at http://windtreepress.com

Publishing History
First Edition
Doctor in Petticoats 2010 (Print and ebook)

Second Edition
Doctor in Petticoats 2012 (Ebook only)

Third Edition
Doctor in Petticoats 2022 (Print and ebook)

Published in the United States of America
ISBN 978-1-957638-36-2

Acknowledgements

Special Thanks:
Oregon School for the Blind
Baker Heritage Museum
Joan Jacobs
Alfred Mullett

Diana Pearson

Chapter 1

1890 Salem, Oregon

He was sick of the darkness, sick of the pitying voices, sick of waiting to see the head of the blind school.

"Mr. Halsey, stop slouching. Just because you can't see how pathetic it looks doesn't mean it isn't."

The harsh feminine voice rippled his skin like a cow grinding its gums.

Sick of being bossed around.

Clay Halsey slumped even more and stretched his legs out in front of him. Turning toward the voice, he spread an insolent grin on his face.

Something hit his legs. Hands slapping against wood echoed through the room followed by a surprised "oomph" as weight landed across his shins.

He reached down and grasped soft fabric in one hand and scratchy wool in the other. The object was the size and weight of Aileen's twelve-year-old son. Squirmed like him, too.

"Put me down!" an incensed young voice spewed. "What's with stickin' your feet out? Don't ya know there's blind people here?"

Great, he'd only been here an hour and already he was wreaking havoc on someone's life.

"Sorry." He held the boy until he stopped flailing. "I'll try to keep my big feet under me."

"Well, ya better if ya plan ta hang around here. I don't like trippin'." The boy's voice trailed away. His shuffling footsteps faded in the distance.

Clay'd been so intent on irritating the matron he'd shut out the sounds around him. The first thing he learned after becoming blind was to use his other senses more.

Why did his older brothers, Ethan and Hank, insist he come here? He hated the harsh scent of lye hanging in the air and not knowing his surroundings.

"Mr. Halsey, the superintendent will see you now."

The matron's deep, commanding voice riled more than Hank ordering him around. What he wouldn't give to be back at the stamp mill being ordered around by Ethan and Hank, and his sister-in-law, Aileen's, Scottish temper blasting at him for sitting about like a log.

A hand gripped his elbow. "I'll lead you to Mr. Griffin's office."

He used the woman's hold to leverage off the hard, smooth bench he'd warmed the last hour. He'd been adamant Ethan leave him at the blind school and let him enroll himself. It was time he owned up to his new life.

The matron's breathing came in coffee fetid puffs at shoulder height. That made her nearly as tall as his height of a couple inches over six feet. She set a slow pace down the hall. I'm blind, not an invalid. He stepped out at his usual pace, and her wide hips brushed against his.

"After your meeting, I'll show you the railing on the halls and how to determine where you are." She huffed to keep up with him. "Whoa. You're going right past the office."

A whoosh of air wiggled his pant leg and rustled his hair. Someone opened a door.

"Dr. Tarkiel." The matron's voice sweetened in a patronizing way.

Clay snickered. Must be an old geezer the woman has a crush on.

"This is our newest student, Mr. Halsey." The matron pushed his arm forward.

He held his palm out waiting for a crippled hand to slide across. Instead, long slender fingers and a firm grip clasped his hand. Warmth radiated up his arm.

"Mr. Halsey, welcome to the Blind Institute. I hope you use all the facilities to your benefit."

The sweet feminine tone and sincere welcome intrigued him.

"A woman doctor?" He couldn't stop the words tumbling out his mouth.

"You're very astute, Mr. Halsey." A light-hearted laugh trailed away from him. Citrus wafted in the wake of her barely audible retreating steps. The eye-watering lye fumes quickly engulfed the sweet lemon scent. The citrus reminded him of the lemon drops his mother had bought with money she earned from selling knit scarves to the mercantile in winter. His mouth watered as he remembered the sweet treats, and his heart ached for the little things his mother did for her sons that as a boy he hadn't appreciated until it was too late.

The matron dragged him forward. "You're lucky she's used to that reaction."

"I didn't mean it in a bad way. I've never met a woman doctor before." Clay cringed. Ever since that damn dynamite had blown up in his face and taken away his sight, he couldn't do or say anything right.

"She's a kind heart. She's already forgiven you." The matron nudged him ahead.

This room didn't harbor the acrid lye of the hallway. Cigar and leather. The male trappings relaxed him. He'd grown up surrounded by brothers.

The matron prodded him forward again. If they weren't standing in the superintendent's office, he'd tell her to quit shoving him around like a piece of furniture. Something bumped the back of his knees, and he folded onto a hard chair.

"Mr. Halsey, welcome to the Blind Institute."

Clay stood and leaned, stretching his hand out toward the sound of the deep, raspy voice. A plump hand with short fingers clasped his. "I'm glad you were willing to take on someone as old as I am."

"Mr. Halsey, at twenty-seven you are not the oldest student we've schooled." Mr. Griffin's voice descended as he talked.

Clay stepped back, touching the chair to the back of his legs, and sat. "I'd like to learn a skill I can use to help my brothers with our stamp mill."

And stop being a burden on them.

"You'll have to start with the basics like all students. Learn how to get around the school, use Braille, and use the typewriter. You'll also work on a trade."

Clay shook his head. "I don't need a trade. I need skills to work in the stamp mill, like the typing. I could type up records, keep lists."

"Well, yes, we'll see how you do and go from there."

The superintendent's condescending tone stoked the already smoldering anger in his gut. He shot out of the chair, his mouth open to speak.

"Mrs. White, show Mr. Halsey around and then to his room." Papers shuffled.

If he hadn't promised Ethan he'd come back ready to be of use to the mill, he'd walk out right now. He didn't need or want this man's pity or dismissal.

The rustle of a skirt and a hand gripping his elbow, so forcefully he felt each finger dig in, signaled the meeting was over.

"Good day, Mr. Halsey."

The finality of the remark rankled. Clay rested a hand on the back of the chair to walk around it and headed for where he presumed he'd find the door. Mrs. White moved him a bit to the right. He crossed the threshold, and the caustic lye-filled air accosted his nose. His nostrils closed, and his eyes watered. So much for feeling camaraderie with the superintendent.

"Mr. Halsey, put your hand here."

The matron's large, rough fingers, guiding his hand, reminded him of his brother's. If he forgot she was a woman, having her boss him around wasn't so bad.

His fingers touched something cool, smooth, and round. He gripped the object and recognition dawned. A handrail.

"This is how the students move along the hallways. Always keep the rail on your right side and there should be few accidents." Mrs. White let go. She walked ahead.

Listening, he realized she had a tack or nail in one shoe that made every other step click. He had to learn to keep his emotions in check, to keep his senses all working.

"How come that boy fell over my feet if he was using the rail?" Clay moved along the hall. Moving about without the aid of another person exhilarated him. He'd managed the small confines of the cabin at the mine and the stamp mill office, but to have space to really walk—his hopes rose. Maybe this school wouldn't be so bad for a short time.

"Donny's been here long enough he rarely uses the railing to get around." She started to puff keeping up with his lengthened strides.

"Why's he been here so long?" His fingers dipped into a notch on the rail. He stopped. "What does the notch mean?"

The click of her shoe faded. "Donny doesn't have anywhere else to go. He teaches the broom-making class." She cupped his elbow. "Turn and walk straight, holding your right arm out."

Her heel clicked beside him as he walked, one arm stretched out. His wrist smacked a corner. Running his hand down the wall, he discovered another rail. Mrs. White let go of his elbow and set off ahead of him.

"This wing is where we hold the classes."

The railing stopped. Clay halted while the woman clicked ahead of him. "Why did the railing stop?"

"That's the reading room. Keep going forward, you'll feel the door and then the rail again."

Indeed, his knuckles slid across solid wood and then bumped into the handrail. A few trips down this hall and he'd know his way around. A smile tugged at his lips. Six months ago he'd thought his world ended. If he studied hard and learned to type, he could be back in Sumpter helping Ethan and Hank with the mill in a few months. Unlike the unfortunate Donny, he had a place to go, and he wasn't going to stay here any longer than necessary.

"The stairs to the dorm are on your right."

His thumb dipped into a long gash with bumps like stairs. "Ethan said I wasn't staying in the dorm."

"If there was another adult male here this semester you would be staying in a room with him, but since you're the only adult, you'll room next to Mr. Smith." Her deep voice dripped with derision.

Clay flared his nostrils and detected lye and the faint sweet scent of straw. "Is Mr. Smith a teacher?"

Mrs. White's steps continued down the hall. He hurried across the space with no handrail and found it again four strides along the hall.

"Mr. Smith is the handyman."

Her superior tone made Clay feel sorry for the man. "Then I'll be in good hands."

"Humph!"

She wasn't tolerant of others less fortunate. What the heck was she doing in a blind school?

A loud creak echoed through the hall. "You're room is out here."

Clay scraped his hand along the wall in front of him, side-stepping, until his fingers curled around a door jamb. He stepped through. A rush of fresh air fluttered across his face.

"My room isn't connected to the building?" If the air hadn't been clue enough, gravel crunched and rolled under his boots, birds chirped, and the bitter scent of fresh-cut bushes traveled on the breeze.

"Mr. Smith is only allowed in the main building when working." Again, her words were forced and sounded as if they stung her tongue.

Was the handyman a criminal?

Metal clanged, wood cracked against wood, and a deep, hoarse voice cursed.

"Mr. Smith!"

The indignation and scorn in the matron's voice raised Clay's eyebrow.

"Sorry, ma'am. Didn't know'd you all was there."

Clay'd never heard the man's drawl or word formation before. He held out a hand. "I understand we'll be neighbors."

Mrs. White cleared her throat. He waited for the man to take his hand. When he didn't, Clay wondered even more about the handyman.

Gravel skittered, and steps retreated. "I believe your valise was delivered to your room when you arrived." Mrs. White's words faded.

He stood, sunshine warming his face, waiting for the handyman to show him to his room. He'd heard only one set of retreating steps. Labored breathing and a sharper tang of cut brush came from in front of him. Mr. Smith was still there.

"How about you show me to my room and tell me about the routine around here? I thought Mrs. White would give me more of a tour."

"Dis away," the deep voice croaked.

Clay tipped his head and tried to catch the sound of footsteps to determine which way to walk. The man wasn't walking on the gravel path. "Mr. Smith, I'm blind. You're going to have to either keep talking so I can follow you or take my arm."

Steps crunched toward him and stopped. "You all sure 'bout dis? Dey never said nuttin' 'bout you all bein' blind."

"It's either you help me or I stand here forever." What was wrong with helping him? Why did the people so far, except the doctor, act like he had a disease? He was blind just like every other student in this school. Maybe coming here was a mistake. If he could get a ride to Portland, he'd catch Ethan and Aileen before they sailed for England. They might be on their honeymoon, but damn, he was blind. They could do anything they wanted in front of him and he'd never know.

The gravel shuffled in front of him. "I's got ta tell ya, I's a nigger and most white folks don't care ta have me touch 'em."

Not that long ago, he might have hesitated to be friends with someone different. He'd taken Miles's word that Aileen was a husband killer and marked by the devil. Hell, it had been the other way around. Miles. His blood boiled just thinking the name. Miles, his friend, had thrown the dynamite that left him in blackness.

Now, he knew what it felt like to be alienated by something not of your choosing.

"That's not a disease." Clay stuck his arm out. "Turn around, and I'll put my hand on your shoulder. You can lead me to my room." His finger tips jammed into a solid wall of muscle. He raised his arm and placed his palm on a wide, muscled shoulder a couple inches higher than his own. Mr. Smith was a large man.

Doctor Rachel Tarkiel stood at the window of the infirmary watching the newest student at the blind school treat the handyman like a contemporary. The regret on Mr. Halsey's face after he'd exclaimed she was a woman fluttered a smile to her lips. He seemed genuinely horrified he'd spilt the words. She was so used to hearing the derogatory comment she found it humorous.

Mr. Halsey was the type of gentleman who flocked around her beautiful sister, Celeste. The type Rachel had once dreamed of marrying. That was years ago as a child, before the accident and before she learned the truth from William. The day he broke their betrothal after discovering her scar was the day she'd set her dream on becoming a doctor and helping others like her.

Mr. Halsey's jacket pulled across his broad back.

He didn't wear a hat. His dark brown hair

shimmered with copper highlights in the mid-day sun. The dandies Celeste favored had hair that just touched their collars. Mr. Halsey's curled over his collar. His brown eyes, though unseeing, sported laugh lines in the crinkles at the corners. His calloused hand had gripped hers with authority and sent tremors of excitement skittering up her arm. She'd have to ask Mr. Griffin about the man. His charming voice, embarrassment, and tingling touch intrigued her.

The men disappeared in the small cottage at the back of the property. Company would be good for Mr. Smith. From her vantage point the handyman's color didn't seem to vex Mr. Halsey. Unlike Mrs. White. The woman needed a dressing down on the way she talked about the man around the students. She put fear in them for no good reason.

Rachel spun away from the window to make a note to talk to Mr. Griffin about Mrs. White's attitude.

Her reflection in the small mirror she used for exams wiped away any coherent thoughts. Trembling fingers bumped along the ridge of scar tissue running from her temple to her chin. She avoided mirrors other than to cover the scar when going out in society.

Planning to only spend time at the blind school this morning, she'd not mixed face powder with lard to conceal the blemish. The staff knew of her scar, and she'd become good at keeping her head turned just enough so people only saw one side of her face. She rarely covered the mark when she remained all day at the school.

Heavens, it was a good thing Mr. Halsey was

blind. If he'd seen her scar, her being a woman doctor wouldn't have bothered him.

Her heart twisted remembering the day, five years ago, when she and William were caught in the rain. He'd wiped at her face before she could stop him, revealing the puckered ugly skin. At night when loneliness shrouded her like a heavy wool cloak, his face screwed up in disgust haunted her. She'd remain a spinster and help others rather than experience the repulsion she'd seen that day in a man who'd professed he loved her.

The next day, hearing him revoke his intentions—she gulped the rising bile—she'd barely been able to face the contempt on a face she'd thought handsome. He'd said she deceived him. Maybe so, but only because she feared exactly what happened. She'd hoped by the time they married he'd love her for who she was, and the scar would mean nothing to him. Celeste was right about men—all they wanted in a woman was beauty or a servant.

She'd lost her beauty twenty years ago. The day remained vivid in her mind. The shouts, the dust, the run-away wagon barreling through the street straight for Celeste. She'd shoved her sister out of the path and froze as the wagon swerved—but not enough.

She cringed remembering the corner of the wagon striking her face.

Falling into the street.

The yelling, her mother's shriek, her sister's tears.

The darkness and waking to a head swathed in cloth and her mother sobbing by her bedside.

And the ache, physical and mental. Her head

throbbed and her mother no longer called her, her beautiful girl.

She'd never regret saving her sister, but she'd forever harbor anger at the cruel injustice. She who had longed for a mate and companion was destined to be a spinster, while her beautiful sister with throngs of suitors scorned the men flocking around her.

Chapter 2

"Mr. Smith, this room will do fine." Clay counted the steps from the door to the far wall, rubbing his leg against the bed on his way across the room.

"Sir, calls me Jasper." The handyman's voice drifted from the doorway.

"Only if you call me Clay." He ran a hand across the bed and slapped the side of a valise. "What's in this room, a bureau or pegs?"

"Both, sir—"

"Ah, I said call me Clay." He shrugged out of his jacket. "Which side of the room?"

"Pegs on the one yer by. Bureau by the door."

Clay stepped forward, his arm extended, and found the wall. Moving his hand in circles chest high and raising it up the wall higher, he found a peg and hung his coat. "When do they serve the mid-day meal?"

"S—"

Clay frowned at the man.

"Clay, you all done missed the mid-day meal.

Ain't nothin' till dinner at six."

He'd eaten little that morning. His knotted stomach hadn't tolerated much more than dry bread and a cup of coffee. "Is there a café close by?"

"You all can't leave the school without a teacher or such with you."

The fear in the man's voice jolted Clay out of his musings of a nice hunk of roast. "I can't go anywhere without someone from the school?" This was a prison.

"It's for you all's safety."

That made sense. But he still didn't like it. He'd guess from the time he spent on the bench, the tour, and visiting it was early afternoon. "Are all the teachers teaching right now?"

"They's not here today. Classes start tomorrow." Jasper's shuffling feet indicated the handyman wanted to get back to work.

"What about the doctor. Is she kept so busy she couldn't escort me to town?"

"Tha's a good idea."

The enthusiasm in his voice led Clay to wonder about the doctor. At their meeting, her voice hadn't mocked but held a lilt of humor and goodnature. While the handyman had said barely a word to the matron, he wasn't afraid of the doctor.

"I'll get her."

"You can just take me to her." Clay reached for his jacket. He slid his arms in and felt a tug on his left hand. Jasper's calloused fingers tugged Clay's hand upward. The scratchy wool of the handyman's shirt prickled his palm. He clamped onto the broad shoulder. When the man moved, so did Clay.

Sunshine warmed his face. The crunch and

roll of gravel under his feet disappeared. His steps were cushioned and hushed by grass. Why did the man go off the path? How was Clay to find his way around if he had to cross grassy patches?

Jasper stopped and moved out from under Clay's hand. Gravel scraped, and something plinked against glass. What was the man doing?

The rasp of wood on wood reverberated from a few feet in front of them.

"Mr. Smith, Mr. Halsey." The doctor's voice floated somewhere above them. "What can I do for you two gentlemen?"

The light-hearted lilt in her voice made Clay smile. "I'm starving and Jasper"—the man beside him sucked in air like a drowning man—"says I can't leave the school without an escort." He smiled and raised his face toward the warm sun. "Would you be interested in escorting me to the closest café?"

Fear bubbled in Rachel's chest. Her makeup sat on her bureau at home. She couldn't go out in public without it. Sitting in a café where people might stop to talk was different than wearing her large floppy bonnet and walking the three blocks to her parents' house.

"My stomach's eating itself. Please."

He stared above her. The boyish smile and his rumpled hair stirred a longing deep and visceral. One she had no right to feel, but one she wished to pursue.

"I'll take you to the kitchen and find something. Mr. Smith, please bring Mr. Halsey to the back door. I'll meet you there."

The handyman grinned, showing large white

teeth, and nodded. She backed into the room and closed the window. No one knew Mr. Smith tossed pebbles at her window when he needed something from inside the school. It had been their little secret. Now Mr. Halsey knew. She'd have to tell him to keep it confidential. She had a feeling he'd like keeping the knowledge. He had the energy of a mischievous little boy.

Rachel left the infirmary, headed down the hall, and met them at the back door. Mr. Smith backed away and nudged Mr. Halsey through the door. She hooked her wrist through the handsome new student's arm, and they strolled down the hall like a couple on an outing. Her stomach fluttered. She'd touched other men as a doctor, but none made her feel giddy. She hadn't been this close to a man since William broke their betrothal. Thoughts of William darkened her heart, and bitterness soured her stomach.

"Jasper doesn't work much with the students does he?" Mr. Halsey's sarcastic comment laced with humor and a raised eyebrow made her laugh.

"No, he's not allowed to interact with the students." She studied his full bottom lip, angular cheekbones, and slightly crooked nose. Her heart stopped, and then palpitated like hummingbird wings.

"Why? He's big but seems like a nice fella."

The question in the man's tone made her study the frown lines on his wide forehead.

"Negroes aren't welcome in this state, Mr. Halsey."

His face jerked in her direction. "Who says?"

She watched his dark brown eyes and wished

she could see into their depths. The blank stare tugged at her heart. "It's the law. They aren't welcome here, but if they don't cause trouble, people don't care as long as they don't own a business or land." She stopped and opened the door to the kitchen, and then led Mr. Halsey to the table in the middle of the room and pulled out a bench.

"Sit here while I find some leftovers."

He tipped his head as he sat. "Are we alone in here?"

"Yes. Mrs. Daniels, the cook, is resting until she needs to make dinner." She moved to the icebox and pulled out leftover chicken from the night before.

"Will she mind our invading her kitchen?" His large hands rested clasped on the top of the table, he stared straight ahead.

"I've been known to come in here and grab a snack when I need one, so she won't think anything of it." Rachel put two pieces of chicken and two rolls on a plate. She carried the food to the table and placed the plate between his arms. She laid a trembling hand on his. He jumped, and then smiled.

"Give me your hand, and I'll show you where the food is on the plate." She moved his warm, pliant hand around the plate clockwise. "Two pieces of chicken are at nine o'clock, and two rolls are at three o'clock. That's the best I could come up with."

"It's a feast compared to waiting until dinner. Thank you." He picked up a chicken leg and took a bite.

Rachel crossed to the stove and poured two cups of coffee, leaving one about an inch from the rim. She placed it directly above his plate. "There's coffee at twelve." She was impressed by how quickly he found the food and the cup.

"How long have you been blind, Mr. Halsey?"

He frowned. "About six months."

"You're dealing well with it."

His frown lines deepened, and he stopped chewing. "Not much choice, now, have I?"

She grabbed a dish towel, brushing his hand with it as she placed it on the table. He wiped his mouth and hands.

"How did it happen?"

He picked up the cup and took a sip. He was so quiet, so contemplative, she wasn't sure he planned to answer. Had she opened a wound he wasn't ready to talk about? She understood the self-doubts and anger about a situation you couldn't change. She'd spent years crying into pillows and wallowing in pity. Until she realized she could help others in her situation.

She sat down next to him and took a sip of her coffee. If he wasn't ready to talk, she wouldn't push. Talking about her own personal scar wasn't high on her list of favorite things.

"Where are you from?"

His body relaxed, and he lowered the cup he'd been sipping from. "Sumpter, a small mining community on the east side of the state." His voice deepened, exuding pride and a touch of longing. Lines curved at the corners of his mouth. His face lit up. Her gaze dropped to his hands. No wedding ring, but that didn't mean anything. Usually only the wealthy shared rings.

"Do you have family there?"

A smile spread across his face, drawing in a dimple on his left cheek and showing fine white teeth. "I have a passel of brothers. Four. And three of them are married. Gil, the youngest, and his wife, Darcy, have a little girl. Zeke's next in line. He and his wife, Maeve, travel a lot as Pinkerton agents. Ethan, the oldest, brought me here. He and his new wife, Aileen, and her two kids are headed to England to settle a family land claim." He exhaled and ran a hand through his hair. "Ethan shouldn't have brought me here while he's gone. Hank has to take care of the stamp mill all by himself. I should be there helping."

His frustration made his motions jerky and furrowed his brow. Rachel placed a hand over his, offering comfort, showing support, not expecting heat to race up her arm and bloom in her chest. "You'll be more help to him when you can read and work a typewriter."

Clay pulled his hand out from under the doctor's. He didn't want sympathy. He wanted to be back at the mill helping his brother. Food wouldn't settle the rumble of unease twisting his guts. Anger seethed through him, tightening his muscles, clenching his hands, and holding him as much a prisoner as his sightless eyes. The only thing that would make his world right again was his sight.

"Since you're a doctor, what are the chances of my sight coming back?"

He wished he could see her face, judge if she told the truth. What color were her eyes? She must have a pleasant face, her voice held compassion and humor. Perhaps small laugh lines beside her eyes?

"How did it happen? I can't give you any answers without knowing the extent of the trauma." Her voice lost its earlier softness. All business now.

"A stick of dynamite blew up about ten feet in front of me. Doc Spangle said the concussion from the blast is what made me blind." He rubbed a hand across his face. "He also said there was a slim chance I could get some vision back, or I could never." He swallowed. "And told me to prepare for the latter."

A faint clicking sounded to his right. He slid his hand over and discovered the doctor tapping her fingernail on the wood.

"Well?" He tried to keep the pleading out of his tone.

"I'd say Doctor Spangle is correct, but I could examine your eyes to see if he missed anything."

Her voice didn't sound hopeful, but he wasn't about to miss a chance to perhaps find out something new about his condition.

He pushed back from the table. "I don't have anything to do this afternoon." He started to stand, but a hand rested on his arm, stalling him.

"I'm afraid I do. With the start of the semester, I have to check out each student and document his physical well-being." The rustle of her skirt and her voice ascending above his head told him she stood. "Are you going to finish the food?"

He grabbed a roll and waved the plate away. "Do you have time to give me a thorough tour of the school? Mrs. White just took me down the hall to the classrooms and out to my cabin." He stood when a brush of wind registered she walked away from him. Her citrus scent hung on the air and dishes rattled a few feet away. He started toward the sound but stopped at the tap of her returning steps.

The snap of a pocket watch to his left brought his attention around.

"I have twenty minutes until the first student arrives. However, tomorrow you will all be taken on a tour of the facilities after breakfast."

She draped her arm through the crook of his elbow. Her small wrist fit perfectly in the curve. He liked that she led him around in such a manner. It was less demeaning than being steered by his elbow or trailing behind the handyman like an old nag.

She kept their bodies from touching. An endearing and aggravating action. He wanted to touch. Had from their first encounter. Her nearness set his body yearning. Not only did he want to feel her size and shape, his body craved the knowledge. But he'd have to be content with her light touches and citrus scent. He enjoyed her company, more in fact, than any other woman he'd encountered, but understood her need to keep a professional rela-tionship.

"I'll show you the dining room and how to get from there to your room."

He followed beside her. She started to ease her hand from his arm.

"Is there a door here?" He stopped.

"Yes, I'll get it—"

He pulled her back and stepped forward with his hand extended in front of him. His palm smacked into the door.

He swept his hand down the cool, smooth

wood and found the round knob. He opened the door and motioned for her to go through. Clay followed, and she slipped her wrist back through his arm, gently tugging him to the left. A smile tickled his lips. Doctor Tarkiel allowed him to move about as an adult unlike his brothers who herded him like an imbecile or small child.

He curved his lips in a smile of thanks and tipped his head Dr. Tarkiel's way. Her intake of breath and tightening grip on his arm proved he affected her in the same heart racing way she affected him.

For the first time since losing his sight, he saw a future.

Chapter 3

Clay kept his hand on the rail and followed the sound of shuffling feet as the group toured the school. At breakfast they introduced themselves. Eight boys, not counting himself, and four girls made up the student body this semester. He and one other boy were new, but they were all herded around the facility as if the staff thought they found comfort in numbers.

He'd have preferred a personal tour by the doctor. She hadn't said when she could give him an examination. He wanted to ask, but didn't want to cause a rift by asking Mrs. White if he could talk with Dr. Tarkiel.

The tour hadn't come upon the infirmary in the maze of halls. The music teacher, Miss Valerie Hubert, had tittered when he asked a question earlier, and he wasn't about to ask her another. He'd put his foot down at having music lessons. He'd come here to learn skills to help his brothers, and serenading the stamps or the mine wasn't going to get them any more gold.

"Everyone into the music room. You'll start each day bringing the love of music into your world."

Miss Hubert's dry squawky voice didn't sound like she could sing any better than a crow.

Clay stopped at the door. "Miss Hubert, I'm not here to learn music. I'll go to the reading room and start learning to read." He continued past the door. A claw-like hand dug into his arm through his flannel shirt.

"I'm sorry, Mr. Halsey, but all students are to have music." The warble in her voice proved no one had ever bucked the rules.

"I'm not wasting time here learning music. That's not a skill I need to help my brothers at our stamp mill." He yanked free of her hold and crossed his arms. He wasn't a child, and he wasn't going to waste time learning to sing. The school needed to cater to older students.

"Is there a problem here, Miss Hubert?" Mrs. White's domineering voice echoed in the hall.

"I'm not taking music lessons." Clay didn't care if they tossed him out. He'd find another way to learn to help at the stamp mill without wasting his time singing.

"Let's go speak to Mr. Griffin." The matron gripped his elbow.

Clay shook it loose and marched across the hall—five strides—grasped the rail, and headed to the superintendent's office. One thing about moving slow on the group tour, it had given him time to sketch a diagram of the halls in his mind and count steps. He knew where to find the superintendent.

The handrail disappeared. He ducked into the office and drank in the aroma of cigar and leather. He walked straight into the room until his outstretched hand bumped the back of a chair.

"Mr. Halsey." The superintendent's voice rumbled from beside him. "Why are you here and not on the first day tour?"

"I'm not taking music lessons. I need to take an extra class of Braille instead." Blazes! He wasn't a child to be ordered around. He was a man, and a man made his own decisions. His face heated with anger. He'd be damned if he wasted his time in a room full of singing children.

"I see." Mr. Griffin cleared his throat.

The click of a door shutting behind him swung Clay around. "Who else is in the room with us?" he asked.

"No one, Mr. Halsey. I had Mrs. White close the door." The man's steps retreated. "You may sit, Mr. Halsey."

Clay gripped the back of the wooden chair in front of him. He wasn't going to sit. He wanted to stay in a strong position. "No, thanks. I don't plan on staying that long." He relaxed his fingers on the chair. "Mr. Griffin, no disrespect to Miss Hubert or the school, but I'm here to learn to read and help my brothers, not sing in a choir. I'd rather put my time to better use."

"I understand, but Miss Collins doesn't come in until the afternoon. The mornings are spent with music and trades."

Damn! Clay didn't need a trade or to learn music. He needed typing and reading. "What about

Donny? Does he take music lessons?"

"No, he's not really a student any more. He teaches the broom-making classes. Why?"

"Then he can work with me on reading while the rest of the students are singing. I assume he knows how to read Braille?" Clay wanted to learn as fast as he could.

"I suppose..." The skepticism in the man's voice rang like a fire bell.

"What? Why do you seem hesitant?" This had to work. Unless the doctor could read Braille and teach him... There was a thought. And not an unpleasant one. His heart picked up pace.

"Donny has a problem with adult males." The man coughed. "This is confidential, but if you want the boy to work with you, you should know his father is the reason he's blind. The man whacked him hard upside the head one too many times."

A vision of Aileen's boy, Colin, came to mind. He and his mother had been victims of her second husband. "I know a little about how to handle a boy like that. My new nephew came from a similar situation."

"Let me have Mrs. White round up Donny." The rustle of the man's clothes and the sharp tang of cigar swirled. A whoosh of lye-filled air wafted around him.

Voices mumbled behind him. He heard the woman snort, then her retreating footsteps.

Mr. Griffin's footsteps tapped past. "Mrs. White will bring Donny here, and we'll ask him if he'll do this." A chair creaked behind the desk. "Please, sit. It could be a while before Mrs. White finds the boy."

Clay tried to read the emotions in the man's voice. Did he like the boy or only tolerate him? He eased around the chair and sat down.

"Will you join the students in the trade classes?" Mr. Griffin's grating tone held censure and resignation.

"I already have a trade. As I said, I help my brothers with the family business. Typing and reading are the skills I need." He leaned back in the chair and crossed his arms.

Footsteps and voices floated through the open door. "I'm getting ready for my class, what's with dragging me down to Griffin's office?" The indignant voice, Clay remembered from tripping the boy, harangued the matron.

"Donny!" The superintendent's firm tone indicated he wouldn't put up with insolence.

"Mr. Griffin may I speak?" Clay didn't want Donny ordered to help him.

"Go ahead, Mr. Halsey."

Mr. Griffin's sighing "good luck" attitude almost made Clay smile. He stood and extended his hand, hoping the matron would point Donny in the right direction. "Donny, I'm Clay Halsey. I'm looking for someone to teach me to read Braille in the mornings while the others are singing."

A calloused hand, half the size of his, touched Clay's palm, and he gave it a firm shake.

"Why're you askin' me?"

The skepticism in his young voice made Clay smile. The boy's distrust reminded him of his nephew, Colin.

"Because the reading teacher doesn't come in until the afternoon, and you read Braille and teach." He wished he could see the boy's face and determine if his words sank in. Damn, losing his sight made him more than physically blind, it made him emotionally blind. He'd give anything to see what emotions played across the boy's face. That way he'd know what to say to get the boy to come around to helping him.

"I'll lose set-up time for my class."

"I'll have nothing to do after our reading class. I can help you prepare the classroom."

The boy laughed, shooting Clay's temper up a notch. "How are you going to help with something you know nothin' about?"

"I'm a fast learner, and I've been working with my hands a lot longer than you've been teaching how to make brooms."

"Gentlemen," Mr. Griffin said, "how about Mr. Halsey sits in your class today, and if you think he can handle helping you, you'll start reading with him tomorrow."

"I agree. How about you, Donny?" He didn't want to waste half a day at the school. The short time he'd been around the boy, he felt a kinship, not only through their blindness but their need to feel useful. He could help Donny feel useful, and possibly help him get over his fear of men.

Feet shuffled, and a groan of regret filled the air. "All right. But if he messes up my room or bugs the other students, I'm not helpin' him."

Clay wanted to strangle the little brat and give him a handshake to seal the deal.

"Donny, show Mr. Halsey to the broom-making area." A hand landed on Clay's shoulder. "Mr. Halsey, good luck," the superintendent said close to his ear.

Clay chuckled. He'd prove all of them wrong. Donny, the superintendent, even his brothers. He'd be back at the mill in time to enjoy the last rays of summer sun.

He followed Donny into the broom-making room. The scent of fresh dried straw with a sweeter undertone wafted around him, bringing back memories of feeding the horses. He inhaled. A tang of dried wood also hung in the air.

"Stay to the right." Donny's voice carried to him from the middle of the room. "Feel along the edge. There are five stations set up." The rattle of corn stalks grew closer as Donny's footsteps approached. "Are you in the first station?"

Clay ran his right palm along a wood surface. "Is there a table?" He felt a low, metal pan. "A pan." His fingers dipped into water. "With water?"

"Yes," Donny said near him.

The straw scent engulfed him as tassels brushed past his face.

"Watch where you're going."

Something hard smacked him in the side, and he fumbled around until his hand was captured.

Donny placed Clay's hand on a pile of round, long, corn-like stalks. "This is the broomcorn we use to make the brooms."

"I didn't know brooms were made from corn." Clay picked up one piece and ran his fingers the length of the stalk. There weren't any ears, and the scratchy leaves were slenderer than corn. The top tassel was stronger, harder than the top of a corn stalk. Seeds sprinkled onto his palm.

"It isn't corn. It's sorghum. But because it

looks like corn when it's growin' and it's used for brooms it's called broomcorn." Donny grasped his wrist again. "Each station is set up with a pile of broomcorn and a seed scraper." Donny dipped Clay's fingers in the water. "And water to soak the straw." He pulled Clay's hand out of the water and placed it on a ball of wound string. "The twine is used to secure the straw to the handle." The boy raised Clay's arm and moved it around in the air until a thin rope twisted around Clay's wrist. "This is used to tighten the twine around the stalks. It's kind of like a pulley, only the rope loops over the rafter. One end is on the person's foot acting as a weight. The other is slipped around the broomcorn, tightening it to wrap and tie with the twine."

Donny untangled Clay's wrist and led him forward. "This is another station. I have to make sure they all have water, broomcorn, twine, and handles." They stopped four strides from the last station. "I was pourin' water when Mrs. White came and got me. There are two more to fill." Donny pivoted Clay to the left, and they walked forward five strides. Clay reached ahead and smacked his knuckles into a table, hip height.

"The supplies are kept on this table. Mr. Smith replenishes them every night and takes away the finished brooms." Donny's voice drifted to the right. "Stay here until I get the rest of the water poured."

Clay ran his hands over the table top, walking first left and encountering broomcorn, and then right and finding balls of twine, small wooden pegs the size of a match but sturdier, and long wooden staffs. Fingering the length of the staff, he discovered two holes the perfect size for the wooden pegs. Water splashed behind him.

Donny knew this room and his trade well. "How did you end up teaching this class?" Clay positioned his back to the table of supplies and listened for Donny's whereabouts.

"I made brooms before I became blind." The scorn in the boy's voice piqued Clay's interest.

"How long ago did you lose your sight?"

"I was eight, I'm twelve now." Water splashed again.

"Why were you making brooms at such an early age?" At eight, Clay had worked alongside his father and brothers in the mine, but never more than an hour at a time.

"Because my drunken father couldn't keep up with the orders." Donny's voice deepened with anger. He stomped toward Clay. "My ma and little sister had to eat. I'd watched Pa enough to know how to do it. And when he was drinkin' 'stead of fillin' orders, I started makin' them."

"If you aren't there to make brooms, how are your ma and sister managing?" Clay thought of his new sister-in-law and how she and her children had scratched to get by until Ethan fell in love with the whole lot of them.

"I get paid for teachin'. I give the money to my ma. They moved here when I came to the school." He snorted. "My pa can rot in hell. He may have taken my sight, but I'm a better man than he is."

"I agree."

The boy's intake of breath made Clay smile. Donny hadn't expected an adult to take his side. Clay pondered what the matron had said earlier.

"Why did Mrs. White say you don't have any place else to go?"

"My money here just pays for a room at a boardin' house for my ma and sister. What my ma can make sewin' helps them some. But they can't afford another mouth to feed. So I stay here." He cleared his throat and sighed heavily. The boy's resignation struck a chord with Clay.

"You won't be here forever. At sixteen you could start up a broom-making shop."

"You think so?" Hope rang in Donny's tone.

"Yes. Now, what can I do? I don't like to stand around."

Donny stepped beside him. "To your left are wooden pegs. Use the small mallet and insert one in each hole on the handle."

Clay smiled. Finally, something he could do. He grasped a handle, found the hole with one finger, poked a peg in the hole, and brought the mallet down. It wasn't the same as pounding a stake in the ground for cart tracks, but each swing of the mallet proved he could do more than sit in the dark and feel sorry for himself. He hoped learning to read Braille proved as easy and satisfying.

$$Chapter\ 4$$

Rachel entered the superintendent's office. She had time to check Mr. Halsey's eyes but hadn't found him in the music room with the other students.

"Dr. Tarkiel, good morning."

His over-enthusiastic welcome and exaggerated smile were always at the ready for her. Even though the state paid for her to be on call to the school, her father gave the school generous donations to make sure she had a place to practice medicine. That her father more or less paid for her to have a doctor's position irritated her. She'd give up her family ties to strike out in her own practice. But until the blind school, no one had wanted a woman doctor with a disfigured face. Even the hospital had turned her down, despite her glowing credentials in surgical applications.

"Mr. Griffin, I've come to ask that you have a word with Mrs. White. She is condescending and rude to Mr. Smith."

His smile drooped, and his eyes lost their welcoming gleam. "Mrs. White has been the matron here for many years and no one has complained about her behavior." He shuffled papers on the desk and avoided eye contact.

"That's because she has bullied everyone into not saying anything. She has a good heart, for the most part. But her prejudices need to be kept to herself. It makes the children frightened of Mr. Smith, and they shouldn't be. He does so much for them and the school."

"Is that all?"

His quick dismissal didn't surprise her given Mr. Griffin's indifference to Mrs. White's treatment of the handyman. She'd have to ask Mr. Smith how he came to get this job when it was evident two of the staff held such bigotry.

"No. Where might I find Mr. Halsey?"

The superintendent jerked his head up, his eyes questioning. "Why are you looking for Mr. Halsey?"

"All students require a physical." She squeezed her hands together in an attempt to not say more to endanger her job. She may hate the fact her father "bought" this job, but at least she wasn't a burden on her family.

"B-but he's a man…"

"Yes, and I'm a doctor who is paid to check all incoming students."

He stared at her like she'd pulled up her skirts and shown her knees. She'd received that look so many times when working with a male patient, her face didn't heat anymore.

"It is no different than a male doctor giving a

female patient a physical."

"He's helping Donny set up for the broom-making class." His gaze strayed to the scar on her face, and then darted away.

"Thank you." She spun out of the stuffy confines of the office and shook out her aching fingers. She may desire a more fulfilling physician's appointment, but she didn't want to lose this one until something better came along. She would never allow herself to be a burden on her parents.

Her heart fluttered the closer she walked to the door of the broom-making room. She'd be lying if she said she didn't look forward to giving Mr. Halsey a physical. Heat flamed up her neck and scorched her cheeks. Heavens! Not in an inappropriate way. She enjoyed his company and the ease with which they could talk. And yes, the way his touch ignited her senses fascinated her.

She stepped in the door and smiled. Donny and Clay chatted like old friends, working side-by-side at a table laden with supplies.

"Excuse me, Donny, Mr. Halsey?"

The two turned toward her voice at the same time. Donny's brow scrunched in concern, but a smile lit Mr. Halsey's face. Her midsection did a slow roll, and heat curled behind her bellybutton.

"Dr. Tarkiel. Have you come to learn how to make a broom?"

The teasing in Mr. Halsey's voice fluttered her insides. "No, you need a physical, just like all the other students."

"Does he have to go now?" Donny whined and frowned. "The students will be showin' up any minute."

She smiled. Never had she seen Donny show anything other than bravado. His whining about taking Clay away was a sign the boy might finally be making steps toward not being afraid of men.

"I promise to bring him back as soon as I'm through."

The lines on the boy's face deepened, and his mouth screwed up in disbelief.

"It can't take that long to see I'm healthy." Clay patted the boy's back and started across the room.

To help navigate Clay to the door, she said, "It will only take about thirty minutes." When he stood in front of her, she moved to his side and slipped her hand through the crook of his arm.

"I'll be back as soon as the doc's through with me," Clay said over his shoulder, and then motioned for her to start walking.

Out in the hall, she studied him. The faded flannel shirt and denim work britches suited him more than the gentleman's coat and trousers he'd worn the day before. The softness of his shirt enticed her to snuggle against him. She straightened her back. That was a most inappropriate thought.

"Does this physical include you looking at my eyes?" His voice dropped, suggesting he wanted to keep their conversation private.

"Yes." She led him back into the main hall and around the corner toward the dining hall.

"The infirmary is near the dining hall?" He tilted his head and his nostrils flared.

She sniffed, inhaling the hearty scent of the noonday stew, and smiled. "Yes, the infirmary door is across the hall from the dining entrance." She stopped, and he stepped forward, searching with his hand until he found the knob and swung the door open. Rachel stepped through the threshold, took his hand, and led him to a chair in the examining room. The heat of his palm and the small squeeze he gave her fingers fluttered her mid-section anew.

"Sit." She placed her palms on his solid chest, moving him back onto the chair.

"I could get used to being bossed around by a woman."

The devilish smile curving his lips sent another flurry of heat and excitement skittering around inside her.

"Wait until I start probing and prodding, then you won't think that." She reached toward the counter for her stethoscope. His large hand grabbed her skirt.

"You'll tell me the truth. No saying things you think I want to hear." His ragged voice pleaded, and his brow furrowed in worry. The sight and sound of his desperation tugged at her heart.

"I'm professionally bound to tell you the truth about your condition." She released his fingers from the folds of her skirt. "I promise you will only hear the truth from me."

"Thank you." He swallowed and his Adam's apple bobbed. "There's days I'd rather be dead than blind, then I meet people like you and Donny and curse myself for being so weak."

Rachel stared at him, uncertain what to say. He couldn't know about her scar. "Why do Donny and I make you curse yourself?"

"Donny's only twelve, yet, he teaches others

how to make a living and provides for his ma and sister, and he's blind like me. You work in a profession that's generally held by a man. Yet, you"—he coughed into his hand, and his face reddened—"you keep your womanly qualities right there where a person knows you didn't take this on because you wanted to be a man."

She bit back the laugh bubbling in her throat. "No, Mr. Halsey, I didn't take this profession to prove I was better than a man. I picked the profession to help others."

His sun-bronzed face flushed a crimson to rival a breathtaking sunset. "I-I didn't mean to say—"

She patted his shoulder. "I understood. I was just teasing."

His body relaxed under her hand. His muscled shoulder heated her palm, and she pulled it away.

"Let's get this examination done and you back to Donny before he comes looking for you." She smiled and slipped the stethoscope into her ears. "He's taken a shine to you. I've not seen him like any men since I've been here." She slipped the wooden bell of the stethoscope down the front of Mr. Halsey's unbuttoned collar.

He grabbed her hand. "What's that?"

"Sorry. I didn't warn you. I put the bell end of my stethoscope down your shirt to listen to your heart." She extracted her hand from his and held the bell against his solid chest.

"What's that got to do with my eyes?"

She leaned in closer to listen, and his heart picked up speed. "The state requires a physical for all students." She listened to the steady glub, glub of his heart longer than necessary. Recognizing her reluctance to remove the bell jarred her into action. She removed the instrument from inside his shirt and backed away. She knew better than to be attracted to a patient. It was one of the reasons the male professors believed a woman couldn't be a doctor. Her weak constitution would allow her sensibilities to override her duty.

Rachel placed the instrument on the table and returned with the percussion hammer. "Cross one knee over the other, please."

Mr. Halsey complied.

"I'm going to tap your leg below the knee. This is a test of your reflexes." She tapped. His foot jumped as well as his body.

"Hey!" He uncrossed his legs. "What's that supposed to tell you?"

The annoyance wrinkling his forehead made her smile. "It shows if your reflexes are sluggish, and that would mean more could be wrong in your head than just your sight." She shifted to his left. "Other leg crossed, please."

She repeated the process. Both sides showed good signs. Rachel put the hammer down, picked up a hand lens, and stepped closer to Mr. Halsey. Even sitting in the examination chair, his tall frame and broad shoulders made an imposing figure.

"I'm going to look into your right eye first." She pressed close, her body brushing his arm as she put her free hand on his face. "I'll hold your eyelid open." Holding her breath to still the quiver of her insides, she leaned in and studied his dark brown iris, and then searched the outer white for any signs of continued blood flow to the eye. Though she detected no damage, she didn't see the pulse of life in the white. She backed away and moved to the other side of the chair.

"I'm going to look in your other eye now." She again placed a hand on his face and opened the eyelid, stilling her fluttering heart as she pressed close. His clean-shaven face had a couple small nicks on the edges of his angular cheeks. The spice of his shave soap lingered on his skin.

She resisted the urge to rub her cheek against his. The heat of his face under her palm and his breath moving wisps of wayward hair fluttered her eyes closed. She pretended for a brief moment he could be her husband. A man who loved her and wouldn't be threatened by her occupation or sickened by her hideous scar.

His breathing quickened. His hand settled on her waist, slid around to her back, and drew her forward. Her hand, holding the lens, dropped to his shoulder, and she opened her eyes. This behavior on both their parts was unconscionable, but her constricted throat wouldn't allow her to utter the rebuke.

Clay sensed the moment the doctor slid from professional to aroused woman. The hand on his cheek caressed rather than held, her breathing quickened, and her scent invaded his senses like a warm summer rain.

He pulled her body next to his. She came willingly, but then stiffened. Her hands moved to his shoulders. She didn't take a step back, but her chest expanded with an intake of breath.

"Call me Clay when we're alone." He didn't pull her any closer. Instead, he reached up to touch her face. What did she look like? His fingers tangled in soft wisps of hair. She backed away, pulling out of his arm.

"I'm sorry. I shouldn't—" Her voice quivered.

"No, it was me. I shouldn't have touched you." The earlier pleasant companionship was now singed like summer flowers after a first frost. All because he hadn't been able to resist touching her. Since their first meeting, warmth grew in his chest at the sound of her voice and his skin tingled at her touch.

Ominous quiet filled the room. Not a rustle of clothing, deep breathing, or retreating steps.

He reached out in the direction she'd retreated. His fingers skimmed across fabric and he heard her step away.

Clay lowered his hand. Regret and loneliness battled to take hold in his chest. "I truly am sorry. I wouldn't want my forwardness to change the friendship we're building."

"It's not you." Her voice quivered again and—it sounded laced with tears.

"Please, don't cry. I'm sorry."

Never had his actions shamed him as they did now. He'd made this woman cry. His arms ached to console her, but he fought the urge, determined not to cause her further sorrow.

She sniffed and a damp hand grasped his. "Don't. Don't think you did this. And I value the friendship we're building as well. I just..." Her hand pulled out of his. She blew her nose, and a half-hearted laugh echoed in the stillness.

"I'm sorry you have to be a part of me making a fool of myself." Her clipped tone proved she'd gained control and revealed to him her strength.

"I've been told if you can't show all your sides to a friend and still be friends, he isn't really a friend." Clay raised an eyebrow, hoping to ease the tension.

She laughed. "I suppose that's true. Well, you caught me at my worst today. I promise to remain professional from now on."

"You don't have to be professional around me all the time. Especially when we're alone, like now." He raised a hand, palm out, acknowledging what his words might convey. "I don't mean we need to drop proprieties. But I would prefer you call me Clay rather than Mr. Halsey. What's your given name?"

"Rachel." Her voice held a smile.

"That's a pretty name." Silence pressed around them again. Why had that comment affected her? Best to change the subject.

"What did you discover in my eyes? Any chance this is temporary?" He couldn't keep the wistfulness out of his voice. As much as he wanted to see again, he wanted to know this woman better. Wished he could see her, gaze into her eyes—see the emotions swimming in their depths.

"I can't give you false hope. Your eyes are clear, but they don't react to light. Time is the only way to tell if you'll improve."

Her professional tone and direct answer doused his hopes. He'd be stuck in this black hole the rest of his life.

"I better get you back to Donny. I'm impressed with the way you two were getting along." Her fingers wrapped around his hand, drawing his arm forward. The moment she started to slip her hand from his, he slid his palm up her arm to her shoulder, gauging her height. The top of her head would come to his shoulder.

She stepped beside him and slipped her hand around his arm.

"I was just seeing how tall you are," he said following her pace.

"The top of my head comes to your shoulder," she said in a matter-of-fact tone.

"And what's your build? You don't walk heavy. And I noticed you have curves."

She cleared her throat. "I'll share later when we're in private," she whispered over the tap of the matron's shoe growing louder.

"Dr. Tarkiel, I thought Mr. Halsey was helping Donny?" The suspicion in the matron's voice didn't bode well for him spending time with Rachel.

"I finished his new student physical and am returning him to the broom-making room."

Did he detect a bit of prickle in the doctor's tone? Clay bit his lip to keep from smiling. It wouldn't do to rankle the matron.

"I'll take him from here." Mrs. White's heavy-handed tone irked Clay.

"Ladies, I can find my way from here." He turned to Rachel. "Dr. Tarkiel, thank you for doing your duty." He unhooked her hand from his arm and stepped to the railing.

He strode down the hall and into the broom-making room, sorting out the incident with the doctor. Could she be feeling the attraction he was? She'd been aroused by his nearness. Her breathing had sped, and her voice had deepened to silky tones. He wanted to discover the woman in her, but he needed her friendship. He missed his brothers and newly acquired sisters. His whole life he'd been surrounded by family. If the only way he could keep the friendship was to ignore the attraction, he'd try.

Damn! Why did he have to find a woman who interested him when he wasn't in any shape to care for anyone? He could barely care for himself.

Chapter 5

Rachel stood at the infirmary window watching Clay help Mr. Smith spade the garden area. His easy movement and quick work of the patch showed he knew hard labor. One spade full at a time, he laid the earth over. The slight drizzle, common for this time of year, trickled off his hat brim. Her heart sped, and she waved a hand in front of her face to dissipate the heat building.

She'd spent the past two weeks avoiding the blind school's oldest student, not trusting the way her body reacted around him. She had to remain professional. If not, she risked her job and Clay's education. He could end up expelled. Visiting with Donny, she'd learned while Clay found reading Braille frustrating, he was making progress. She didn't want to stand in his way of learning. Of returning to his family.

"Get to work," she told herself and reluctantly moved from the window. Upon her arrival this morning, Mrs. White had brought her a student with a rash on her arms and upper torso. She opened the medical book and began reading, again. There had to be a logical explanation for the rash. The child wasn't feverish or otherwise showing illness.

If she couldn't find the answer in her books, she'd have to visit her mentor and the one local doctor who didn't disregard a woman physician.

A loud crack rang against the window. She jumped and spun around to face the glass in time to see a spatter of gravel strike the pane.

Rachel ran across the room and shoved the window up. Mr. Smith hopped from one foot to the other.

"Mr. Halsey, he done falled!" The man stared at her, his eyes round and scared.

Air whooshed out her lungs and her knees trembled. Clay was hurt!

"I'll be right there!" She grabbed the leather bag with her instruments, charged out of the room, and ran down the hall to the outside door. Mr. Smith met her there, loping alongside as she continued at a jog.

"I done told him not ta climb the ladder in the rain. He just laughed and started up. He don't knowed this area. Things get slick with this here rain."

They rounded the corner of the tool shed. Her knees nearly folded at the sight of Clay. His head sat at an odd angle against the last rung of the ladder and one leg lay askew.

Disregarding the mud, she dropped to her knees beside him and placed a hand on his chest. The slight rise and fall reassured her. He was alive!

"Clay? Clay, can you hear me?" She patted his cheek, but he didn't respond.

"Go get Mr. Griffin to help carry Clay to the infirmary." She didn't look up at the handyman. She focused her attention on the blood seeping through Clay's pant leg. An open fracture.

With care, she ran her fingers over the back of his head. No open wound, but a large bump had already formed. She settled his head and back flat on the wet grass. Running her hands down his body, she searched for more breaks and straightened his limbs until she came to the broken leg.

She cut away the bottom of his pant leg and surveyed the jagged bone sticking through his blood-drenched underdrawers and the hole in his flesh. Her gaze wandered to his face, and her chest squeezed. She'd set many bones during her year of practicum, but the thought of what she'd have to do to— She pushed her irrational thoughts away. She was a doctor. He was the patient and nothing more. She'd need Mr. Smith's help to set the leg.

Heavy footsteps and huffing approached. Mr. Smith, followed by Mr. Griffin, dashed around the corner of the building.

"He's unconscious and his leg needs to be set. Mr. Smith, pick him up under his arms, please." Rachel shot a glance at Mr. Griffin. His face blanched, and he froze, staring at the wound.

She pointed to the uninjured leg. "Mr. Griffin, grasp that leg. Hold on at his upper leg so the two of you carry most of his weight." She held the injured leg, one hand on either side of the gaping hole in his shin, to keep the bone from doing any further damage.

"On the count of three we'll all pick him up and head to the infirmary." She glanced at her bag. Someone could come back for it. "One, two, three."

They all stood at the same time and proceeded to the school. At the building, Mrs. White held the door open. Rachel nodded her thanks, and they continued to the infirmary. In the room, she directed them to place Clay on the wooden table near the windows. She'd need the help of the gray daylight along with the gas lighting to sew up the laceration.

When Clay was settled on the table, she faced the men. "Mr. Griffin, please retrieve my bag. I left it by the ladder. Mr. Smith, I'll need your help setting the bone."

Both men stood still as the furniture, staring at her.

Mr. Griffin stepped forward. "I think it would be best if I helped set the bone."

"I saw the way you paled at the sight of the injury. I can't have you fainting halfway through the procedure. And Mr. Smith is stronger. I need him to hold Mr. Halsey down should he come around while I'm working." She waved the superintendent away. "Go get my bag."

"Mr. Smith, help me get Mr. Halsey's trousers off, and then wash your hands." Her hands shook reaching for the opening on Clay's trousers. He was just a patient.

Mr. Smith pushed her hands aside. "I can do that. Get yer stuff ready."

She sent him a weak smile and stepped to the cupboard for supplies.

Gather up your emotions. She couldn't let her

feelings for Clay hinder her aid. She was a doctor first. Mr. Smith grunted, and Clay moaned, but she remained at the cupboard pulling out a basin, antiseptic soap, peroxide of hydrogen, needle, suture, rolled cotton bandage, and adhesive bandage. She stacked the supplies on a tray.

"What about his long johns?" Mr. Smith asked from behind her.

Rachel picked up a pair of scissors and glanced over her shoulder at the table. "I'll cut the one leg above the wound." She pulled the garment away from his knee and carefully cut the fabric around his muscular thigh, then down the front, laying the cloth open under his leg.

She picked up the soap and motioned for Mr. Smith to follow her to the wash basin. Mr. Griffin entered carrying her bag.

"Thank you. Place it on the desk." She returned to washing her hands, standing shoulder to shoulder next to Mr. Smith.

Mr. Griffin cleared his throat.

She exhaled and threw him an impatient glance. "Yes?"

The man didn't say anything. Just shot a meaningful glance at the handyman, then at her and shook his head. Rachel rolled her eyes. She didn't have time for the superintendent's bigotry.

"We have things under control, Mr. Griffin. Thank you." She dried her hands and handed the towel to Mr. Smith. He glanced at the other man, and then at her. She smiled and nodded. He took the cloth and dried.

Mr. Griffin huffed something under his breath and left.

Clay moaned.

She rushed across the room to the table. "Clay? Clay, you have a broken leg. Mr. Smith and I are going to fix it." He didn't respond.

She had to treat him like any patient and quit showing emotion. Squaring her shoulders, she picked up the chloroform and a towel. She dripped the liquid onto the towel and handed it to Mr. Smith.

"Hold this above his nose. It keeps him sleepy while I work on the leg."

The man nodded, took the towel, and held it above Clay's nose.

"Good." She used her fingers to probe the area around the broken bone. A clean break. But with an open fracture of the tibia, the fibula was broken, too. She hoped the smaller bone would move into place when she set the larger one. "Hold him down, I have to pull the bone back and seam it in place."

The big man nodded and placed his hands on Clay's shoulders. Rachel grasped Clay's long, slender foot and slowly pulled, easing the bone back into the flesh and turning the foot to match the broken ends together.

Clay cursed and moved his head from side to side.

"Hold the towel over him, again." The bones in place, she doused the sterile cloth with the peroxide of hydrogen and scrubbed away all debris. She didn't want to chance an infection.

Happy with the state of the wound, she placed a hand on Clay's chest to register his breathing. His rib cage moved in a steady rhythm. She glanced at his color and toward Mr. Smith.

"You're doing a fine job keeping him sedated." She smiled at the handyman and picked up a needle and suture. He nodded but didn't take his eyes off the needle in her hand. "I'm going to stitch the wound closed. He may flinch, but unless he moves his leg, don't give him any more chloroform. I'd like him coming back around soon."

Mr. Smith nodded.

Rachel held the skin together with her fingers, blood oozed around the skin and trickled down his leg. He'd been lucky the bones hadn't severed a main artery. Fifteen stitches closed the gaping flesh. She stepped to the basin, washed her hands, and returned to the table to clean up his leg and the stitches.

Deep mumbling and his hands twitching at his sides confirmed he'd started to come around. The leg needed to be made stationary.

"Mr. Smith, hold his leg still while I talk to him." She switched places with the handyman and leaned over Clay's face.

"Mr. Halsey? Clay?" Apprehension bubbled in her chest. While she knew a professional demeanor was necessary, she also knew a patient responded better at a more personal level.

His long dark eyelashes fluttered, and his full bottom lip quivered as he moaned.

"Clay, it's Dr. Tarkiel, Rachel. You fell and broke your leg. I have it set, but we still need to stabilize it." She brushed the wisp of wet chestnut bangs off his forehead.

"It hurts," he whispered.

The sound of his voice squeezed her chest.

His pain had become her pain. She placed a palm on his cheek. "I know. If you're awake enough to swallow, I can give you some medicine to help with the pain."

"Yes," he hissed between his lips. Furrows formed on his brow and his color paled.

"Keep holding his leg," she said to Mr. Smith and hurried to her medicine cabinet. She tapped powdered laudanum into a glass and added water. Stirring the tonic, she returned to the table.

"Drink this. It will ease the pain." Rachel slid a hand under Clay's head, raising him enough to sip the liquid.

His nose wrinkled, and he shook his head at the glass. "That's awful."

"But it will take away your pain. Try again." She held the glass in front of his mouth again. His reluctance to drink the foul taste was a good sign.

He drank the remainder.

Rachel settled his head on the table and filled a basin with water. She unrolled an adhesive bandage and placed it in the basin. Picking up a square bandage, she sprinkled laudanum in the middle and placed it over the wound. Mr. Smith held Clay's leg off the table while she wrapped a clean bandage from his ankle to below his knee. She placed two long flat strips of wood on either side of the leg and wrapped the whole thing with the soaked adhesive bandage. She still marveled at the genius who'd thought to press the white plaster of Paris powder into bandages to make casting material for broken bones.

She rubbed each layer, smearing the plaster together and sealing the layers. The cast was an inch thick when she smiled at Mr. Smith.

"That should keep him from doing harm while the bone heals."

Mr. Smith shook his head. "He's a hard man ta keep still, Doctor."

"He isn't going to be a problem for a couple days." She walked to the smaller room housing two spring cots and retrieved a pillow and blanket.

"I'm going to leave him on this table until he comes around again. When he does, I'll need your help to move him to a cot." Rachel placed a pillow under his head and tucked the blanket around Clay's prone body.

Mr. Smith touched the doorknob. "Jus' give a whistle out the window."

"I will." She walked across the floor and took his free hand, squeezing his large fingers. "Thank you. There's not another person in this school who could have helped me."

Surprise crossed his wide features at her words of praise. He cleared his throat, withdrew his hand from hers, and strode from the room.

Clay mumbled, and she hurried back to his side. The laudanum would keep him sedated and pain free for a couple hours, but she feared he might roll off the table. She tucked a pillow on either side of him and set to work cleaning her instruments.

"Doc Tarkiel?"

She jerked her head toward the door. Donny stood in the threshold. "Yes, Donny?"

The boy ventured into the room. "I heard Mrs. White and Mr. Griffin talkin' 'bout Clay. Is he here?" His soft almost shaky words were far from his usual gruff, intimidating attitude.

"Yes. He broke his leg. I have him sedated at the moment." She held out a hand. "Come over here."

The boy walked toward her. She grasped his hand, led him to the side of the table, and placed his hand on Clay's arm.

"He's sleeping right now."

"But he's gonna be all right?" Lines marred his smooth, youthful face.

"He'll be fine, but you'll have to give him lessons here for the next month. He won't be able to do much moving around until I take the cast off his leg." She squeezed the boy's shoulder. The man had touched so many lives at the school in a short time. Her heart thudded in her chest. Including hers.

"Will he be ready to read tomorrow?"

"I don't know if he'll be able to concentrate enough to read, but I know he would enjoy your company."

The boy's smile grew and he patted Clay's arm. "I'll be by in the mornin', Clay." Donny grasped her hand and shook it. "Thank you, Dr. Tarkiel."

She held back a laugh. "For what?"

"For helpin' Clay."

"It's my job, Donny. To help everyone at the school." She glanced down at the slumbering man. But helping Clay brought a special joy.

"I know, but just thanks." His blank gaze shimmered with unshed tears. The reality of how much the man had come to mean to the boy in two short weeks shook her. She peered down at Clay. What have you done to put Donny and me under your spell?

Donny's feet scraped the floor as he left. Rachel pulled a chair alongside the table. She picked up the book on diseases she'd been reading earlier, sat in the chair, and studied the sleeping form. The top of his head went past the six foot table, and his shoulders spanned the width. It was a miracle he hadn't done more damage from such a fall.

Her gaze rested on his face. When awake his square chin, wide jaw, and crooked nose revealed him to be a man who knew how to take care of himself and others. Asleep, as he was now, he reminded her of an innocent boy. She swept a lock of hair off his forehead, touching his wide smooth brow. He mumbled, and his face lolled her direction.

The urge to lean over and kiss his slightly parted lips overwhelmed her, and she moved toward him. His head jerked the other direction, and she yanked her body back in control.

Shaking herself mentally, she forced her attention to the book. Little Sylvie's rash took precedence over her curious infatuation with Clay Halsey.

Chapter 6

His head weighed as much as a cornerstone on the stamp mill. His leg throbbed from his ankle to his hip. Clay tried to wiggle his toes. Pain shot up the side of his leg.

"Gah!" Where was he, and why did his leg hurt like blazes?

"Clay? Clay, it's me, Dr. Tarkiel." A small hand wrapped around the fingers of his left hand. Who was Dr. Tarkiel? Why were they in the dark?

He blinked. His eyelids were open, why was it dark? Where was he?

His dry throat strained to press words through his numb lips. "Where am I?"

"You're in the infirmary." The sweet voice stirred happy thoughts. The intimate tickle of fingers pushing hair off his forehead unnerved him. Who was this woman? Where the hell was the infirmary? They didn't have one in Sumpter.

He swallowed. "Where?"

"The infirmary?" Her tone held skepticism—

and a warble of fear?

He nodded and wished she'd turn on a light. How could a room be so dark?

"At the blind school in Salem." With ease she held up his wrist, the pads of her fingers finding his pulse point.

"Why? Why am I here?"

"You fell off the ladder helping Mr. Smith. You put a fair-sized bump on your head and broke your leg." She replaced his hand. A cool palm rested on his forehead.

"No. School. Why am I at a blind school?" He shifted his head toward the warmth of her nearness, squinting as he tried to see a silhouette in the darkness.

She inhaled loudly, and her hands stilled. "Because—" Her voice descended and a chair scraped across the floor. "What do you remember before the fall?"

"Zeke and Maeve came to visit. Ethan's courting the widow Miller, even though Miles—"

Miles threw dynamite at him.

"Damn!" Clay tried to sit up. His head ached, and two small, but firm, hands held him down.

"Stay down. Rest for a few minutes. Then I'll call Mr. Smith to help move you to a bed."

"There's lights on, right? I'm just a pathetic blind man." He banged his head down on the hard surface below him. Pain was easier to bear than the despair engulfing him.

"That's no way to talk!"

Her tone reminded him of his sharp tongued sister-in-law.

"You are not pathetic. Donny has been helping move you along faster in your reading, and Mr. Smith has found your help outside most useful. If you hadn't been bull-headed and climbed a ladder in the rain, you'd still be out helping him." A chair scraped the floor and steps retreated.

Clay raised a hand the weight of a sledgehammer to his face and wiped it over his unseeing eyes. Was he really learning to read? And was he a help to someone? He tried to remember why he'd climbed a ladder. A breeze washed the scent of lemons, tangy and fresh, over him. His mind connected the woman who scolded him with the scent.

A shrill whistle rent the air. He jumped. Pain sliced up his leg. Blazes! He'd never had a broken bone before. A broken nose from a fight over a girl in primer school, but never more than that. He didn't like the pain or the thought of being laid up.

"Mr. Smith is on his way. I have a bed in the infirmary ready for you. It won't be as comfortable as your bed in the cottage, but you'll need around the clock supervision for a couple of days. Some people don't respond well to laudanum." She pulled something away from his sides. Cooler air washed over his body.

"I don't want laudanum. My uncle wrote letters to my pa about the use of the medicine during the war." He winced the instant she tugged at his injured leg.

"I've already given you a small amount."

Heavy footsteps approached. "Mr. Smith. Help me get him into a sitting position, and then we'll walk him into the other room." Her small hands pushed up under his shoulders, elevating his torso and reflecting lights through his head.

"Blazes!" He gripped his head to still the spinning lights. His stomach roiled and dizziness hit.

"He hit his head pretty hard." Rachel moved to catch Clay's slumping body. "We'll have to carry him to the infirmary." She scowled at the damp clothes covering his torso. She'd hoped to get him out of the dirty garments.

Mr. Smith nudged her aside and scooped the man, nearly as large as his big frame, into his arms and carried him to the other room like a child.

"Thank you! Let's get him out of his shirt. I don't want him catching consumption from wet clothes." The damp undershirt had to come off, too. Rachel drew the sheet and blanket up under his chin.

She pivoted from the bed and caught Mr. Smith watching her.

"Ain't proper you fussin' over him."

"I'm a doctor. I'm trained to fuss over people. I have one more favor to ask of you." She walked into the main room. "I'll write a note to my parents letting them know I'll spend the night here. If you would take it to them, I'd appreciate it." She picked up a quill and dipped it in the ink pot.

"You sure?" Mr. Smith's hands fidgeted with the flap on the front pocket of his overalls.

"You know my family aren't bigots like the staff at this school. If it makes you uncomfortable, go to the back door, and give the note to our cook, Matilda." She blew on the ink.

Rachel folded the note and handed it to the handyman. "If he does well tonight, I'll ask you to stay here with him tomorrow night." She patted the big man's arm and smiled. "I do understand proprieties."

He smiled back and shuffled out the door.

Rachel scanned the room making sure all was tidy. Her stomach growled. She should have had Mr. Smith ask Mrs. Daniels to bring up a tray for both her and Clay. Until he was lucid, she didn't dare leave him alone.

The tap of Mrs. White's shoe stopped in the doorway. Rachel didn't want a confrontation, but she could see by the fists planted on the woman's ample hips one was in the making.

"Mr. Smith says you're staying the night."

"Please, Mrs. White, lower your voice. You'll disturb my patient." Rachel crossed her arms and peered at the woman like her mother stared down politicians. "I had to give Mr. Halsey laudanum for the pain, and until I see how he reacts to it, I can't have anyone else watching him."

"This isn't proper." The woman's nostrils flared.

"I am a doctor. It's no different than if he were my patient in a hospital. I'd still remain to make sure all was going well."

"I can stay with him."

"You're not a doctor, and you're needed near the dorms. I don't know what you're worried about. He has a heavy cast on a leg that has to be giving him a great amount of pain. Mr. Halsey will be in no shape to make advances." Rachel laughed at her own humor. No man would make advances toward her. Even a blind one would eventually discover her disfigurement.

"You joke, but I know men. They can work their way until you let your guard down, and then you're ruined." Mrs. White's eyes fogged over.

This was a woman who'd been hurt by a man. Intrigued, Rachel felt an unexpected connection with the matron. They'd both been spurned.

"I can guarantee Mr. Halsey won't be in any mood to use his charms on me tonight." She settled an arm around the matron's shoulders. "Would you ask Mrs. Daniels to send up a tray with dinner for me and some broth for Mr. Halsey?"

The matron nodded as Rachel maneuvered her to the door.

"Thank you. I do appreciate your concern. If he does well through the night, I'll have Mr. Smith stay here with the patient at night."

The other woman's eyes rounded, and her mouth shifted from a surprised "o" to a stiff line of disapproval. "It isn't proper for that man to be in this building all night."

"Then I guess I'll have to move in until Mr. Halsey's leg is healed." Rachel stifled a laugh at the war of emotions wrinkling the matron's brow and contorting her lips. "We'll see how things go, and I'll discuss the matter with Mr. Griffin tomorrow." She waved Mrs. White down the hall.

Bed springs creaked. She rushed to the small infirmary. Clay's open eyes stared at the ceiling, and his body wrestled with trying to sit up.

"Clay, lie still." She put her hands on his bare shoulders, pushing gently to make him lie back. The covers slid to his waist. His broad muscled chest, dusted with dark curls, sped her heart and warmed her face.

He grasped her hand. "How long am I gonna be stuck in this bed?"

The heat of his hand flashed up her arm and fluttered in her chest. "A-at least two weeks. After that we'll see how you're doing." She cupped his cheek in her free palm. The day's growth of whiskers pricked her palm, emphasizing his maleness and coiling heat in her mid-section. "Donny's coming by tomorrow to visit and continue your lessons here." He smiled at the name. "Do you remember where you are?"

He nodded. "The blind school. Ethan brought me here over two weeks ago. I climbed the ladder to help Jasper repair the shed roof. Can you prop me up?"

His grip on her fingers softened, and his thumb moved across the back of her hand. Warm shivers ran in waves through her stomach and up her back. His touch raised her temperature and sent shivery tremors of excitement through her body.

"Let's wait until your dinner arrives. With your head wound, I'd rather you stay still for a while longer." She leaned over him, grasping the covers to pull them back over his stunning body.

He raised his hands and captured her head between his palms. Instinct jerked her back, but his hands gently held her in place.

"Don't." His raspy voice stopped her backward motion. "Dr. Tarkiel, either your laudanum has made me lose my senses, or my curiosity is finally getting the better of me." His hold relaxed. His fingers roamed over her loosely pulled back hair.

She kept her naturally curly hair short around her face to help conceal her scar. His hands started forward, and she pulled back again.

"Please. I won't do anything inappropriate. My fingers are my eyes."

She grasped his hands, drawing them down. "I have brown curly hair, the color of scuffed shoes. My face is oval, no distinct cheekbones. My nose is neither large nor small and sits above small lips. My eyes are brown."

Clay frowned. She painted a very dismal picture of herself. "Do you always describe yourself so plainly?"

She sighed. "I will always tell you the truth. I've accepted my plainness."

He started to shake his head, but the movement flashed pain in his temple. "No one is plain. Every person I've ever met has some characteristic that sets them apart from others."

"Like your crooked nose?"

He didn't miss the teasing in her voice or her attempt to turn the conversation from herself. "That might have happened for the wrong reason, but it sets me apart from my brothers who all have the same color hair and eyes. We're each just an inch or two shorter or broader shouldered than the next one. Gil, the baby of the family, is six foot, and has the narrowest shoulders. But dang if he doesn't have the prettiest face." He snorted. "'Course we don't tell him that. We've been telling him he's the ugliest. Keeps him humble."

Rachel's laughter soothed his aching head like a warm tonic.

"I imagine growing up with—how many brothers?"

"Including myself, five." He rubbed his thumb over their clasped hands still resting on his chest.

"And Gil's the smallest? My heaven, how big is the biggest?" Her weight settled on the side of his bed. Her thigh and hip warm against his hip and side.

"Ethan makes an imposing sight. He's six-four and his shoulders scrape most doorways when he walks through. I'd guess Jasper is about his size."

"My! You Halseys are big men. I feel sorry for your mother feeding and clothing you."

Sadness washed over him. He'd been a young man when his parents were killed, but he still ached for the arms he remembered snuggling in when he was ill or scared. "She didn't live to see us grown."

"I'm so sorry." She clutched his hand tighter. Her stomach rumbled.

"Have you missed eating because of me?"

"I asked Mrs. White to have the cook send up food." She let go of his hands. A moment later something in the vicinity of the doctor clicked. "Dinner is almost over for the students. We should have our meal soon."

The bed rose, and her warmth disappeared, cooling the heat coiling in his system.

"Where are you going?" He enjoyed her company. More than he'd enjoyed anyone's in a long time. And he didn't want to be left alone to think about how he'd spend his time confined to a bed.

"I need to tidy up the outer office and get things ready for tonight."

"Tonight?" Did he need more medical attention?

"I'll spend the night in the infirmary with you."

His heart pounded and blood rushed to a rising appendage. He eased a hand under the covers, capturing the beast her comment brought to life. Her statement eased his pain more pleasurably than the laudanum.

Chapter 7

If not for her embarrassment at how her words came out, Rachel would have found Clay's antics amusing.

"I don't want you left alone, and because you are sedated, I want to remain close in case there are complications." She sat on the bed four feet away from Clay. It creaked, and his head shifted her direction. "There's another bed I'll rest on through the night."

"You really know how to burst a fella's dreams." The smile curving his lips was devil-ishly charming. Heat swept through her body and ignited a blaze of desire. She shook her head to expel the image. When he wasn't feeling sorry for himself, he was quite the charmer.

"You can dream all you want, but it won't come true."

"Doc." Mr. Smith's deep voice boomed from the other room.

She stood. "I'll go see what Mr. Smith wants.

Rest, that's what helps bones heal."

Mr. Smith stood in the middle of the room holding a satchel. "Yer ma sent these things along." He held the satchel out.

Leave it to her mother to think of sending clean clothes. Always conscious of her appearance and those of her daughters. With a scarred older daughter who refused to socialize, her mother taught her younger beautiful daughter all the fine points of being a lady. This suited Rachel just fine.

She took the satchel. "Did she say anything?"

"She done said you best be home for a dinner tomorrow night." Mr. Smith nodded toward the other room. "Mr. Halsey, he feelin' better?"

"As well as he can with a broken leg. You may go in and see for yourself if you'd like." Rachel put the satchel on the table and opened the clasp to see what her mother had sent. She didn't want to attend the dinner tomorrow night. There would be people—men—William had told about her "deformity". She could always tell. They stared at her face all evening trying to find the scar under her make-up and couldn't keep a decent conversation going due to their preoccupation.

The rumble of male voices drifted from the other room. Footsteps stopped at the doorway.

"How is Mr. Halsey?" Mr. Griffin asked.

Rachel faced the superintendent and smiled. "He's as he should be considering he has a broken leg and a lump on his head." She noticed a notebook in his hand.

"I need to take down his statement as to what happened." Mr. Griffin headed to the other room.

"Mr. Smith is visiting, so you'll get both accounts."

The man hesitated. Didn't he want Mr. Smith's account as well? He continued into the room. Curious, she followed the man and stood at the doorway.

"Mr. Halsey, it's Mr. Griffin. I need to write down how your accident happened." The man barged in, interrupting Clay's conversation with Mr. Smith.

Rachel frowned. One more mark against the man in her mind.

Mr. Smith backed away from the bed and stood, his eyes downcast. Mr. Griffin sat on the empty bed and opened the book. He pulled a pencil from his breast pocket.

"Now, why did you climb the ladder? Did Mr. Smith ask you to?"

Rachel wanted to protest the accusation, but her gaze traveled to Clay first. The angry line of his mouth and the red tinting his ears indicated he understood the direction the man headed.

"Mr. Smith was still in the shed getting the shingles when I took it upon myself to climb the ladder. I figured he could hand the bundles up to me and save time. It's hard to misstep on a ladder and a shed roof isn't that steep. I've helped shingle before and figured another person on the roof would make Mr. Smith's job go faster." He ran a hand over the back of his head. "I didn't consider the moss being slick on the roof."

"So, you're saying you found the ladder and climbed it of your own volition?" Mr. Griffin questioned, his eyebrow arched.

"I followed Mr. Smith to the shed. He'd said

he was going to patch the roof and told me to go in my room and practice reading." A crooked smile formed on Clay's lips. "Instead, I found the ladder leaning against the building and climbed it."

Rachel smiled. She could see him doing just that. He was a typical male. Rather do physical things than reading and paperwork. Other than Mr. Smith, her life had been filled with men who were intellectually tough. She liked the physical toughness of Clay mixed with his intellect. Her gaze scanned his bare shoulders. Her heart picked up speed.

Mr. Griffin slapped his book closed, jammed the pencil in his pocket, and jerked to his feet. "Mr. Halsey. I'll have this printed in Braille and ink and get your signature." The superintendent glared at Mr. Smith and breezed past Rachel without a word.

She entered the room. "You didn't tell him what he wanted to hear."

Clay's head jerked her direction. "He didn't want to hear the truth."

"Don't jump on me. I know you told the truth." She flashed a smile at Mr. Smith. "Considering Mr. Griffin is on a witch hunt, I'll stay here every night until Clay is ready to return to the cottage."

The handyman shook his head. "Doc, you're respectable. I'm nothin'."

"I'd feel less respectable if you were tossed out of here for nothing and I could prevent it." Her voice squeaked from the ball of anger clogging her throat.

"Jasper, I don't mind the doc hanging out with me."

The grin and slight waggle of Clay's eyebrow

swept away her anger and sent a wave of heat rushing from her toes to her hair.

"You best not be thinkin' those things," Mr. Smith growled and glared at Clay.

Rachel glanced from one man to the other and laughed. One was dead serious, and the other was joking. "How have you two been getting along the past two weeks?" She walked over to Mr. Smith. "Clay's fooling with you and me. He won't be getting out of that bed for several days and even after that, I'll be able to run faster than he will." Clay frowned at her last comment, and Mr. Smith nodded, his stern expression wavering.

"Doctor Tarkiel," Mrs. White called from the other room.

Rachel left the two men and hurried to the woman who held a tray covered with a tea towel.

"Your dinner." The matron sat the tray next to her satchel on the wood table near the window. "When did you have time to get clothing?"

"Mr. Smith brought it after delivering the note to my parents."

The woman sniffed. "Well, Mr. Griffin is looking into Mr. Halsey's fall."

Rachel bit back the words she wanted to say and squared on the woman. "Mr. Smith had nothing to do with Mr. Halsey's fall. Mr. Halsey told Mr. Griffin that. So I'd appreciate it if you didn't start spreading false rumors."

Mr. Smith walked out of the other room. The matron's mouth fell open wide enough Rachel could have reached in and pulled out her molars.

"You need any more help, Doc?" he asked, not glancing at Mrs. White.

"I think we'll be fine for the night, but if you could check in before breakfast, I'd like to change the bedding and could use your help." She smiled, giving the handyman her full attention. He nodded and left the room.

The matron shook her head. "Doctor Tarkiel, you shouldn't be so friendly with him."

"Why? He's a person just like you and me." Rachel leaned closer and whispered, "I know for a fact their blood is just as red as ours."

Mrs. White straightened and hustled out of the room. Rachel burst into giggles. She shouldn't have said that, but the attitudes of the superintendent and the matron dangled her good manners on a short fuse.

She picked up the tray and headed into the other room.

The aroma of food swirled around Clay, and his stomach growled.

"Dinner's arrived."

Rachel's no-nonsense tone told him the visitors had ruined the bond he and the doctor had started to forge.

"It smells good. Mrs. Daniels's cooking sure beats the slop Hank makes." He tried to scoot to a sitting position. The movement aggravated his leg, slicing pain upwards. Nausea rather than hunger clenched his gut.

"You get broth tonight." Her voice came from beside his bed.

Fingers fluttered across his brow. The sensation lighter than the wings of a butterfly but affected him like a sledgehammer slamming into his chest.

"Feel like trying to sit up some?"

"It would make drinking the broth easier."

Her small hands helped him lift his shoulders off the bed. A soft cushion grew behind his back. Her citrus scent wafted around him, tickling his nostrils and heating his body. Need swirled in his gut.

He reached out. His palm cupped what felt like her small, hard, round shoulder. "You have a gentle touch."

Her motions stalled. "Thank you."

Her breathy words danced across his face. Her shoulder slipped from his hand and dishes clattered.

"Mrs. Daniels put the broth in a mug. Do you want me to feed you or just drink it yourself?"

"I'd enjoy you feeding me, but I don't want you waiting to eat. Put the mug in my hands." Clay extended his hands and a warm smooth object filled them. He brought the mug to his mouth and hesitated, inhaling the meaty aroma. He'd anticipated his stomach rebelling; instead, it emitted a slow easy rumble of hunger. He sipped the soup and swallowed. The broth slid down, appeasing his stomach. He smacked his lips. A feminine giggle fluttered on the air.

"Are you eating?" he asked, tipping his head.

"Yes."

"So while you eat, tell me about your family." He'd told her about his, and now he wanted to know more about the woman and why she became a doctor. Most people frowned on a woman in a man's occupation. What had motivated her to ignore society and pursue a life of medicine?

"My father is a judge, my mother loves being the center of attention at functions, and my sister, Celeste, gives my mother competition these days."

Her flat monotone delivery piqued his interest. Why did she show so little emotion when talking of her family?

"She's become the most sought after young woman in Salem."

Did her dreary tone mean she wished men sought after her or had she tired of her mother and sister's rivalry?

"And you? Do you like the social life and have many suitors?" He worked to keep his tone non-committal, but inside his heart stopped. He hoped she didn't have a string of suitors. Why, he wasn't sure, but this woman renewed his excitement for the future. Something he hadn't considered since losing his sight.

Her soft laughter floated to his ears like the song of angels. "Heavens, no! My family can enjoy the politics and the parties. Give me a good thick medical book to read and I'm happy."

"Only medical books? I would think someone with your wit and compassion would be the center of charity work." Stillness hung in the room like a mist. He strained to hear anything. "Did I say something wrong?" Damn! He wanted to see her reaction so bad his headed pounded from the strain. Frustration at the darkness and inability to read her expressions clenched his hands and triggered a pain down his injured leg.

"You didn't say anything wrong. I just— I have my reasons for staying out of any social settings." Sadness wrapped the softly spoken words.

What could be a reason she hid herself away with medical books? And tried to convince herself it was what she wanted?

"I don't hear you eating." He sipped his broth, listening for her to resume eating. He'd keep their conversation on neutral ground.

"Tell me about the school staff."

"Mr. Griffin has been the superintendent here for five years. Mrs. White came here as the matron when her husband died three years ago. And the teachers are both in their second year here. Mr. Smith has been here less than a year." She'd slid back in control. Her tone rang clear and precise, stating less than useful information about the staff. He wanted descriptions. He also noticed she didn't mention herself.

"I meant what do they look like, so when I'm talking to them I can visualize them. I see Jasper as a big bear, Mrs. White a sturdy woman with a sour disposition, Mr. Griffin a small, round man with a scowl, Miss Hubert, like a crow, and Miss Collins a tall thin woman who is forever smiling."

Rachel's laughter floated through the air, sprinkling him with good humor.

"So, I'm way off in my images?" He smiled and took another sip of the broth.

"Yes and no." Her giggles subsided. "Mr. Smith at first sight is very imposing, but he's kind and gentle. I wish Mr. Griffin and Mrs. White would just let him do his job and forget his skin is a different color."

"How did he get the job here when the two main staff members don't trust him?" The question had plagued him for several days, but he hadn't wanted to ask Jasper.

"Same way I got mine." She sighed and mumbled, "My father."

The defeat laced in her words throbbed in his chest, and he ached to console her. "I don't understand. How did your father get you and Jasper jobs here? Especially you."

"I attended the Woman's Hospital Medical College of Chicago. Most of the other medical colleges are men only. After graduating, I spent the required year under a woman physician in Chicago, then came back to Salem. After three years of schooling and one year of practicum, all I could find was a nursing job." She spit the last statement out as though forcing it through clenched teeth. "My father knew the physician who'd been on call for the Blind School was overworked and offered my services to Mr. Griffin, along with an endowment for the school." She snorted. "My position here was bought. I could have been some person who'd never been trained and I'd have received this job."

He wanted to jump off the bed and wrap his arms around her. Console her wounded pride and learn more about the passionate woman he heard in her words and felt in her actions. "I don't believe that. Mr. Griffin must have seen your credentials and your worth."

"All he saw was money for the school and another person to help with the students." Dishes rattled. "Are you through with the broth?"

Clay drank the rest of the liquid and held up his cup. Her fingers brushed his, igniting the sparks he tried to suppress. Each small gesture and innocent touch fueled his desire for her. The mug disappeared. Her scent wafted away with her footsteps.

He'd bet she placed top in her class and had high hopes of securing a practice with a physician about to retire. Surely in a town the size of Salem such an opening had existed. Her light steps returned.

"Would you like me to remove the pillows so you can rest?" The clipped words sent a message. She'd finished her visit.

Well, she may not talk, but he could still get close to her. "Yes, this leg hurts like a son-of-a-gun." Citrus circled his head, and the heat of her body drew close. His body lowered a pillow at a time, and he drank in her nearness. She tugged on the last pillow. He reached up, found her hand, and brought it to rest on his bare chest. The coolness of her hand on his skin surged heat to his shaft. His desire for her doubled. Did she crave him as he craved her?

He'd give up his family to see her emotions reflected in her eyes.

Her breath hitched as her fingers splayed across his skin.

"Will you come back and visit with me when you finish your duties?" Her hand pressed down, pushing to get away. He wrapped his fingers around her dainty wrist and stopped her retreat. "No one's brought me a book to read, and I'm bored."

"You need your rest." The words came out on a breathy sigh.

His lips itched to slip into a satisfied smile, but

that would only make her pull away.

"If I rest, when you come back will you visit with me?" He ached to slide his hand up her arm and draw her down beside him, but she was skittish of close contact.

"Y-yes."

Her hesitation made him laugh. "You're just going to tippy-toe back in here and go to sleep." Clay opened his hold, freeing her.

She straightened but didn't move away from the bed. "The thought had crossed my mind." The sheet tugged across his chest. Hands gently tucked it around him. "Rest."

Her footsteps retreated.

He inhaled and smiled. Doctor Rachel Tarkiel was an intriguing puzzle. She shied from close contact when he initiated it, yet, she touched him at every opportunity.

She said she preferred being alone, yet when she talked of her family her tone had been bittersweet, as though she yearned to travel in the circles they did.

Clay slid his hands behind his head and smiled. He had a penchant for solving puzzles.

Chapter 8

Rachel ran a hand over her heated brow and peeked back at the man smiling smugly. Did he know the affect his naked chest had on her? When he'd placed her hand on his hard pectorals dusted with dark brown curly hair, her knees nearly buckled. The heat that surged through her and exploded in her pelvic area brought desires the like she'd never experienced.

She stood in the doorway staring at his sheet covered form. What was it about this man that brought her body to life? Did he feel the same? Spinning from the room, she stared at the satchel on the table. No way would she undress anywhere near that man. He may not be able to see, but she'd feel his presence. Just thinking about disrobing in the same room shot heat to her cheeks and neck. She fanned her face.

Rachel grabbed the tray of dishes and headed out the door. She needed time to herself and her wayward thoughts. In the kitchen, she took her time washing the dishes. Everyday chores had a way of easing tension. The simplest of tasks done with rote actions allowed her mind to untangle her emotions. She dried the dishes, placing them in their respective spots.

Crossing to the stove, she filled one pitcher with warm water from the reservoir and pumped fresh water into another pitcher.

She carried the pitchers back to the infirmary, setting the warm water on the counter next to the wash basin and the other in wait for her patient. Who evoked emotions she shouldn't harbor. She would remain in this room until she was certain he slept. She'd grudgingly told him she'd visit, but in truth, the more she learned about him the deeper he burrowed into her emotions.

Used instruments sat in a metal bowl of hydrogen peroxide. She pulled them out one by one, drying and wrapping them in clean cloth. Her thoughts wandered again to the man in the next room.

She'd keep a friendly distance. Once his leg healed and his stay in the infirmary ended, she'd make it a point to go the other direction when she saw him. Encouraging more than a formal relationship would only make things worse when he left.

The thought of him leaving weighed heavy on her. He was the first person since her accident who'd treated her like a normal woman. Of course, he couldn't see her hideous scar. She sighed. If he could, he'd shun her like all the others.

She'd missed several years of school due to the scarring and countless visits to doctors in her mother's quest to make her pretty again. During that time she'd lost touch with the few children who had been her friends.

When the doctors said nothing more could be done, her mother had hired a tutor. That's when she learned the art of stage makeup and began hiding her scar under lard and powder. There wasn't a day during her schooling she didn't get up earlier than everyone else and spend an hour making her face look normal. To keep her secret hidden, she remained aloof to anyone who tried to befriend her. Loneliness was easier than revealing her scar. She'd worked hard to graduate at the top of her class. All that mattered was becoming a doctor and helping others.

Upon her return to Salem, she'd hoped to form old alliances and meet new individuals and had, until William revealed her scar and deceit to anyone who would listen. Her hands shook as she put the instruments away in the cupboard. How could she have even considered marrying such a callous, hurtful man? She poured warm water into the wash basin.

The gas lights filled the room with a soft friendly glow. She glanced out the window at the sparkling night. The rain and clouds had moved on, leaving a dark sky filled with twinkling silver stars. Rachel returned her attention to the wash basin and quickly cleansed her face, neck, and hands. The pins used to hold her hair dug into her scalp. She pulled her hair out of the bun and brushed the dull brown strands. She didn't plan to put on her bed clothes, but she would braid her hair.

Clean, her hair braided, she turned the knob on the lamp, lowering the flame, leaned on the windowsill, and stared at the stars. A lifetime ago she'd made a wish on a falling star. She snorted. Her wish for a loving husband and family would never come true. Her mother's warnings that no man wanted to marry a career woman had turned her to medicine. If no man wanted a smart wife or one set on a career, she didn't need to bother with a husband.

A deep snore drifted from the other room. She glanced at the door. When she was engaged to William, why hadn't her heart raced at his nearness the way it did thinking of Clay? She'd been engaged for six months, and never once had she responded to him like she did to the man she'd only known a few weeks.

The blinking stars blurred and wobbled. Her head drooped, and her eyelids grew heavy. She pushed away from the window and stared at the hard wood table. Sleep here or curl up on the cot next to Clay. Even in her tired state her body heated at the intimate thought of sharing the same room with him.

She shuffled across the floor and into the other room. The cot creaked when she sat down. She held her breath. Clay didn't awaken. She didn't want to visit, she wanted to sleep. Careful not to make noise, she untied her boots and set them on the floor. Rachel slid in under the covers, settled her head on the pillow, and tried to ignore the manly snore coming from the next bed.

"Doctor Tarkiel! Doctor Tarkiel!"
Mrs. White's panicked shout drove Rachel

straight out of the bed onto her stocking feet. The bed next to her creaked and swearing ensued.

"Mrs. White. Here." Rachel found the gas light on the wall and turned the knob, lengthening the flame. The matron stood in the doorway, Sylvie's small body sagging in her arms.

"She's not breathing!" the woman wailed.

"Put her on the bed," Rachel ordered, running past the woman to the other room for her instruments. She grabbed the bag and towels and hurried back to the child.

She dropped to her knees alongside the cot and opened the child's mouth. Her throat had swollen shut. Rachel opened her bag, grabbed a scalpel wrapped in sterile cloth, a small piece of rubber tubing, and peroxide of hydrogen. She tucked a towel under the child's neck, poured the liquid over the skin, and used the scalpel to make an incision an inch long through the skin and trachea tube. Inserting the tubing, she watched the small chest. Sylvie's body shuddered and her chest expanded.

Rachel exhaled.

Air had reached the child's lungs.

"That's it, Sylvie, take in all the air you want." Rachel smoothed the child's hair and felt her forehead. No fever. "You're going to be fine." She glanced up at the white-faced matron.

"Tell me what happened." Rachel dabbed at the blood trickling down the child's neck. She gently spread petroleum around the incision and placed small strips of cloth over it.

"Marcie came and got me, said Sylvie was making strange noises." Mrs. White let out a long gush of air. "When I got there she was gagging, and I headed down the stairs with her. Right before I got to your door she went quiet and limp."

"You did the right thing by bringing her right down." Rachel stood and put an arm around the woman's shoulders. "If she'd gone without air any longer, I couldn't have saved her."

"What's wrong with her?" Clay's question made them both jump.

Rachel swung to the cot and the man leaning up on one elbow. "She came to me this morning with a rash. Tonight her throat closed off. But she doesn't have a fever or any other symptoms. I've been reading my medical journals, but I haven't found anything." She studied the girl. Her unseeing eyes were open.

"Sylvie—" Rachel sat on the side of the cot. "It's Dr. Tarkiel." She picked up the child's small hand. "I had to put a tube in your throat so you can breathe. Please don't touch it. When your throat isn't swollen any more, I'll take it out." Small fingers squeezed her hand.

"You're in the infirmary. Mr. Halsey is in the bed next to you with a broken leg. Tomorrow morning you two can entertain each other with stories. Right now, I want you to try and sleep."

Sylvie nodded and closed her eyes. Rachel tucked the child's hand under the covers and kissed her on the forehead. "That's a good girl. Sweet dreams." She gathered her instruments and bag from the floor and stood. Mrs. White remained at the end of the cot.

"Go back to sleep, I'll keep watch over her now." Rachel drew the woman into the other room.

"I've never lost a student." The matron's shaking statement ended in a whisper.

"You aren't going to lose one. Sylvie is fine now. Go back to bed." Rachel put an arm around Mrs. White, leading her out of the infirmary and into the hall. "She'll be fine. Go on."

The matron shuffled down the hall in her flannel nightgown and bare feet. Seeing the matron so distraught over the child warmed Rachel's heart to surly Mrs. White.

She slipped back into the infirmary, placed a chair against the wall between the two beds, sat, drew a blanket over her body, and closed her eyes.

Clay heard Rachel settling in. How could she sleep on a chair? He lay awake listening to the slight whistle of the child and the slow deep breathing of the doctor. The chair creaked, and Rachel moaned.

He reached toward the sound. His knuckles skimmed over her hair. He twisted, grimacing from the pain shooting up his leg, and used his hands to determine her position. She leaned sideways. He slipped the closest arm around her back, grasped the arm farthest away from him, and gently tugged.

She mumbled, pulling back.

"Shh, Lie down here and get some sleep." He spoke softly. "You've had a busy day. Lie down."

"Sylvie."

Her soft feminine mumble tugged his lips into a grin. She wiggled from his grasp starting to stand. He found her hand again and tugged.

"She's fine. Lie down. Rest."

She plopped onto his body. He winced at the

pain of her weight forcing his injured leg downward.

Her head rested on his chest, one arm across his middle. He grasped her leg pushing down on his injured one and draped it over his thighs. He breathed in the citrus scent of her hair and waited for the throbbing in his leg to abate. The weight of her limbs comforted him in a way he hadn't expe-rienced since childhood. Her warm curves pressed against him, fitting to his body perfectly.

Clay brushed a hand over her silky hair. Dull brown, she'd said. It was too downy and sweet smelling to be a dull brown. He traced her small ear hidden under soft, short curls. His fingers fol-lowed her velvety skin up along her hairline, down the middle of her forehead, so smooth and warm, over a small bump of a nose and pouty, supple lips. He traced the pointed edges at each side. What would it feel like to taste them? A puff of warm air misted his fingers, and she mumbled.

Clay continued his exploration, moving down her chin and the side of her face. The pads of his fingers ran over a ridge. He held his breath and traced the ridge from just above her jaw all the way to her temple. The narrow pucker of skin lay two finger widths from her hairline and ran the length of her face. A scar? How had it happened? And when?

This was why she pulled back from his touch and gave such a disparaging view of herself. Had someone left this scar on her? If so, he'd find that person and make him pay. His hands fisted. He flexed his aching knuckles and squelched his rage. It wouldn't do to show how her disfigurement riled him. His limbs gradually relaxed, and he pondered how to help her overcome her poor view of herself. How did he bring up the topic of her scar without upsetting her?

Clay wrapped his arms around Rachel's middle and clasped his hands, holding her from rolling off the bed. Her warm breath puffed across his chest. His heart expanded at the latest knowledge about the woman. He was falling for Rachel's caring nature, her witty conversation, and her touch that heated his body like no other. He'd give up on ever getting his sight back if he could end each day with her wrapped in his arms.

Chapter 9

"Doctor Tarkiel!"

The shriek jerked Rachel out of a deep sleep. She shoved her body off the bed and dizziness struck. Her eyes sprang open at the warm skin and hair under her hand. She glanced down. Clay's bare chest lay beneath her hand, and her leg sprawled wantonly across his blanket-covered thighs.

Embarrassment and a curling of heat in her abdomen shot her off the bed. She stumbled and nearly fell onto the child in the adjacent cot.

"I-I, please don't say anything to Mr. Griffin." She righted herself and raised a pleading hand to Mrs. White.

"She was falling off the chair. Rather than have her fall on the floor, I held her on the bed and let her sleep."

The monotone ring of Clay's voice nearly twitched her lips into a smile.

"I didn't know I was sleeping on—with—

him." Rachel took a step toward the matron. Mrs. White's narrowed eyes and crimson face gave no indication of forgiveness.

"It won't happen again. I'll have a cot put in the other room for tonight."

"You'll not stay here tonight. I will." Mrs. White glared at Clay and walked to the child's cot.

Rachel's face heated with rage rather than embarrassment. "I will remain here until I deem the patients no longer need monitoring." No one would toss her out of the infirmary. Mrs. White may think she ruled the school but she wasn't about to rule how things worked in here.

She slid a glance to Clay. He listened intently but didn't butt in. Any more comments from him would send the matron to the superintendent.

The matron's lip curled in a sneer. "How well did you monitor your patients last night?"

Rachel's cheeks flamed. She should have awakened rather than slip into the Clay's arms. She glanced at the handsome man, his bare chest teasing her senses.

"I was exhausted and evidently short of someone yelling"—she gave the woman a direct stare—"I required the sleep. My patients are well, and had they needed me, I would have heard them."

The matron motioned to the child and pointed to the other room. Rachel agreed, her cheeks heating again. This conversation should be held out of the young girl's hearing.

Rachel followed the woman into the next room. She crossed the threshold and Mrs. White spun on her.

"I saw the way you were sprawled all over that

man," she hissed. "What if someone other than me had walked in?"

"I didn't know I was sleeping in the same bed with him." Rachel crossed her arms and glared at the woman. What she did was her own business and no one else's. "I don't know how I ended up on his bed and had no idea I slept with a man." The intimacy of the situation heated her blood. Had he just lain there, allowing her to use him as a mattress? Had he run his hands over her? Desire ripped through her body. She lowered her lashes, hoping the woman hadn't caught sight of the carnal feelings building inside.

"Please ask Mrs. Daniels to bring up breakfast for the patients and me." She took a step toward her patients and pivoted back to the woman. "When Mr. Smith comes in, have him come see me."

Mrs. White's outraged face deepened in color. She marched out of the room mumbling under her breath.

Rachel sighed. How long would it be before Mr. Griffin stormed up here and tossed her out?

No time to worry about that. She had patients to tend and they were her first priority. She marched into the room and found Clay sitting with his bare back against the wall. His powerful chest sprinkled with curls made her breath catch. She'd spent part of the night sleeping on that broad expanse. And so tired she didn't know it.

"Are you going to lose your job because of me?"

The apology in his soft spoken words warmed her. She stepped toward him, but stalled her feet and shifted to the child.

"I don't know." She sat on the edge of Sylvie's bed and inspected the child's incision. "I hope you're feeling better, Sylvie. Open your mouth, please."

The swelling in her throat had gone down, which pleased Rachel. What had made it close up, and what had caused the rash? A visit to Dr. Runkle would be prudent.

Clay's deep voice broke into her thoughts. "You were moaning and sounded uncomfortable so I tugged your hand and you just flopped onto my bed. I only wanted to make you comfortable."

"What? Oh, I know you didn't mean any harm." She glanced at the man. Worry furrowed his brow and tipped down the corners of his full mouth. Quivers of desire vibrated in her lower abdomen and heated the juncture of her legs. She drew her gaze back to the child. "I'll deal with the repercussions later. Sylvie needs attention now."

She patted Sylvie's arm. "Your throat is open again. I'll take that rubber tube out and sew you up as soon as Mr. Smith arrives to help." The child shivered and shook her head. "Shh." Rachel drew Sylvie's small body into her arms. "You'll be good as new once the tube comes out and I stitch the incision closed. You won't feel anything. Mr. Smith will help you sleep while I make you better."

"Sylvie," Clay said, "you want to sit with me while Doctor Tarkiel gets ready? I know some pretty good stories."

Clay's soft tone melted Rachel's heart. "She can't talk, but she's nodding." Rachel stood and carried Sylvie to the other bed. She placed the small child on the cot next to Clay. His size made the child appear even smaller. He wrapped an arm around Sylvie and smiled.

"Hi, Sylvie. I don't think we've met before. I don't take all the same classes the rest of you do." His hand rested lightly on her blonde curls. "Do you like fairy tales?" Her head bobbed and a smile spread across his face. "I suppose being a girl you like ones that have princesses as opposed to dragons." She nodded. "You're lucky my ma told my brothers and me both."

Tears burned Rachel's eyes as she watched Clay interact with the child. He would be a wonderful father. She spun from the sight and into the main room, fighting the emotions he stirred up in her. He wasn't looking for a scarred wife, and she had a career to build. Even if her heart longed to share her life with someone like the man telling the tale of Rapunzel.

"Dr. Tarkiel?" Mr. Smith called from the doorway.

"Mr. Smith. I'll need your assistance with Sylvie this morning." She shook away her dreary thoughts and set about preparing the necessary tools. The handyman stood at the door, his hat in his hands. "Come in and wash your hands. I need you to keep Sylvie asleep while I stitch her trachea."

His eyes widened.

"You'll be fine. It's the same thing you did while I set Mr. Halsey's leg yesterday. You have steady hands and a constitution of steel. That's what I need."

Mr. Smith straightened and squared his shoulders. He crossed the room, placed his hat on a chair, and began washing his hands.

"Everything is ready. I'll get our patient." She stepped into the room.

"And the prince and princess lived happily ever after." Clay's soothing voice ended the story. His large arm curled around the child's body, cradling her next to his side. Sylvie held his other hand, playing with his fingers. The soft smile on his lips knotted Rachel's throat and wrapped her heart in a blanket of warmth. She swallowed the lump and walked to the bed.

"Sylvie, we're ready."

The child clung to Clay.

"It's okay, Sylvie," Clay said. "Dr. Tarkiel and Mr. Smith worked on me yesterday and I'm still alive."

Though the chuckle in his voice was lost on the child, it made Rachel smile. Clay patted Sylvie's head, and she wrapped her small arms around his neck.

"You want me to come with you?" he asked, his hand still resting on her small head. She nodded. "Okay—"

"It isn't a good idea for you—" Rachel cut off her words when Clay locked her in a glare.

He swung his uninjured leg over the edge of the bed, dragged the heavy cast across the mattress, and placed it on the floor, wincing. He clutched the child to his chest and stood. They both wobbled.

"Mr. Smith!" Rachel stepped to Clay's side, grasping a solid arm and holding his body in an upright position. The handyman dashed through the door and gripped Clay's other arm.

"Sylvie won't let me help her without Mr. Halsey. We need to get them both into the other room."

The handyman rolled his eyes and shook his head. He placed an arm around Clay's shoulders and helped steady the two as they shuffled into the main room.

Clay held the child and pushed his aching body across the floor. He'd had little experience with children, but he found the last hour or so holding Sylvie and telling her stories brought happiness to him unlike anything he'd yet experienced. Her thin arms gripping his neck and the patter of her heart against his chest spurred a wish to have children of his own—a wish he'd all but given up on. He'd assumed when he became blind he'd never be a father. But maybe—just maybe he could. The thought seeped in and started to take root. Being blind would make fatherhood a challenge, but he'd protect anyone he loved with the same fierceness he'd displayed before he lost his sight.

His leg ached, his bruised body ached, but he wouldn't let this child down. A hip high table bumped against him.

Clay set Sylvie down and removed her arms from his neck. "I'll sit right here and hold your hand."

Something touched the back of his knees. He hoped it was a chair, because his weak body wasn't going to hold him up much longer. Perspiration cooled his forehead. He wiped it with his free hand and sat down. "Thank you," he whispered at the flutter of cloth against his bare arm. Citrus filled his senses.

"You're welcome."

Rachel's quiet reply eased some of his pain and curved his lips in a smile. Maybe she'd forgiven him for pulling her onto his bed.

"Sylvie, relax, honey, and just breathe in and out."

Rachel's soft melodious tone reminded Clay of his mother's voice soothing him when he was ill.

The child's hand slowly relaxed in his. He listened to the sound of Rachel's even breathing, the rustle of her skirt, and the clink of instruments as she worked. A sweet scent mixed with Rachel's lemon aura. His eyes grew heavy.

"Mr. Smith, you may remove the cloth and help Mr. Halsey to the other room."

The authoritative tone shook Clay awake. "I have to be here when she wakes up." He tightened his grip on the child's hand. A Halsey always kept a promise.

"Mr. Smith will help you to the commode in the other room. While you are using the facilities, we can move the beds together, and you can hold her hand until she wakes. But I want you back in bed. You aren't well enough to remain up for long periods."

Jasper's rough hand gripped his arm, lifting him from the chair.

"Doc, it ain't proper him wanderin' around with no clothes."

"Once you get him settled on the commode, run out to his cottage and bring him back a n-nightshirt."

Clay grinned at her stutter. The practical, efficient doctor appeared flustered talking about night clothes. It was comical considering what he wore at the moment.

"I don't own one," Clay said, raising an eyebrow and enjoying the fact his comment would fluster her.

"H-how—what do you sleep in?"

The rise in her voice tickled him. "My drawers."

"Well, then, bring him a fresh set, tops and bottoms."

"Doc, it ain't proper for me to rummage through his things. Mrs. White, she don't like me messin' with nothin' that ain't mine." The reluctance in Jasper's voice rang like a church bell at a funeral.

"I might need Jasper." Clay faced the direction Rachel's voice sounded. "You have my permission to find me some clothes you deem decent."

Jasper pulled him away from the table. He didn't like having to lean on the man, but his strength had faded considerably. The trek back through the door to the room with his cot had to be a mile or better. That's what it felt like the way his good leg shook and the bad leg throbbed.

"Pull down your drawers and sit." Jasper's gruff impersonal tone didn't help his confusion.

"What are you talking about?"

"The commode's behind you. Sit and you know..." The man's steps retreated.

"Hey, I'm not sitting in the middle of the room am I?" He might want to get personal with the good doctor, but having her walk in on him in this state wasn't what he had in mind.

"Yer behind a screen. If ya hurry she won't come in afore yer done."

Chapter 10

Rachel didn't care for the idea of going through Clay's personals, but she also knew if Mrs. White or anyone else caught the handyman going through a student's things he'd lose his job. She pressed her shoulders back and walked out of the infirmary, leaving Mr. Smith to watch over her patients.

The gravel crunched under her feet intensifying her already strung nerves as she walked to the cottage Clay shared with Mr. Smith. She stepped into Clay's side of the cottage.

The wool jacket he'd worn the first day hung on a peg along with the wool trousers. A comb, toothbrush and powder, straight razor, strap, and shave soap lay in a perfect line atop the bureau beside a photograph of five men, a petite woman, and a boy of about twelve or thirteen. She held the shave soap to her nose, inhaling the spicy scent, and studied the photograph. The smallest of the men and the woman held hands in the middle of the group. A boy stood beside the woman and two men flanked both sides. Clay stood alongside a man slightly taller than he. The amiable smile he aimed at the photographer she'd only witnessed once. The brightness in his eyes she'd never see. Her heart longed to know the man he was before losing his sight. Would he have accepted her, scar and all?

The scent of the soap trickled through her musings, reminding her of the man and why she'd entered his room. She glanced down at the personal items again. He might like these. She scooped the toiletries into her apron pocket.

Her gaze lingered on the wide bed. She could visualize his large frame sprawled across the mattress. His shoulders filling the whole cot in the infirmary came to mind. The only way for two to sleep on the small bed would be for her to sleep on top of him. Her cheeks heated, shooting a rush of flames to her extremities.

She fanned her face and pulled open the bureau drawer. Mrs. White sleeping in the infirmary would be a good option considering the way Rachel's body responded to Clay. She ran her hands over the neatly folded flannel shirts. Three. Two pair of denim work pants lay beside the shirts. She opened the next drawer. Dark wool socks were stacked in between one set of full body long johns and two sets of underdrawers.

Rachel grabbed a pair of socks, one pair of underdrawers, opened the top drawer and grabbed a flannel shirt. She shoved the drawer closed. Something in the drawer slid and thumped. She reopened the drawer and reached under the clothing.

Her fingertips brushed the binding of a book. The scuffed brown leather cover of the small journal showed wear.

She shouldn't peek inside, but she longed to know everything about Clay.

Opening the book, she stared at neatly printed block words, numbers, and line drawings. A third of the book held mechanical diagrams and descriptions. What had he been trying to build when he lost his sight?

A bird squawked, and she slapped the book shut, slipping it back under his clothing. She gathered the items and hurried back to the infirmary.

Mr. Smith had moved Sylvie onto a cot. Clay wasn't in sight. "Got him cleaned up and waitin' for his clothes." The man took the garments from her arms and disappeared behind the screen.

She hastened to the restless child waking from the chloroform. "Shh, Sylvie. Lie still, you're going to be fine."

A clatter of dishes in the other room popped her to her feet, and she rushed to see who'd arrived. Mrs. Daniels stood next to the examining table. Steam curled up from a large platter of dishes sitting on the table.

"I brought the food you asked for. How is that dear child, Sylvie?"

The older woman had cooked for the school longer than any of the current staff had been in residence. Her shoulders hunched slightly and her short carriage appeared frail. Guilt assaulted Rachel over the woman carrying such a large heavy platter.

"She's on the mend. But I have to find out

what is causing her rash." Rachel motioned to the door. "You can go see her as soon as Mr. Smith gets Mr. Halsey settled in bed."

The handyman stepped out of the room. "He's in bed and holdin' the child's hand."

"Thank you for all your help Mr. Smith. I don't know how I'd handle Mr. Halsey without you." Rachel crossed the room and smiled up at the man. "I have one more favor. I need to keep Sylvie here for another night or two. Could you bring a cot into this room for me to use?"

He stared at her a moment, and then nodded.

"Thank you." The farther away from Clay she slept the better. She was intrigued by the way her body responded to him, but she had to keep a professional distance. The handyman shuffled out the door, and Mrs. Daniels picked up the tray.

"Let me get that. You go on ahead and see Sylvie." Rachel smiled and eased the tray away from the woman. She followed the cook into the room. Her heart rammed against her ribs and air whooshed between her lips.

Clay sat up in bed, one flannel clad arm stretched out, and his large hand held Sylvie's small one. The smile on the child's face was infectious. Sylvie grinned from ear to ear as if the two shared a private joke. Rachel's gaze returned to Clay. The two day stubble darkening his face, his crooked nose, and the arch of one brow gave him an intimidating appearance, contradicting the gentle way he held Sylvie's hand.

"Dear, how are you feeling?" Mrs. Daniels asked, nearing the child's bed.

"Like I was thrown in front of a train."

Clay's comment stopped the cook. She glanced at him, a smile cracking her thin face.

"You don't look like it, Mr. Halsey." Mrs. Daniels snickered and patted Sylvie's left hand. "I brought you some broth, and when you're feeling up to swallowing more, I'll have some fresh cookies."

"I can swallow fine." The laugh lines around his eyes crinkled.

"You, sir, will get cookies when you learn to mind your manners. You know full well I'm talking to Sylvie." Mrs. Daniels's voice chastised, but she winked at Rachel.

Rachel glanced at Clay's crestfallen expression and slapped a hand over her mouth to stifle the giggle bubbling.

"I have your breakfast, Mr. Halsey." Rachel set the tray on the chair beside Clay's bed.

"Real food, not just broth?" The longing in his voice made her smile.

"Real food." She picked up the plate. "Hold out your hands." He complied, and she placed the plate on them.

Clay settled the warm plate on his lap and raised his right hand for an eating utensil. A cold metal object met his palm. Rachel's warm slender fingers wrapped around his fist.

"Scrambled eggs at three. Ham, already cut into bite sized pieces, at six. Bread at nine." She moved his hand around the plate as she spoke. Her firm but gentle hold launched visions of her gripping another part of him and jolted his senses like a jab with a hot pitchfork. He jerked, and she released his hand. He resisted the urge to find her hand and draw it back.

"Thank you." He stabbed at the ham. She remained near, and her citrus scent played tag with his already inflamed desire. He'd hated to wash when Jasper handed him a rag and soap earlier. Her scent had remained on his skin from sleeping on him. He'd dozed off and on while she slept sprawled across him as if he were a mattress and not an aroused male.

He shoved food in his mouth to refrain from speaking. He hadn't heard the cook leave, and talking intimately with Rachel while the child was present wouldn't be a good idea. But they would have to talk.

Skirts rustled. "Here you go, Sylvie. Let's prop you up and I'll feed you the broth with a spoon. Small amounts at a time would be best for your throat."

Rachel's soft voice laced with authority made him smile.

"Doc Tarkiel?" Donny called from another room.

"In here," Rachel's voice sang out. Clay smiled. Even when she raised her voice it flowed like a sweet song.

The cadence of Donny's hesitant gait entered the room.

"How's Clay?" Donny asked, his voice a bit shaky.

"I'm fine. Soon as I finish eating, I want to continue reading." Lazy footsteps approached his bed.

"Donny, don't sit in that chair." Mrs. Daniels said. Hurried, ratta-tapping steps rounded the end of Clay's bed and stopped. Dishes rattled. "Now you can sit."

"What'd you do to break a leg?" Donny's tone held uncensored boredom mixed with curiosity.

"I fell off the shed roof." Clay took a bite of the mushy eggs. He hated mushy eggs, but that seemed to be all they served here.

"How'd you get up there?"

The awe in the boy's voice lodged the bite in Clay's throat. He coughed and managed to swallow.

"By being stupid."

A snicker drifted from his left. The pitch and feminine tone was Rachel's.

"What's so amusing, Dr. Tarkiel?"

"I find it amusing that you would readily admit to being stupid. Which I find quite accurate in this instance."

The lilt of her words brought a smile to his face.

"It takes a big man to admit when he's done something wrong."

Clay's dimple tugged on his cheek from the huge grin he sported. Someone other than Rachel coughed. He released his aching facial muscles and finished the food on his plate.

"I'll take that, Mr. Halsey," Mrs. Daniels said near his head. He raised the plate, and someone snatched it from his hands. "Would you like coffee, water, or milk?" the cook asked.

"Coffee."

A warm object weighed down his outstretched palm. He slid his fingers up the side and found the handle of a coffee mug.

A spoon clattered to his left. "Mrs. Daniels,

could you sit with these three for a while? I need to change clothes and consult with Dr. Runkle about Sylvie's condition."

"I still have dishes to wash and the midday meal to prepare." Dishes clattered and the cook's tapping gait faded.

Rachel's sigh whispered through the room. "Donny, would you go find Mrs. White? I must visit with Dr. Runkle. She'll have to keep an eye on you three while I'm gone."

"Aww, does it have to be her?"

Donny's attitude matched Clay's sentiments. Anyone but the matron. He didn't like her high-handed tactics or her attitude toward Jasper.

"I'm sorry, but she's the only other staff available."

Something heavy and square plopped on Clay's lap. He flinched and jerked his injured leg. Pain shot from his ankle to his hip. "Wha—"

"Here, hold the books while I go look for her." The chair scraped the floor. Donny's lazy gait faded from the room.

"Are you okay?" Rachel's smooth gentle hands whisked the hair from his forehead.

"Just a twinge when the brat dumped the books on my lap." He'd get even with the kid. Her hand drifted down his face. Her intake of breath and hastily withdrawn hand accelerated his heart. Did he affect her as she did him?

"I-I'm going to step behind the screen. T-to clean up and change," Rachel stammered. "You two tell stories."

He could tell a story and still strain to hear her every move. Her footsteps retreated from the room, and then hurried back.

"You can start talking any time," she ordered, and Clay chuckled.

He cleared his throat. "So Sylvie, do you want a tale about a fierce dragon?" He slid his hand up the child's arm to her face, cupping the small head in his hand. Her soft curls rubbed his palm as she shook her head. He laughed. "I guess that means another girl story."

A faint snicker drifted from the corner. "You take too much delight in me telling girl stories," he said to the corner of the room.

"I think it's telling that your mother of five boys took it upon herself to tell you all stories and not just ones about dragons and knights."

The splash of water meant she had her dress off. What part of her body could she be washing? What would it feel like to aid her in undressing? Run his hands over her soft skin? Heat pooled in his gut.

Sylvie pulled on his hand. He cleared his throat and pushed the lustful thoughts aside.

"Once upon a time there was a girl named Cinderella..." He told the story, making up what he couldn't remember. His ears strained to hear Rachel's movements, but the click of the matron's footsteps caught his attention first.

"Hurry, that huffy matron is coming," he whispered loud enough for Rachel to hear.

Footsteps approached. The odd click of Mrs. White's shoes and the adolescent shuffle of Donny entered the other room.

"Mrs. White, thank you for helping out." Rachel's cheerful voice didn't portray any stress.

Clay smiled. Sylvie tugged on his hand, and he had to think back to where he left off in the story. He picked up the tale as Rachel and the matron's voices drifted away.

If he weren't laid up, he'd offer to walk with her to see this other doctor. The only good to come from his injury was being able to spend more time with the intriguing doctor. And he planned to make the most of his time.

Chapter 11

Rachel patted the side of her face, making sure the make-up felt smooth. Her mother had packed the face powder and small container of lard to mix it in. Dr. Runkle, who'd cared for her after the accident, knew of her scar, but she refused to walk around town without the make-up. Though she wasn't vain like her mother and sister, she didn't like witnessing the pity or horror in people's eyes.

She crossed Dr. Runkle's front porch and knocked on the door. The physician had retired several years before her return to Salem. She'd hoped he would share his practice with her upon her return. But due to a heart attack which left his left side paralyzed, he'd given it over to another doctor before she finished her schooling. The new physician didn't approve of women practicing medicine.

Dr. Runkle opened the door, leaning heavily on a cane. "Rachel, what a wonderful surprise!" His gravelly voice shook more than the last time they'd visited. Hands, gnarled and knobby from arthritis, waved her into the dark interior of his simple single-story home.

She'd been in his home as a patient and a colleague. She ambled down the hall, allowing for his slow movements, and entered his office. The room overflowed with books on shelves and tables just as it had the day he told her mother nothing more could be done for the scar marring her oldest daughter's face.

Rachel inhaled—musty books, stale cigar smoke, and liniment assailed her nostrils.

"Is this a social or professional call?" he asked, shuffling to the chair behind his desk. Rachel sat in a wooden chair in front of the desk.

"Professional. I have a student at the blind school who broke out in a rash two days ago. Last night her throat closed up and I had to perform a tracheotomy. The swelling was down this morning, but I don't know what's causing her symptoms. She isn't feverish and doesn't exhibit any symptoms other than the rash and swelling." She ruffled the curls around her face.

"Sounds like there's something in the school irritating her. Either something she breathes, eats, or comes in contact with. You're going to have to find out all you can about where she lives, and then figure out what it is that's different."

Rachel leaned back in the chair. "Thank you. I've been reading my books and couldn't find anything that made sense."

"Sometimes it isn't what you find in the books but what you've encountered that helps you diagnose."

She smiled. "That's why I came to you. With your years of knowledge, I figured you'd know what I needed to do." She started to stand.

His fading green eyes stared at her. "How's it going over at the school?"

"It's going as well as can be expected. Besides the child, I set a broken leg yesterday on an adult patient. He climbed on the roof." She smiled as she thought of how Clay had responded to Donny's question that morning.

"A blind adult? What was he doing on the roof?"

"Helping the handyman. He doesn't take all the classes the younger students do." She hoped her disclosure didn't bring bad light to the school.

Dr. Runkle shook his head. "I take it this man hasn't been blind for very long?"

"No, he's still testing his limits on what he can and can't do." She thought of his audacity of pulling her onto his bed, and her heart accelerated. He also tested her self-control with his charm.

"He should keep you busy during his stay at the school." The old man chuckled.

In more ways than you know. "We're all hoping this last escapade will teach him."

"I doubt it." Laugh lines around his eyes crinkled. "Any man who would climb onto a roof when he's blind is not a man to let his condition limit him."

"Thank you for your help." Rachel stood. "I don't want to leave either patient for too long. It's hard telling what kind of trouble they might get into."

Dr. Runkle placed his hands on the desk and

pushed as though to stand.

"I can find my way out." She smiled brightly at the gentleman and hurried down the hall and out onto the street.

Rachel thought of the doctor's words as she wandered back through town toward the school.

"Rachel!"

She stopped and scanned the boardwalk. Her sister and a state representative sat at an outside table in front of a café. The man, Wayne Wright, had been keeping time with Celeste on a regular basis.

Celeste smiled at the man as he stood, took her gloved hand, and kissed her knuckles. She watched a sparkle light her sister's green eyes as the sun shimmered on the blonde ringlets cascading down her back from under a fashionable hat. Her sister had to be the most beautiful woman in Salem. Even women stared at her.

Rachel waited until the man moved on and took the seat next to her sister.

"Are you going to make the dinner party tonight? Mother will be livid if you don't." Celeste waved her hand, and a waiter arrived with two cups of steaming tea and a plate of biscuits.

"I'm afraid you'll have to tell mother I won't be there. I have two patients in the infirmary and can't possibly attend dinner." And she didn't want to attend. She hated her mother's social gatherings. She hated the gossip that always seemed to flow, and since her break up with William she seemed to be the usual subject.

"You're away from them now. Surely, you can be away for a few hours tonight." Celeste raised her tea cup and sipped.

"I was on my way back from Dr. Runkle's. I needed his opinion on one of the patients." She picked up a biscuit and nibbled. It had a spicy sweet flavor. She shouldn't be lolling here with her sister. "I need to remain at the school night and day for a few more days. At least until I figure out what's causing a rash on Sylvie."

Celeste's glazed-over eyes indicated her boredom hearing about Rachel's trials as a doctor at the school. Celeste and her parents only cared about politics. It was too bad women couldn't vote, no doubt Celeste would have been the first in line. Instead, she and their mother used their wiles to help influence political decisions and sway votes.

"Thank you for the tea, I really need to hurry back. Give Mother my regrets." Rachel stood. "And thank her for sending extra clothes yesterday."

"She isn't going to be happy about tonight." Celeste raised an eyebrow. "You really can't hide from your social obligations."

"I'm not hiding. I have professional obligations to attend to tonight."

Celeste shook her head. "Keep telling yourself that and you'll be a spinster."

"I could do worse." Like be in a marriage with no love.

Celeste snorted in an unladylike fashion. "Nothing is worse than being alone."

"I won't be alone. I'll have my family, friends, and patients." Thoughts of the comfort and security she'd experienced in Clay's arms that morning heated her neck and warmed her cheeks. After the initial shock wore off she'd realized, even with the short amount of sleep she'd had, she'd slept deeper and woken more rested than any night since the accident.

"But at night you'll lie in bed alone."

"What do you know about having a man in your bed?" She studied her sister. As far as she knew, her sister had yet to bed with a man. Celeste didn't need to go that far to get a man to do her bidding.

A sparkle lit Celeste's eyes. "Only what married friends have said."

"Do you have a man in mind for yourself?" Jealousy burned in her chest. Even though no man would marry her it rankled to think her younger sister would soon marry.

"Not one who gives me the time of day." Celeste's usually bright demeanor darkened.

Ah, so her sister had her sights set on someone who didn't cater to her charms. This could be interesting to follow.

"I really need to go. Give my regrets."

Rachel strode away from the café, playing the conversation over in her head. Discovering who Celeste had her eye on would almost be worth the discomfort of attending a couple of her mother's parties. It couldn't be the man at the café. He'd looked ready to sweep her off her feet.

Her stomach clenched. Regret washed over her like a dark shroud. She'd never have the satisfaction of being swept off her feet. Few men liked a wife who had career goals. Married women physicians she'd conversed with who had open-minded husbands had mentioned it was unwise to have children since they were in constant contact with diseases that could harm their offspring. This was the one concern about her profession that made it easy to concentrate on her career and forget about marriage and a family.

The blind school sat on two large lots several blocks from the downtown activity. She walked up the front steps, eager to start questioning Sylvie about her home life.

Mr. Griffin met her at the door of the building. "Where have you been? Mrs. White was needed to help a female student."

"I was consulting with Dr. Runkle about Sylvie." She pulled off her bonnet. "I'm sure Mr. Halsey could handle Sylvie. He's quite good with children."

"You know the policy. The only time the students are left alone is at night when they're sleeping." Mr. Griffin matched her hurried steps to the infirmary.

She crossed the threshold and smiled. Clay's voice floated to the outer room. Sylvie must have talked him into telling another fairy tale. How many did he know?

Rachel dumped her bonnet and gloves on the counter and crossed to the infirmary. Clay leaned against the wall, one arm holding Sylvie's small body on the cot next to him. The books Donny brought sat on the chair by his bed. The child smiled and nodded, lost in the story.

Rachel swept her hand toward the two, showing Mr. Griffin he had nothing to fear.

"Hello, I'm back."

Clay finished his sentence and nodded, smiling. "We'd begun to think people forgot we were here." He leaned his cheek against Sylvie's blonde curls.

Rachel's heart thumped at the sight of the large man so sweetly holding the child.

"We didn't forget about you. I need Sylvie to scoot over onto her bed so I can ask her some questions." She walked to the side of Sylvie's bed and helped ease the child out of the hard strong arm Rachel knew could cradle gently. Heat crept up her neck as her thoughts roamed to waking in his arms that morning. She glanced briefly to the door hoping Mr. Griffin had left. He hadn't. Why did he linger and watch?

Clay wiggled, lowering his body to a flat position. He sighed and closed his eyes. Was he relieved to not have to babysit, or just to change position?

She walked around the beds to his side and tugged the sheet up to his chin. The urge to lean down and kiss his forehead tugged her body forward, but Mr. Griffin coughed and she pulled back.

The sound of Clay's breathing and the steady rhythm of his chest rising and lowering proved he'd fallen asleep. She set the books on the floor and carried the chair around to Sylvie's side.

She sat, gathering one of Sylvie's hands in hers. "Can you speak now?"

The child placed her free hand over the bandage on her neck and bobbed her head, making Rachel smile.

"Where does your family live?"

The child forced a hoarse whisper. "Jacksonville."

Rachel glanced at the superintendent. "What

can you tell me about your family?"

"I'll get her registration form." Mr. Griffin disappeared out the door.

A sigh slipped through Rachel's lips, and her body sagged with relief. Apparently, Mrs. White hadn't told him about finding her sleeping with Clay.

"Sylvie, take your time and tell me about your family." Rachel held the child's hand and hoped she could learn something valuable.

"We move around a lot. Pa's a lumberjack." Sylvie's hand relaxed, and she closed her eyes. "There's me and my two brothers. Ma does wash for the single men."

Mrs. Daniels shuffled into the room carrying a tray laden with lunch.

"I brought your food before the rest arrive in the dining hall for lunch. That way you don't have to wait so long to be fed." She patted Sylvie's head and glanced at Clay.

Rachel peeked at him. His eyelids eased open, and he stretched his arms lazily. His corded muscles flexed, stretching the flannel sleeve around his upper arm. Her mouth grew dry watching the male action. Shaking her head, she smiled at the cook.

"Thank you. I'll get these two started on their lunch." Her conversation with Sylvie hadn't enlightened her at all. Mrs. Daniels nodded and shuffled back out the door.

"Mr. Halsey? Are you awake enough to eat?"

"Yeah. How long have I been napping?" He put his hands on either side of him, grimaced, and pulled his body to a sitting position. His uninjured leg drew up, his knee making a tent out of the covers.

"Not very long." She picked up a cold glass of milk. "Sylvie, would you like your milk first?"

The child shook her head. "I don't like it. Mrs. White makes me drink it, but my ma said it made me sick when I was little."

Rachel stared at the glass of white liquid. Could this be what was making the child sick? "I'll tell Mrs. White not to make you drink it, and let's see if that makes you better."

Sylvie nodded and smiled.

"Here's your plate." Rachel set the plate of food in the child's small hands. "Mashed potatoes are all you get just yet. Chew it real good before you swallow."

"I will." The child touched the bandage around her neck.

Rachel picked up the tray, stood, and set the tray on the chair. She carried a plate and cup of coffee around to Clay's bed.

"Coffee or food?" she asked, grinning at his outstretched hands.

"Food."

She placed the plate in his hands.

"Same as Sylvie?" he asked.

"No. Roast at three o'clock, potatoes at six, and bread at nine." An urge to sit on the edge of the bed started her knees trembling.

"Go eat, we'll be fine." He took a bite of bread and stared forward.

"Coffee's on the floor." Rachel set the cup down and scurried back to Sylvie and her lunch. Her body trembled and her eyes strayed to watch Clay eat. She'd witnessed other men up close, had taken care of many at the hospital at the college and during her year of practice with another doctor. Never before had she experienced the disorientation and stimulation looking at Clay generated.

One more night. Make sure Sylvie continued to recover, and then she'd tell Mr. Griffin to allow Mr. Smith to sleep in here with Clay. She didn't trust herself.

Chapter 12

Clay scowled and swung his legs over the side of the bed. He'd been stuck in this infirmary for two weeks, only traveling far enough to use the commode.

He needed fresh air. Pushing to his feet, he put a hand out to the wall to steady his swaying body. A wave of dizziness made him light-headed. Damn, lying around made a body weak.

"What do you think you're doing?" The stern yet quizzical question made him smile.

"I need fresh air. Some sunshine on my face." Rachel's citrus scent wafted around him, and her small hands grasped his arm. Ever since the night he held her in his arms, she'd stayed her distance, but they were alone now. She was his only anchor to keep him from toppling over if his legs gave out.

"You can't go outside in your drawers. Sit back down and I'll fetch a pair of your trousers and have Mr. Smith walk you out to a chair in the back lawn."

He lowered his body. "Will you sit with me?"

"I have things to do." Her tone was curt, but her hands lingered on his arm. Her touch and fragrance heated his body.

"Say yes. You know you want some sunshine, too."

"I have bandages to roll."

"Bring them outside, I'll help you. I need a break from reading."

"Sit down. I'll get your trousers and Mr. Smith." Her scent and steps faded away.

Mrs. White hadn't told the superintendent about finding the doctor in his bed, so that wasn't why she kept her distance.

She'd left his care at night to Jasper, and Donny hovered during the afternoons, leaving him without a chance to question her about the scar he'd found. Was it red and ugly? Was that really why she worked at a blind school, because her patients couldn't see the scar? And why she avoided social situations?

He wanted time alone with her, away from all the prying eyes and ears at the school to really get to know Doctor Rachel Tarkiel.

Heavy footsteps resonated through the room and the floor vibrated under his feet.

"That was fast," he said, reaching his hands out for his britches.

"Doc says you want to set outside." Jasper's deep voice grumbled about three feet in front of him. Rough cloth scraped Clay's fingertips.

He grasped the top and slid his feet into the legs, wrestling the pant leg over the hard heavy bandage. Inhaling, he gave his weakened body a moment to rest and his dizziness to settle. He slowly stood, leaning against the wall and pulled the garment up his thighs and secured the waist.

"Yes, I want to sit out in the bright sunshine and breathe in the fresh air. I'm tired of the lye and whatever it is in this infirmary that makes my lungs ache." He sat and held out a hand. "Did you bring my boots?"

"Yeah."

His hand slapped against worn leather. He tipped his toes in and tugged the boot over the foot of his uninjured leg.

"Guess the other foot has to go bare." He'd fingered the knee to ankle bandage encasing his leg. A boot wouldn't fit.

He pushed to his feet, again leaning on the wall while his dark world settled. "Ready."

"You sure?" Jasper's strong hand grasped his arm.

"Yes. Go slow, I'll be fine." Clay clenched his jaw and started forward. His uninjured leg wobbled. He reached out to steady himself, and his knuckles rapped a door jamb. He'd made it out of one room. Jasper turned him slightly to his right. His heavy bandaged leg dragged. He used all his energy to force his leg to pick up the weight.

The pungent scent of lye swept over him. Jasper turned him right again. How many steps to the outside door? His strength diminished with each step he fought to take. Maybe going outside had been a bad idea. Sweat dampened his forehead and trickled down his temple. Both legs wobbled and ached.

Jasper stopped and stepped away, leaving Clay

gasping for air and willing his weary limbs to stop quivering and hold him erect until the man came back.

A door creaked, wafting fresh air over Clay. He breathed deep, and a new surge of energy charged through him.

Jasper grasped his arm and led him forward. Gravel poked Clay's stocking-clad foot for two steps. Grass cushioned his steps for three more strides. Sun warmed his face and he breathed in the sweet scent of flowers in bloom.

Jasper's hands shifted him and pushed down. "Sit."

Clay had no choice. Between the man's strength and his shaky legs, his backside landed harder than he liked on a solid seat. He gripped a wooden arm with one hand. His other hand splayed across a smooth wooden surface. He sat on a bench. Maybe Rachel would join him after all.

"Thank you, Jasper." Clay sucked in the fresh air and willed his hammering heart to slow. Recovering would take time if his weariness from this short walk were any indication.

"You gonna be all right here?"

"I'm fine. Unless you have something I could do with my hands while I sit here?" The citrus scent he associated with Rachel swirled around him, warming him in places she'd best not know.

"I brought the bandages you offered to roll."

Rachel's brisk and formal tone amused him. He smiled. "Good. I hate sitting around doing nothing." He expected her to sit next to him. Instead, something hard brushed his arm and crunched like dried twigs beside him.

"On the bench beside you is a basket of cloth strips. Find an end and start rolling." Her scent rippled around him, and her skirts rustled. "There's another basket on the ground by your right foot. Place the rolled bandages in that basket."

Clay pulled a folded letter out of his shirt pocket. He'd received it the day before but hadn't asked anyone to read it to him.

He held out the unopened envelope. "Could you read this letter to me?"

"I-I'm sure you wouldn't want me to see your personal mail."

Her stammer and low whisper surprised him. Why would she worry about reading a letter that had to be from one of his brothers?

"I can't read it, and other than you, Jasper, and Donny, I don't want anyone else knowing my business."

Paper crackled. "Do you know who it's from?"

"No. I figure one of my brothers. I doubt Ethan since he should be sailing toward England. That leaves three other possibilities."

"It's from Hank."

He nodded. "Figured as much, he'd be the only lonely one."

"Oh, thank you, Jasper." Her skirts rustled.

"'Dear Clay.'"

Her sweet voice was head level. Jasper must have brought her something to sit on.

"'I wasn't sure if you are up to writing letters yet, but thought I'd fill you in on the stamp mill and what I know about Gil and his family and Zeke and Maeve.'"

Clay listened to the lilt of her voice and only

half heard the news of his brothers. He wished she were on the bench beside him instead of the basket of rags.

Her voice stopped.

He shifted his injured leg and waited.

"You could roll the bandages while I read."

Clay picked up the end of a rag and started rolling.

"'The miners have been flocking in here wanting to schedule days to run their diggings through the mill. There are days we could have put in double the stamps.'" She stopped. "Could you explain to me what a stamp mill does?"

Rachel stared at the transformation on Clay's face. His mouth lifted at the corners. His shoulders squared, and his back straightened. The stamp mill was definitely the Halsey brothers' pride and joy.

"It has five stamps which are large heavy stones attached to long poles that move up and down like pistons." He moved one hand up the same time the other went down. "In a motion like this with each hitting at a different time. Small pieces of rock drop under these and are crushed, revealing the flakes and nuggets of gold."

"From the letter it sounds like you do this for other miners?" She wanted to learn all she could about Clay and how he planned to fit in when he left. Knowing he would be safe with his family helped, but he had to feel needed as well.

He grinned. "It was Ethan's idea, but we all agreed. We use Sundays to collect our own gold. The rest of the week we allow the other miners to cart their diggings in. We receive a percentage of what comes from their rock."

"So if there isn't any gold, you don't get any-thing? Isn't that a lot of work for nothing?" She wasn't greedy, but she believed in getting paid for her time.

Clay grinned and nodded. "It's rare a miner brings in rock that doesn't have gold in it. We have men working for us, and they have to get paid."

"What was your job before you lost your sight?"

"I helped build the mill and lay the ore cart railing. It had barely started when all hell broke loose." His brow furrowed, and his mouth straightened into a disapproving line.

"What happened?"

He sucked in air and exhaled. The white knuckles on the hand holding the rolled bandage relaxed, and the wrinkled, scrunched cloth fell from his hand and landed in his lap.

"A person, I thought of as a friend since grammar school, tried to kill a child, assaulted the woman Ethan loved, tried to blow up a mine, and blinded me." He shook his head slowly. "I didn't have a clue he had such a mean streak in him."

Wanting to move the discussion away from the accident, she asked, "After you lost your sight, what did you do at the mill?"

Sarcasm wreathed his laugh. "Nothing, if my brothers had anything to say about it. But I'd sneak out to the mill and work on the gears and stuff at night when it was shut down." He almost smiled before his lips tipped down once more. "Until one of the workers wanted to know who was coming in at night and greasing the gears. They figured it was me and shipped me out here."

She placed a hand on his knee. "What do you want to do when you go back?"

His hand covered hers. The weight comforted her and conjured up visions of the same hand roaming about her body. Heat ignited in her belly.

"I want to work alongside my brothers, building all our futures. I have some ideas how to make the mill more productive in the winter when the stream is frozen."

"Are those the drawings I saw in your journal?" She hoped they had become good enough friends that he wouldn't think her a busybody.

"Yes, I had it just about figured out when I lost my sight."

"Dr. Tarkiel, you have a visitor," Mrs. White said.

Rachel jerked her hand off Clay's knee. She spun toward the pathway and groaned. Celeste stood beside the matron. Her frilly off-the-shoulder dress and fancy hat reduced the matron to the servant class.

"So, this is why we hardly see you." Celeste's gaze traveled up and down Clay. She extended her hand. "I'm Celeste Tarkiel, Rachel's sister."

Rachel stood, taking Celeste's hand and drawing her to the chair she'd just vacated. "Celeste, this is Clay Halsey. The student who recently broke his leg."

Celeste's eyebrow rose as she took the offered seat. Rachel still held Clay's letter. She shoved it in her apron pocket. Grabbing the basket on the bench, she sat next to Clay.

"It's a pleasure to meet you, Miss Tarkiel. Rachel talks about her family quite a bit."

Clay's deep smooth voice tipped Rachel's lips in a smug smile. For a miner he could talk just as smooth and sappy as a politician.

"So, do the two of you spend a lot of time together?" Celeste's tone rang with accusation and innuendo.

"Not as much as I'd like." Clay's smile and comment warmed Rachel's heart. She hid the smile tickling her lips and set her face in her professional expression.

"Mr. Halsey, you've been told before not to be so forward."

"I can't help it, you're so interesting." He reached over and placed his hand on her arm. His actions and seductive voice fluttered her heart.

Celeste's mouth dropped open, and then snapped shut.

Rachel stared at her sister. How could she get Clay to remove his hand without being rude in front of Celeste? He must have felt her tremors, because his brow furrowed, and his hand moved to his leg.

"Why are you visiting me here?" Rachel asked, wondering if Mr. Smith would come by so, she could have him take Clay back into the infirmary.

"It was such a lovely day I went for a walk. And do you know who I ran into? Madge New-comb. She was going on and on about what a shame it was you were tucked away here in this blind school and not getting out and socializing."

Rachel groaned and swept a glance at Clay. Of course he'd perked up to listen. "I don't really—"

"I told her you would be at the Fourth of July celebration. After all, it is an election year, and Father will be expected to speak. You never miss his speeches." Her sister shot a glance to Clay and took a breath to go on. "She wanted to know who would escort you—"

"I don't need an escort, and I'd rather you didn't gossip about me with your friends." Anger gurgled in her stomach. Heat streamed up her neck, infusing her cheeks. How dare her sister presume to speak of her to others? Her business was just that—her business.

"I'm escorting her."

Clay's declaration nearly shot Rachel off the bench. She twisted on the seat, her knees bumping his. Her heart bounced around inside her ribs like popcorn in a kettle.

"You have a broken leg." She couldn't control the warble in her voice.

"A Fourth of July celebration would be on July fourth. That's still a month away. You said this should be healed in six weeks. What better way to celebrate getting this heavy thing off my leg than escorting a beautiful woman to listen to her father speak?" He placed his hand on her knee and squeezed. "I could use some time away from here, and so could you."

Her heart palpitated. Eagerness to get away from the school and be with him flushed her whole being. But what if it only made her wish for things that couldn't be?

"That sounds like an excellent idea!" Celeste clapped her hands. "Wait until I tell Mother. She'll be beyond ecstatic to know you have an escort."

"B-but I haven't—"

"Just say yes." Clay spoke the words so quietly

she almost didn't catch them. He gave her knee another squeeze. His familiar touches and the sincerity in his request melted her. She had no resistance to this man and his charms.

"What about the staff here? What will Mr. Griffin say?" She wanted to go. But a niggling in the back of her mind said their relationship would change outside the security of the school.

"He'll say it's about time you have some fun," Clay said sarcastically and smirked.

"I think it's a wonderful idea." Celeste stared at Clay, her gaze sweeping over him like he was a Paris gown.

Rachel stood and clutched the basket of bandages to her middle. "Mr. Halsey and I will discuss it further. Don't tell Mother anything until we've made a decision."

Clay shoved to his feet beside her. "We have made the decision. We'll be there."

Celeste glanced from Clay to Rachel. "I do believe, big sister, you have found your match."

Rachel's jaw dropped open and her hands clenched the basket. Not only was Clay forcing her to go to the celebration, now Celeste had fallen into cahoots with him.

Celeste laughed and stood. "Mr. Halsey, it was a pleasure meeting you, and I look forward to seeing both you and my sister at the celebration." She strode back to the school.

Rachel snapped her mouth shut and fidgeted. Should she run to her sister and beg her once more not to say anything, or lay into the man standing beside her grinning like he'd been handed a fistful of money?

<h1 style="text-align:center">Chapter 13</h1>

Clay knew he'd get a tongue lashing. He'd spoken up when she would have rather he kept quiet. But dang if escorting her to a celebration didn't seem like a great chance for them to get to know one another outside the school. The opportunity couldn't have fallen into his lap any better.

"I don't understand your sister's appeal to men." That should throw her thoughts in a tizzy.

"I beg your pardon?" Rachel's voice squeaked. The basket bumped him in the hip.

"She has a screechy voice and a penchant for gossip. Listening to her intrude in other people's lives with that voice would send me scurrying to the highest hill."

"Most men see only her beauty. They're mesmerized before she opens her mouth and all they hear is a choir of angels."

He couldn't tell if she mocked her sister or believed what she said. "Your voice is a choir of angels and your beauty shines through in your gestures." He reached out, touched her arm, and slid his hand down to her hand clutching the bottom of a basket. "I really want to spend the day with you away from here. Please, say you'll go."

"I'll think about it." She pulled her hand away from his touch.

He smiled and sat back on the bench. "Give me the basket and finish Hank's letter." He reached out with both hands. "Please."

The basket crunched back on the bench beside him. The rustle of her skirts stopped where he pictured another chair sat. Paper crackled, and she cleared her throat. Her clear crisp voice began reading again, and his mind wandered to the possibilities of their outing. He had to build up his strength so he wasn't hobbling around when the bandage came off his leg.

"'We all miss you and hope to hear from you soon, Hank.'"

Clay jerked his attention back to the moment. Dang. He hadn't heard the end of the letter. She'd think him a fool if he asked her to read it again. Or...perhaps she'd think him sentimental.

"Could you read that last part one more time?"

She sighed and started reading again. This time he kept his mind on the letter.

"Thank you for re-reading the last part." He craned his head to listen for Jasper's whereabouts. "I asked Jasper to build something for me. Is he somewhere close?"

"I don't see him."

Rachel's no-nonsense reply made him smile. Would she treat him even more distant now that they had a tentative outing?

"Would you look for him while I finish rolling the bandages? The item will allow me to write a letter to Hank." He picked up the end of a bandage and began rolling.

The crunch of footsteps faded. He worked fast, rolling the bandages and setting them in the basket by his foot. He was anxious to try out his invention. If it worked, he'd see if Mr. Griffin would allow other students to use it.

Rachel found Mr. Smith working in the shed. The clean tang of fresh wood filled her nostrils. Wood shavings spilled over his boots like tan snowflakes. She knocked on the open door.

He glanced over his shoulder and his hands stopped whittling on a flat piece of wood the size of a ledger. Evenly spaced slats allowed elongated openings the width of the board.

"Mr. Halsey asked me to find you. He wanted to know if the item he asked you to build was finished."

The handyman faced her, holding the board. "He's a right smart fella. He told me how to make this so's he can write a letter and make lists." He waved the board in the air. The item intrigued her.

"How will that work?" She stepped into the shed.

He placed a solid board the same size as the first on the work bench. "He can put a piece o' paper on this"—he swiped a hand across the solid board—"and place this here board with the openings on top, matching the edges. Then he can write in the cut out spaces."

Her heart beat rapidly. What a wonderful idea. And it would help so many other blind people. "It's marvelous!" She ran her fingers over the smooth wood, dipping her finger into the open groove and sliding it along the straight line. "Is it finished? He received a letter from his brother and wants to write back."

"I jus' have to add a strip a leather to hold the pieces together."

He cut a three inch wide length of leather and fit it on the long side of the board. Awl in hand, he tapped through the leather and into the wood and inserted small wooden pegs into the holes. He flipped the boards over, pulled the leather over the other board, and repeated the process.

She studied the finished book he held out to her.

"Oh, no. You should present it to him. You have remarkable craftsmanship."

Jasper smiled and motioned for her to exit the shed in front of him. She did, leading him to Clay, his hands folded on his lap, a full basket of rolled bandages at his feet.

They both stopped in front of him. Clay tilted his head in a way she'd learned meant he focused on their movements.

"Is it finished?" he asked.

"Yes. And Mr. Smith did a wonderful job on a remarkable idea." She couldn't keep the admiration from her voice. His idea and the handyman's workmanship had created a truly superb invention

Clay held up his hands. Mr. Smith placed the wood tablet in them. Clay's hand roamed over the surface. His fingers dipped into the open spaces and slid along the straight groove. His grin grew and grew. His dimple deepened. Her heart stuttered.

"Jasper, this is exactly what I'd envisioned. You did an excellent job." He held up a hand. "Anyone have paper and a pencil?"

"I'll go get some." Rachel held up the front of her skirt and hurried into the school. She was as excited as Clay to see it work.

"Where are you hurrying to?" Mr. Griffin's voice carried down the hallway.

"Mr. Smith just made the most wonderful invention from Mr. Halsey's idea. I'm getting him paper and a pencil to try it out." She rushed into her office and grabbed the items. When she returned, Mr. Griffin fell in step beside her.

She hurried across the grass to the bench. "Here you go." She placed the items in Clay's hands. He opened the boards like a book, settled the paper on the bottom board, matching the edges to the edges of the board, and flipped the top back in place. With a finger, he found the top open space, slid his finger along the opening to the left, and then set the lead end of the pencil in the slot.

In block lettering he wrote, Dear Hank. He pulled the finger trailing along the slot behind the pencil out and slipped it into the slot right below and wrote a sentence.

He raised his head and smiled. "Jasper, it works great!"

"Was your idea," the handyman said, grinning as broad as Clay.

Rachel's chest squeezed with happiness and pride. The two had made a wonderful gift for blind people.

"Let me see that." Mr. Griffin stepped forward, snatching the board book from Clay's lap and studying it. He stared at Clay, then at Mr. Smith, and back down at the boards. "You two came up with this?"

"I thought it up. Jasper made it." Clay held out his hands.

When Mr. Griffin continued staring at the boards, Rachel took them away and placed them in Clay's hands.

Mr. Griffin pivoted to Mr. Smith. "Could you make more of those?"

Mr. Smith nodded and grinned. "How many?"

"Let's start with ten. Students who have been blind since birth and don't know the alphabet can't write, but those who have similar situations to Mr. Halsey should find these quite useful." Mr. Griffin shook his head. "Bring them to my office when you finish."

Mr. Smith nodded, and Mr. Griffin wandered back to the school.

"Clay, this is—" Rachel pulled the basket off the bench, sat down, and put her hand on Clay's arm. "I'll ask my father which lawyer would be best to work with to get this idea patented."

"Patented?"

"Yes, a patent. That way no one else can steal your idea. And you can make these to sell."

"My own business?" His eyes widened, lifting his eyebrows. His handsome face brightened. "Jasper, how do you feel about moving to Sumpter?"

Rachel stared at the handyman. How wonderful, Clay would share this with the man.

"I-I's never been there."

"Well, as my partner, you'll have to move there to help me run the business. You'll be in charge of manufacturing this tablet."

Mr. Smith's grin spread across his face, showing white teeth and a sparkle in his eye. "You all sure that's what you all want?"

"Yes." Clay rubbed his hand over the board. "I'll write to Hank and tell him we're starting a business and to look for a place we can manufacture these books."

Rachel picked up the basket of rolled bandages and placed it in the empty basket. "I'll leave you two to work all this out, and after lunch I'll visit with Father about the lawyer."

The excitement and energy the two men emitted swirled happiness in her chest. They made a good team. With Clay's inventiveness and Mr. Smith's skills they could make any number of worthwhile things.

"Rachel"—Clay cleared his throat—"Thank you." His eyes gazed at her. Her face heated, and her heart raced. If only he could see her.

"I haven't done anything." Her hands clutched the baskets to keep from touching him.

"You believe in both of us. That's what counts."

She pulled her gaze from the man who day by day grew in her heart and glanced at Mr. Smith, who grinned and nodded.

Rachel smiled back and ducked her head, hiding her embarrassment as she hurried into the school. Both men held a special place in her heart. Mr. Smith because of his kindness and help and Clay... When he returned home it would be like losing a piece of herself. She'd never held the feelings and connection with another that she'd developed with this man. Over the past weeks, the more she learned about him the more she wanted to spend time with him.

She stumbled into the infirmary and quickly set to putting clean sheets on his bed. Grabbing his pillow to pull the case off, she stopped and inhaled shave soap and his unique scent. She clutched the pillow and dreamed of walking arm in arm with Clay through the crowd at the Fourth of July festivities. Women would watch them with envy. He would be the most handsome man there. Pride straightened her back and desire tightened her breasts. In the dark, fireworks bursting overhead, would he kiss her?

<h1 style="text-align:center">Chapter 14</h1>

Clay stood in his room in the cottage. He didn't want to wear the hot, wool suit jacket to the festivities, but he didn't want to disappoint Rachel by dressing like a worker rather than someone of her status.

"Ya better hurry or they's gonna come and leave without ya," Jasper said from the door.

"Is my hair staying put?" He should wear a hat, but then he wouldn't know when to take it off in the presence of ladies. Rachel would understand, but would her family?

"Ya look like a dandy."

The mirth in Jasper's voice made some of Clay's nerves flee.

"I do? Then I shouldn't look out of place in the mob Dr. Tarkiel's family entertains." Clay walked to the door. "Take me to the front of the school. Dr. Tarkiel said we'd wait for her family's buggy together."

Jasper fell into step alongside him. A hand on

Clay's elbow guided him around the school building.

When Rachel had said her father insisted on picking them up so they all arrived at the festivities as a family, he was a bit apprehensive.

At least during the short ride to the park he'd have a chance to visit with her father and see where the man stood on his daughter's choice of escort.

"Steps," Jasper said. "Four."

They were at the front of the school. After the announcement he would escort Rachel to today's gathering, he had asked Jasper to take him walking every day, rain or not, so he would be strong enough to escort her wherever she wanted to go during the festivities.

"Oh my!"

Rachel's exclamation made him stop.

"What?" He hurried toward her voice. "Is something wrong?"

"No, you're—"

"What? Jasper, did I forget my britches?" He patted his legs in mock seriousness.

Rachel giggled. "No, you look wonderful."

His heart picked up its pace and he reached out for her hand. She placed it in his. He stepped closer, running his palm up her arm over cool soft skin. A scrap of fluffy cloth covered her shoulder. His hand continued up the gentle curve of her silky neck. The warmth and texture fanned his embers of desire. With tentative fingers, he caressed her upswept hair and ran the tips of his fingers over her face. He'd picked the right side of her body so she wouldn't shy away from his touch when he came near the scar. Her allowing his touch raised his hopes of stealing a kiss or two during their outing.

"You are beautiful." The whispered words for her ears only.

"You all's ride's coming," Jasper said from a distance.

Rachel's small hand drew his from her face. She maneuvered them around, her hand through the crook of his elbow, and started across the porch.

Walking upstairs was easier than going down. He concentrated on her forward motion, putting his foot out when she pulled and stepped down.

"Bottom," she said before he positioned his foot for another downward step. They walked along a crunching graveled path and stopped. The clomp of shod horses, jangle of harnesses, and crackle of wheels rolling down the street grew louder.

Rachel's hand clutched his arm. He placed a hand over it and squeezed. Why was she so nervous? This was her family, people who loved her. Maybe she had second thoughts about being escorted by a blind man?

The noise ceased. The creak of springs ripped through the stillness.

"Rachel." A man's deep voice filled the quiet, and she released his arm.

"Father." The warmth in the one word told Clay which parent she favored. She clutched Clay's right hand and extended it palm in. "Judge Tarkiel, I'd like to introduce, Clay Halsey."

His hand met an equally sized, firm grasp.

"Judge Tarkiel, it's a pleasure to meet you. Rachel speaks of her family often."

"You have us at a disadvantage." Judge Tarkiel's deep authoritative voice rang with accusation. "We've heard little of you other than Celeste's visit to the school."

"Rachel has been busy with her duties at the school." Clay jumped to her defense. He unclasped his hand and motioned for Rachel to climb into the carriage. His stomach flinched with nerves wondering how he would get in without floundering like a fool.

Rachel's fingers wrapped around his hand, drawing him forward. "It's a beautiful day. I'm glad you have the top down on the buggy, Father." She stopped and draped Clay's left hand over the smooth wood on the side of the vehicle. She took his right hand and he felt her rise in the air. Two steps up.

Gratitude stopped his lurching guts. She gave him a visual of how to proceed. Keeping his hand on the side, he swung to face the buggy and raised his foot until he bumped the step, then placed his foot on it and stepped up. He repeated the movement and stood in the buggy. A tug on his sleeve drew him to sit on a plush bench. The sway of the buggy and more rustling of skirts meant the judge had climbed aboard and settled.

Clay held out his hand. "Mrs. Tarkiel, it's a pleasure to meet you."

A small, rather bony hand, slipped briefly across his palm. Not knowing where Celeste sat, he nodded. "Miss Tarkiel, a pleasure, again."

Rachel's hand slipped into his. He squeezed

gently. The buggy moved and a slight breeze ruffled his left side and back of his head.

"Mr. Halsey, we know so little about you. Are you a local?"

The judge's question didn't bother Clay. He'd have thought less of the man if he didn't question him and his intentions toward his daughter.

"My brothers and I own a mine and stamp mill in Sumpter."

"It supports how many of you?"

"I have four brothers, three are married. One's a marshal, one is a Pinkerton, and Ethan, Hank, and I run the stamp mill and mine." He shrugged. "We haven't had to scrounge for food the last five years. We had some lean ones right after our folks were killed, but Ethan, he's the oldest, held us together and kept us fed."

"So you don't have any relatives other than your brothers?"

He presumed the woman speaking was Mrs. Tarkiel as it wasn't Celeste or Rachel.

"We have some cousins in the east. Ethan exchanges letters with them. But other than my brothers and their families, we're it."

The buggy slowed and the chaos of voices and movement filled the air as they neared Wilson Park.

"Father, look at all the people!" Excitement vibrated in Celeste's voice.

Rachel's fingers gripped his hand like a hawk holding its prey. Her panic vibrated into him. One sister relished the excitement and crowds, while the other feared them.

He rubbed his other hand over hers, trying to

relax her muscles. He leaned close and whispered. "My having problems navigating through crowds should keep us on the edge of things."

The buggy came to a stop and shifted as the judge stood. Clay waited while the buggy jiggled and settled. Once he determined the judge had disembarked, he stood and ran a hand along the edge of the buggy to the opening and slowly stepped down first one rung and then to the ground. At the bottom, he held onto the side and raised a hand.

Rachel's small fingers wrapped around his as she climbed down and stood by his side. He offered his hand to the next woman. Celeste. The hand wasn't bony and only touched him briefly before she alighted. Next, Mrs. Tarkiel, her thin hand clasped his tightly as she descended. The sandalwood scent and heavy footsteps of the judge closed in, and he claimed his wife.

Voices called to the judge and his family. Rachel's hand slipped through his arm, and they started forward. He patted her hand and forced a pleasant expression on his face, even though he had no idea what they were headed into, and his stomach twisted tighter than hemp rope.

Rachel stared into the mass of bodies moving like the undertow in the ocean. Her heart raced in her tightening chest. She didn't want to be swallowed by the crowd. Clay's hesitant steps mirrored her feelings. He appeared in control, but his crooked elbow tightened more and more and he clutched her hand tight to his side. The visual of all the bodies scared her. What was it like to be blind walking into this chaos?

Following her family around all day would be

utter foolishness. Especially when neither one of them wanted to be in this crowd.

She urged Clay to the left. When they broke free of the throng of people greeting her family, she slid her hand down to Clay's and drew him to the outskirts of the mob. A huge sigh relieved the tightness in her chest, and she smiled at Clay. He dutifully followed her and relaxed when they no longer were among the gathering. His smile grew.

"Where are we?" he asked, pulling on her hand and stopping her.

"Under trees that ring the area where people have gathered for the speeches."

"Are we alone?" He raised an eyebrow and she giggled.

"Unless someone comes looking for us, yes. We can sit here and watch without being crushed among the hoards who wish to make themselves known to my father and other politicians."

"I've waited to be alone with you since the first day I blundered."

His free hand cupped the back of her head. His large warm fingers heated her body from her neck down. He was going to kiss her. Her heart thrummed in her chest, and her breath caught. She'd dreamed of a moment just like this ever since he declared he'd escort her today.

His lips brushed hers lightly, teasing. She pressed forward. His lips curved against hers.

"I'm going to savor this," he whispered, once again teasing her with a slight brush of soft skin against soft skin. She leaned against him, wrapping her arms around his middle, reveling in his hard body against hers. He tilted his head, covered her mouth completely, and licked the seam of her lips.

She gasped at the intimacy, and he entered. Her legs weakened at the sensation of his tongue inside her mouth. His taste was something she'd never expected—intoxicating, addictive, and sweet like a sugar cookie. She moaned, and his arms clutched her tighter.

Horns blared. The sound jolted her to where they were. She leaned her head against Clay's chest and listened to his beating heart.

"The horns mean the opening ceremony is beginning. And Father will speak."

"Do you want to get closer to hear?"

His husky voice made her smile. He'd been affected by the kiss as well.

"I would like to hear what he has to say about the upcoming election."

"Lead the way." He twined their fingers together and fell in step beside her.

She led them along the edge of the crowd, moving as close to the erected stage as she could. Her father stepped up to the podium and scanned the assembly. How he found her hovering on the edge of the crowd she'd never know. His gaze dropped to her hand clasped in Clay's, and he frowned.

Her father's disfavor confused Rachel. He usually stood behind her decisions. She didn't get caught up in the politics like her sister and mother. She and her father had a different bond. When he wanted to get away from the politics and fade from the center of attention they went fishing or for buggy rides.

He started speaking and the mob hushed.

Eloquent phrases about the town, the country, and the upcoming elections flowed for thirty minutes. All the while her mother and sister stood on either side of him smiling like two Greek goddesses carved from marble.

When her father finished the crowd cheered.

"I can see why your father is held with such high esteem. He has vision for this town and state."

Clay's comment filled her chest with pride. She stood on her tiptoes and kissed his cheek. "Thank you."

"Miss Tarkiel, who is this man with whom you behave so familiarly?"

Rachel whipped around at the accusing male voice. She groaned. William. Of all the people in this crowded park, why did she have to run into him?

"Clay Halsey, I'd like to introduce you to William Stanley."

Clay extended his hand. She'd felt him stiffen at the man's words. How did she convey William meant nothing to her without blurting the whole betrothal mess to him?

William shook hands. She had to hide a smile behind her hand at the way he flexed his fingers after the greeting.

"Halsey." William studied Clay.

"Stanley." Clay continued to hold her hand, his thumb caressing her knuckles.

"You in politics?" William asked.

"No. Mining." Clay said.

"Is your family here, William?" Rachel couldn't for the life of her figure out why William was interested in Clay or her for that matter. He'd made his thoughts perfectly clear the day he tossed her aside.

He shook his head and continued to stare at Clay. "They went to Portland to visit my grandparents." He waved a hand back and forth and a wicked smiled split his long face.

Rachel inhaled, and Clay stiffened.

Clay didn't like the way Rachel vibrated with fear. What had this man done to her?

"Let's go," He tugged on her hand. "Nice meeting you," he tossed over his shoulder, leading Rachel away from the stage and crowd. Damn, he felt like a coward hurrying away, but he couldn't protect her from things he couldn't see. And it rankled.

Thirty paces away, he stopped. "Is there a bench we can sit on somewhere?"

"Is your leg bothering you?" She drew him ten more steps to the right and placed his hand on the solid arm of a bench. Clay sat, tugging her down beside him.

He held both her hands. "What did that man do to you?"

"I-I—"

"I felt the fear in you and you flinched. Did he try something with me standing there?" God, I hate being blind. Frustration pounded in his head. How was he to protect her if he couldn't see what others did?

"No. He waved a hand and realized you were blind and then..."

"What?" What had he done that caused her to flinch? He'd felt her agitated body as soon as she'd seen the man. He'd find the truth about the man and make him pay for upsetting Rachel.

She squeaked, and he realized his hold on her hands crushed her fingers. He raised her hand to his lips and kissed them. "I'm sorry. I hate the fact I can't shield you from danger because I can't see it."

"He wasn't harmful. He just—he had this wicked smile." She inhaled deeply. "You should know. I was betrothed to William before I went back east to school."

The knowledge the other man had courted and held her in his arms swirled jealousy hot and vile in his guts. "I see. He's bitter you went to school and changed your mind." He couldn't keep his jealousy from tainting his words.

"No. He called it off before."

The sorrow in her voice made him wonder if she still loved the man. The thought ripped his guts liked a rock shattering under a stamp.

"And you still love him and he throws that in your face." Clay's chest ached like someone had driven a stake into him. The kiss under the trees earlier—he would have sworn she'd been involved as much as he.

"No! I never loved him." She sighed. "I realize that now." He barely heard the last muttered sentence. The words filled him with hope.

"Then why does he bother you?"

She pulled her hands from his and started to slide away. He reached up, placing his hand on the scarred side of her face. It was smooth, but had a funny feel. She pulled back.

"Where's your scar?"

Rachel sucked in air and started coughing. He pulled her into his arms, crooning and rubbing her back.

She caught her breath and stiffened, trying to pull out of his arms.

"H-how did you know about my scar?"

"I felt it the night you slept in my arms." He settled her in the crook of his arm and leaned back against the bench, drawing her back as well. "How did you get the scar?"

"When I was ten there was an accident. A-a run-a-way wagon. I shoved Celeste out of the way, but it struck me."

Her tale tugged at his heart. Her bravery had left a scar. One, he now realized, that was deeper than the welt he'd run his fingers over.

"Why would Stanley break your betrothal? If he loved you, he wouldn't have noticed the scar."

"When I'm out in public I use stage makeup and lard to hide it. He didn't know I had a scar. I was going to wait until we were married—"

"That's wrong. A couple getting married need to know everything about each other, the good and the bad."

He knew that wasn't what she wanted to hear, but he wanted to make it clear there would be no secrets between them. He mentally shook himself. When had the thought of marrying this woman or any woman jumped into his head?

She sniffed and her shoulders shook. Had he made her cry? Clay touched her cheek. His finger came away wet.

"Shh..." He pulled her head against his chest and kissed her hair. "I wasn't judging you. If you had really loved Stanley, you would have told him the truth and not hid the scar."

Clay kissed the top of her head and inhaled her citrus scent. "What did he say when he broke it off?"

She mumbled against his coat, and he had to strain to hear. "He said because I hid a hideous scar from him it made me a liar, and he refused to marry a liar."

"He didn't love you anyway. You can't marry if you don't love the person. It makes both people miserable." He raised her face. "Besides, if you were betrothed to him, I'd have to beat him up." He lowered his lips and found hers willing and sweet.

She drew back. Her finger slid down his nose. "Is that how this happened? Fighting over a girl?"

Clay laughed. "Yeah, when I was six."

"So, you have a string of besotted girls you've left mooning over you?"

The laughter in her voice warmed and expanded his chest.

"There you two are." Celeste's grating voice broke into their cocoon.

Chapter 15

Rachel straightened, putting distance between her and Clay at the sound of her sister's accusing voice. "Why are you looking for us?"

"Father asked me to round you up to join us at the family tree. But if you prefer to be alone..." Celeste's eyebrow rose, and her gaze flitted from Clay's arm around Rachel's shoulders to their clasped hands. Was that a ring of jealousy in her voice?

"I didn't realize the speeches were over." Rachel pulled her hand from Clay's and straightened her skirt. Was her makeup smudged? She'd behaved brazenly, but they'd sat on a bench far from the gathering.

Clay twined his fingers with hers, stood, and drew her up beside him. "Let's join your family. I'd like to learn more about you."

She heaved an exaggerated sigh even though she wanted this man who knew her worst to know more about her. He smiled and squeezed her hand.

Rachel motioned for Celeste to lead the way. Holding hands, she and Clay ambled along behind her sister. Celeste called out to people they knew, drawing their attention to the threesome. It didn't matter, William would have made sure by now everyone within their circle knew her escort was blind.

Her father's gaze took in her fingers entwined with Clay's. His lips formed a rigid line. Her mother's brow wrinkled. Please let them see beyond Clay's blindness. Celeste folded her legs under her on the blanket next to their mother.

Rachel sat beside her father and gently tugged Clay down on her other side. Once they were all comfortably seated, her mother poured lemonade into glasses.

"Mr. Halsey, have you been blind from birth?"

"Mother!" Rachel glared at her mother and shot a sympathetic glance toward Clay.

"I have a right to know all I can about a man who is being"—her mother's gaze lowered to their clasped hands—"forward with my daughter."

Clay didn't flinch at the statement and held her hand when she tried to pull it away. A polite smile tipped his lips. She felt his nerves as his grip tightened.

Clay straightened his shoulders. "Mrs. Tarkiel, no, my blindness happened from an accident eight months ago. I'm getting used to maneuvering around in the dark." He squeezed her hand and moved his head as though scanning the group of people seated on the blanket.

"Judge Tarkiel, I'd be pleased if you would allow me to court Rachel."

Happiness swelled her chest causing a wonderful ache. She knew he liked her, but they hadn't talked of anything beyond their day to day existence at the school. She trembled. Did she want to be courted? Something that led to marriage? Her body heated at the thought. She knew the mechanics of conjugating a marriage. She'd planned to never marry, to be happy with a fulfilling career as a doctor. She stared into Clay's handsome face. Could she be fulfilled if she didn't see where their feelings for one another might take them?

His thumb caressed her joined hand. Sparks raced up her arm, and her breath caught. Yes, she wanted to see what her life might be like with Clay in it. But they had much to talk about.

"A rational man would not consider a courtship between his daughter and someone like you."

Her father's voice pulled her out of her thoughts. His tone and disrespect tightened her chest. Her heart ached at such harsh words from a man she loved and respected.

"Father, how could you say something so—so cruel?" She placed her free hand on Clay's arm, showing her solidarity to him.

Her father swept his hand toward them. The waft of air he conjured puffed against her face, and Clay reached in front of her as though blocking a blow.

Her father's eyebrow rose, but he continued. "I know nothing of this man and wonder how he plans to support you when it is obvious he can't hold a proper job."

"The school is teaching me to read Braille." Clay leaned forward, his tone controlled. "I can still write. I'll always have funds from our stamp mill."

"Gold dwindles. Look at all the rushes that left behind ghost towns."

Her father smiled at her mother and sister as though he'd made an eloquent speech. Rachel couldn't believe her father was so rude and uncompromising. She had a career that would sustain them as well. She started to say as much.

"When the gold dwindles we'll procure other metals from the rock, and when that goes, we'll have already invested in other opportunities. There's talk of a railroad from Baker City to Sumpter to help haul logs out of the mountains. Hank is already looking toward investing in that. We aren't backwoods riffraff, Judge Tarkiel. My brothers and I are well learned and have proven it takes a lot to take us down."

Rachel smiled at Clay's grit and the way he countered her father's objections.

"I'd hoped you'd be reasonable about me courting your daughter. But whether you accept or not, I still plan to see Rachel. I'm heading back to Sumpter in a month. I'd like Rachel to come with me, meet my family, and see if she could live there."

Her mother gasped and started shaking her head. Celeste's eyes lit with disbelief, and her father's face reddened.

"You'll not take my daughter anywhere!" Her father roared. Rachel's neck and face heated as the people near them gawked at the group.

"Father, control your voice." Rachel stared at Clay. When had he planned to tell her this? He squeezed her hand. "If I decide to go it will be my decision. Since this is the first I've heard of it, I'd like the courtesy of having a chance to discuss it with Clay."

"I'd planned to discuss it with you today." Clay shrugged and sent her an impish grin that fluttered her stomach. "Sorry I blurted it out in front of your family."

"I-I'm speechless. I think it's something we'll need to discuss in private." Rachel gave his hand a squeeze. So many thoughts raced in her head she felt dizzy just sitting.

"You're not considering traveling alone with this man?" Her mother's voice rose an octave. "You'd scandalize our name. And you'd never find a decent husband."

Rachel stared at her mother. "If I traveled with Clay to his home, it would be no one's business but mine. And if I traveled with him, it would be because I had feelings for him."

Her father opened and closed his fists as though he wished to grab Clay by the neck.

She couldn't believe the anger and fright—yes, the fright she saw in her parents' eyes. Why were they frightened of Clay?

Rachel caught movement beyond Celeste. She smiled and nodded. The man walking to them would stop the conversation and hopefully give her and Clay time to talk.

"Look out, Celeste, here comes Representative Wright." She'd expected her sister to turn a bright smile on the man, but instead her gaze went to their father, her eyes asking for help.

"Don't worry," he mumbled and stood. "But this conversation isn't finished," he said, pointedly glancing from Rachel to Clay and back. He walked to the representative Rachel thought had caught her sister's heart and stopped him several yards away.

"Why is father keeping him from you?" Rachel wanted nothing more than to wander off with Clay to discuss his proposal. But her sister had become agitated which was so unlike her usual in-control manner.

Their mother patted Celeste's arm. "Rumor has it Representative Wright plans to ask your sister to marry him today."

Rachel caught her sister's hand. "That's what you wanted isn't it? To marry a politician, and he's been courting you for two years."

Celeste's gaze traveled from Clay to Rachel and to their still entwined hands. "You two have known each other what, two months? And you show more affection to one another than Wayne has shown to me in two years." Her gaze drifted to the crowd. "I feel more for someone else I barely know than I do for Wayne."

"So you're avoiding the man rather than tell him you don't want to marry him?"

Clay's accusing words crumpled Celeste's already faltering façade. Her face scrunched as tears glistened in her eyes. She jumped up and hurried away.

Rachel pushed to her feet.

Clay held onto her hand. "I didn't mean to hurt her, but a man needs to know where he stands."

She squeezed his hand and slipped her fingers free. "I know." She understood his double meaning and hurried after her sister. She was new at being in love, but maybe she could help Celeste.

Clay cleared his throat. He was pretty sure only Mrs. Tarkiel remained sitting under the tree. He already knew the woman wasn't happy her daughter had feelings for him—a blind man. Would she or her husband give him a chance to prove he cared about Rachel?

"I know you'd prefer your daughter marry a politician," Clay said, "but she prefers not being the center of attention."

"Mr. Halsey, just because her appearance is inadequate doesn't mean she should settle for anyone less as a husband."

Clay ground his teeth and counted to ten. "I'm sorry you feel my sight is what makes me a man and that Rachel's looks make her a woman. I can tell you, from my observations, Rachel is more beautiful than any woman I've ever encountered."

"How would you know? You can't even see her."

"Because I don't judge a person by the outside, I judge her by the inside."

Mrs. Tarkiel huffed.

"Your daughter has more compassion and love inside her than anyone I've ever met. You should come to the school some day and see how the children and staff love her and the wonderful care she takes of them."

Footsteps approached. "Good, I wanted a word with you without Rachel around," Judge Tarkiel said, his voice the volume of an intimate conversation. Clay felt the man settle on the blanket.

"I'm afraid I said something that upset Celeste, and Rachel went to console her." Clay wasn't proud he upset the woman, but he also felt it was his place to speak up for a man who was being strung along.

"I see." The two words rang with reprimand. "Not only do you think you can drag my oldest daughter off to the wilderness, but you also feel it is your place to offend my youngest daughter?"

"I was merely stating a fact. Men don't like to be strung along."

Clay hoped the emotions he felt for Rachel were reciprocated. The hostility emanating from her parents would be hard to ignore.

"Neither do women. I want you to stop encouraging Rachel. She had her heart broken five years ago, and I'm sure her nurturing qualities are the only reason she is showing interest in you."

The man's tone imparted he actually believed his daughter took pity on a blind man. The kiss they shared was not a kiss of pity. He'd know if it was, wouldn't he?

"Judge Tarkiel, I don't feel pity for your daughter, and I'm pretty sure what she feels for me isn't pity."

"Mr. Halsey, you aren't listening—stay away from my daughter, and if you take her to Sumpter, I'll find a legal course of action to take against you."

Rachel found Celeste sitting on the bench she and Clay had occupied. She sat down and put a hand on her sister's arm.

"Tell me about the man you like."

Celeste blew her nose into a frilly handkerchief and stared at her through tear-dotted, light brown lashes.

"He has black hair, and his features are so masculine it makes my stomach flutter. He comes from a farm but has such wonderful ideas for the state."

"So, he's a politician. I figured you wouldn't want to leave the circle of friends you have." Rachel smiled at her sister's nod.

"Yes, he's held a seat as a representative for one term and will surely be re-elected again this fall."

"Does he know how you feel? Have you two talked?"

"He—when I try to talk to him he frowns and turns away." Celeste grabbed her hand. "But when I look at him—I feel more"—she fanned her hand in front of her face—"than I felt the one time Wayne kissed my cheek."

Rachel smiled. She knew the heat of desire. It scorched her every time she looked at Clay or he touched her. She nodded. "Then you need to find a way to talk to him. Who is he? Maybe I can help."

"Jeremiah Folsum." The reverence with which she said the name was reminiscent of Rachel's feelings for Clay.

"Isn't he the man father talked so highly of last fall?"

"Yes."

Rachel had an idea. If her father knew of Celeste's interest in the man, she was sure he'd help arrange a meeting.

"You have to tell Wayne you aren't interested in him. Today."

Celeste cringed.

"It isn't fair to keep stringing him along. He's a nice man."

She nodded. "But what do I say?"

Rachel took her sister's hand. "That your feelings aren't strong enough to make a happy marriage."

She thought of the man sitting under the tree with her parents. Her feelings for him would keep their marriage strong no matter what came between them.

"Come on, let's return to the family and have some dinner before the music starts up."

They rose, and Celeste threw her arms around Rachel. "I'm happy you've found a man who loves you." She pulled back. "I never liked William, he ordered you around too much and you let him." They linked arms and sauntered back to the tree. "I like that you stand up to Clay."

Rachel thought about her sister's words. She'd allowed William to bully her for fear he'd leave if she didn't. Yet, she'd recognized the bond between her and Clay wouldn't break even if they argued. Her gaze landed on the man who had captured her heart. Would he also allow her to continue practicing medicine?

The air around the three on the blanket sparked with animosity.

"Ahh, my daughters have returned." Her father's gaze traveled over Celeste, and then landed on her. "We need to talk." He stood, and Clay started to stand as well. "Now, and alone." Her father glared at Clay, who didn't look happy either.

She put a hand on Clay's shoulder and squeezed. "I'll be right back."

The stormy set to his face worried her. What had her parents and Clay talked about while she was with Celeste?

Her father stomped over to the area allotted for parked vehicles. He stopped near their buggy and faced her. His jaw clenched as he stared the length of her, his gaze stopping at the makeup covering her face.

"I want you to stop giving that man false hope." Her father's voice came out as a growl.

"What do you mean?" She fluffed the hair near her scar, and he moved his gaze to her eyes.

"Stop showing him attention when it's misplaced pity. He's getting the wrong ideas."

Rachel clenched her fists and stared at her father. His face had reddened again. She could tell he held his anger in check. "I don't pity Clay. He's a strong man with a quick wit and wonderful innovative ideas."

Her answer only enraged her father. He stepped forward, taking her arm. His fingers bit into her muscle. "I'll not have you marrying a man who can't look out for you."

"Clay can take care of me." She wrenched her arm from his grip and rubbed the smarting area.

"I forbid you to see him. Go to him, put him in the buggy, and our driver will take him back to the school." His voice escalated, and his finger pointed to the tree where Clay, her mother, and sister sat as unmoving as boulders.

She hated scenes. She glanced at her father. He knew it and used the knowledge to his advantage. Should she disobey, he would make the rest of the evening miserable for both her and Clay. Anger boiled in her stomach. She was a professional woman. Her father had no right to order her around like some school girl.

If she didn't live under his roof, he couldn't do a thing about who she saw or what she did. She lowered her eyes so he wouldn't see the rage or rebellion simmering.

"I'll bring Clay to the buggy if you do something for Celeste. One of us should be happy today." She told her father about Celeste's infatuation with Representative Folsum. His eyes took on a gleam she knew well. He liked the idea of the match.

Her heart was heavy over the deceit she was about to pull, but he gave her no choice. One thing she'd learned from Clay; she didn't have to cower to others. She walked sedately across the grass to Clay. Her father went in search of their driver.

Rachel didn't look at her mother or sister. "Clay, would you walk with me?" She tried to make her voice sound natural, but Clay's head swiveled and his eyes narrowed. The worry furrowing his brow begged her to lean down and kiss him. She restrained, grasping his hand when he pushed to his feet.

Without a goodbye to her mother or sister, she placed her hand in the crook of his arm and wandered slowly toward the buggy.

Chapter 16

Clay knew by the sound of Rachel's voice and the grip she had on his arm something was wrong.

"What did your father say?" He stopped.

"Keep walking. We're going to get in the buggy and drive away. Smile and act like we're strolling and happy." Her stature straightened. "I'll explain everything once we're moving," she whispered in his ear.

He didn't like the mystery surrounding her actions. "Why didn't you tell me to say good-bye to your mother and sister?"

"I'll explain later. Quiet, here comes father and the driver." Her edgy tone and grip on his arm unsettled him. What was going on?

"Clay, I'm not feeling well, do you mind escorting me home? I'm sure you wouldn't want to stay here without me, so Ray will drop you off at the school." Her words rang too sweet, too condescending. He started to question her, but she slid her hand into his and whispered, "Just agree."

Playing whatever charade she'd led him into fought against everything he'd ever been taught. The desperation in her plea hooked him as firmly as mercury latched onto gold.

"Father, thank you for finding Ray." Rachel placed Clay's hand on the buggy like earlier and held his other hand, stepping into the vehicle. Clay followed feeling like a coward and thief stealing away. He sat next to Rachel, who immediately grasped his hand.

"I'm sorry you're going to miss the fireworks," Judge Tarkiel said without the least bit of remorse in his tone.

The buggy jiggled, harnesses jingled, and they jolted forward.

Rachel's warm breath misted against his ear and neck. "Father forbid me to see you anymore and told me to take you to the school and come back to the festivities." She gripped his hand tighter. "I don't like deceiving him, but I won't stop seeing you."

Clay set his lips on hers and kissed her. "He told me to stop seeing you. That you only cared about me out of pity."

"You don't believe that do you? You're one of the strongest men I've ever met." She pressed her lips to his. Her tongue timidly eased into his mouth. He moaned and deepened the kiss, wrapping his arms around her, drawing her against him. He wanted this woman and nothing would keep him from her.

She eased away. "Ray, stop here."

"Miss, your father said to—"

"I don't care what my father said. Let us out

here. I want to walk with Mr. Halsey back to the school. Then I'll walk home from there."

Rachel's haughty tone intrigued Clay. He'd not heard her use the regal attitude before.

The vehicle stopped. Clay stepped down and held his hand up for Rachel. She grasped his hand and hurried down. Her arm circled his.

"Ray, on second thought. Would you be so kind as to go to the house and ask Samuel to pick me up at the blind school in two hours?" Rachel's words purred with sweetness. If she'd asked Clay to crawl through a barrel of knives in that tone he'd do it.

"Yes, Miss. I'll feel better knowing you aren't walking the streets after dark." The jingle of the harness and clomp of the horses faded.

Rachel pulled on his arm to move him forward. Clay set his feet. "What are you up to?"

"We need time to talk. Alone. My father made it clear he doesn't want us to talk at all, so I figure we'll wander toward the school and talk. There's no one about since they're all at the celebration." She squeezed his arm, and he fell in step with her lazy pace.

"Sending him to get you a buggy for later was a wise choice. I wouldn't want you wandering around after dark, either." Fear clenched his stomach at what could happen to her.

"I don't plan to use the buggy, but it was a good way to keep Ray from heading back to my father too soon and telling him I didn't follow orders."

Clay stopped and faced her. "I don't like you deceiving your father. Or any of your family."

"They've given me no choice. I'm a grown woman with a career. They can't tell me who I can or can't be with." Rage shook her voice. "I'll not be threatened or have you threatened." She twisted to stand beside him. Her arm, linked with his, urged him onward as she began to walk. "I'll sleep at the school tonight. Tomorrow, I'll find a boarding house to move into. I'll not have my father dictating what I do and who I see."

"When we get to the school, I'll give you money to get two train tickets to Portland. We'll take the next train north then catch the next one to Baker City. There's no telling what your father might try if we wait a month."

He liked the idea of leaving right away. He'd bet every piece of gold in the stamp mill Judge Tarkiel would find a way to get him thrown out of the blind school if he couldn't keep them apart.

Her steps stalled. "What about your family? Shouldn't you give them notice you—we're coming?"

"I'll telegraph Hank when we get to Portland." Her steps faltered. "What's wrong?"

"We're getting close to the school, and I don't want our time together to end."

His stomach rumbled. "We missed the picnic. Is there anywhere around here we can get a meal?"

"Everything is closed, and everyone is at the park." Disappointment rang in her words.

"What about the school? Didn't they take the students to the celebration?"

Her steps quickened. "Yes! They should have left by now. They'll all be gone until after the fireworks. We'll get food from the kitchen and have our own picnic in the backyard."

Clay smiled and hurried along beside her. The crunch of gravel under his feet and the sweet scent of the lilacs oriented him. They were moving around the side of the school. Rachel stopped at the back of the building. He caught a whiff of the freshly sawn boards Jasper and he had cut to mend a corner of the school. Heat carrying stale food scents and lye wafted out when Rachel opened the door by the infirmary and kitchen.

They turned into the kitchen. His stomach rumbled at the aroma of fresh baked bread hanging in the air.

"Wait here." Rachel slipped from his grasp. Cupboards thumped and dishes rattled. "This should do. Hold out your hands."

He did as directed and grasped the handle of a pitcher in one hand and wrapped the other around a basket handle.

"We're set." Rachel slipped her hand in the crook of his arm and started walking.

Cool air and the tang of fresh cut wood surrounded him as his feet crunched on gravel. The sun no longer warmed his face. In the short time they'd stepped inside, the day had drawn to an end and evening sounds abounded. Crickets and frogs serenading from the pond beyond the outbuildings wrapped contentment around him.

"Wait a minute." Rachel stopped. The sound of a cloth snapping and a pulse of air signaled she planned to sit on the ground. "You can sit now." She guided him two steps forward and relieved him of the pitcher.

Clay sat, placing the basket in front of him. He

reached first on one side and then the other. "Sit beside me."

The rustle of her skirts and her soft citrus scent lured him to his right. He reached out, circling his arm around her shoulders and drawing her into an embrace.

"Whatever happens, I will find you." He sealed his promise with a kiss.

Rachel leaned into his solid chest. She wrapped her arms around his neck, and he pulled her onto his lap. No one, not her family or anyone else, ever made her feel as whole and worthy as this man. He was the first person to not scoff at her career and to not pity her for her scar. His acceptance of who she was humbled and excited her. His touch, voice, and charm sent her senses spinning in a dizzy, delicious spiral to her heart.

His hands roamed reverently over her back and sides. His thumbs barely grazed the sides of her breasts. She pressed closer, pushing her bosom against him, hoping to appease the tingle in her nipples.

He pulled back, drawing in air like a man running a race. His chest heaved. She placed a palm over his racing heart. His hand rose to touch her face. She pulled back.

"No. Never pull away from my touch." He wiped at the makeup and lard covering her scar. "Take this stuff off. I want to touch you."

She clutched a corner of the cloth she'd spread on the ground and wiped the concealment from first his thumb and then her face.

He reached up, his fingers tracing the line. Clay leaned forward, and to her surprise, he spread small kisses the length of her disfigurement. "This is a sign of your bravery and large heart."

Her chest ached from his loving actions and tender words.

His hands cradled her head. She stared into his shadowed face. The growing darkness sheltered them. Clay's face moved closer. His lips brushed hers. The tip of his tongue traced her lips, and she opened, allowing him entry. He swooped in setting her body on fire with his growing intensity. His hand roamed to her hip and up her side, resting under her breast.

She leaned closer, pushing her breast into his hand and moaned at the sensation of his palm holding the weight and his thumb rubbing her nipple through the cloth separating their skin.

A warm ache rippled in her pelvic region. The new sensation so overwhelmed her, she straddled his lap and rubbed the area against him, trying to appease the throbbing.

"Rachel...I want you." Clay's hoarse voice and his hands fumbling with the buttons on her dress yanked her from the need of haze clouding her wits.

What was she doing? She grasped Clay's hands, stopping their exploration of her breasts.

"Not here, not now." She kissed the backs of his hands and set them palm down on her thighs. The heat of his hands beckoned her body to move against him again. She sucked in a breath, stilling the urge. His body shuddered under her.

"You're right." The tinge of frustration in his husky voice shot heat through her again. His hands squeezed her legs and moved up to her waist, sending shivers of desire racing to her center as her shaky fingers buttoned her bodice. "This isn't the place or time." He leaned forward his forehead against hers. "But we will make love, and you won't want to stop."

His statement spun brazen thoughts in her head and renewed the throbbing between her legs. "Is that a promise?"

Clay chuckled. "Yes, and Halseys don't break their promises."

His deep velvety response nearly melted her into a puddle of wanton need. Rachel slid off his lap and busied herself putting food on a napkin. She still tingled and every nerve was sensitive to the cool evening breeze.

"Eat."

His hand captured her wrist, his fingers lingered before sliding down to take the offering. "Thanks."

He began eating. She stared at Clay in the fading evening light.

"There are things we need to discuss before I follow you to Sumpter." She picked up half a sandwich and fiddled with the edge of the crust. She wanted to follow her heart and jump at his offer to join him in Sumpter. But she couldn't without knowing his long term expectations.

"I agree. I had intended to discuss the future with you before blurting it out to your family."

He placed a hand on her leg. The heat of his contact didn't ignite desire as before. The touch enveloped her in security and companionship.

"We haven't had a lot of time alone, and they weren't being all that congenial." She covered his hand with hers. "I've never felt as secure with any-one as I do with you. But I need to know." She took a deep breath. Please, say yes. "Will you allow me to continue my medical practice?"

He entwined their fingers. "Yes. We could use a doctor in Sumpter. The nearest one is Baker City, a half a day's ride northeast." He tugged her hand drawing her near. "I'd never ask you to stop help-ing others. Your huge heart is one of the many things I admire about you."

Tears blurred her vision. This man would al-low her to live as she wished. If she hadn't already lost her heart to him, his conviction in her would have done it. Rachel wrapped her free arm around his neck, pressed her body into his, and kissed him with all the emotion swirling in her heart. Draw-ing back, their lips barely touching, she whispered, "Thank you."

His arms circled her body. "You're welcome," he murmured and kissed her with the same aban-don she'd given him. Molten liquid flowed to her extremities and ignited the pulse of need in her center.

"Miss Rachel? Miss Rachel?" The sound of her father's driver jolted her body like a dip in a freez-ing river.

"I have to go to him. Tell him I'm spending the night here." She pushed out of Clay's arms, her heart pounding with fear. If her father got wind of her antics, there was no telling what he'd do.

She handed Clay the remainder of the food. "Take this. Finish eating. I'll see you in the morn-ing." She stood, drawing Clay to his feet.

"I won't leave you alone. We need to face your

father together." Clay caught her arm.

"Please, I'm going to tell the driver to go home. I'm spending the night here. But considering I can't seem to keep my hands to myself, I think it's best if we part now."

"Miss Rachel?" The driver's voice grew louder as the man made his way around the building.

"Please." She kissed Clay's cheek. "We'll finish our discussion tomorrow."

His qualities of loyalty and fighting wrongs were what she loved about the man. However, her father knew too many men who, for some coins, wouldn't mind beating up a blind man.

She hurried away from him toward the driver's voice. Once they boarded the train to Sumpter her father could do nothing. Even he would have to abide by her choice or risk losing his daughter.

Chapter 17

"Where is she you, son-of-a-bitch?"

Clay sat straight up in bed. Who the hell was yelling? Blazes! His stomach roiled, and dizziness swam in his head. He couldn't have been asleep long.

"Who the hell are you?" he growled, swinging his feet to the floor and taking a stance to defend himself even though he only wore his drawers.

"Where's my daughter?" Whiskey bathed breath whooshed into his face as the voice registered. Judge Tarkiel.

"Last I knew she went to talk to your driver and told me she was spending the night in the school." He clenched his fists. The man thought so low of him that he believed he'd bed his daughter the same night he'd been told to stay away from her?

The man cleared his throat. "When Samuel returned saying Rachel planned to spend the night at the school, I—well, I thought—"

"It's pretty obvious what you thought. Did it ever occur to you I care about your daughter and wouldn't do anything to harm her? And you ordering her to not see me might just make her a bit rebellious?"

"That's why I thought she was—"

"I do see what you thought. You told her to leave me and feared she'd do the opposite and go to bed with me. You don't know your daughter very well." Clay sat on the bed and scrubbed his face with his hands. He wanted to go back to sleep, not battle with Rachel's father.

"Since your daughter isn't here, and I'm pretty sure she's sound asleep in the infirmary, why don't you go on home and not rouse the whole school looking for her? When I see her in the morning, I'll tell her to contact you."

"I don't want you telling her I barged in here thinking..." His voice trailed off. "Just because you weren't in bed with my daughter doesn't mean I condone you courting her. Stay away. I'd suggest you head back home soon and forget Rachel."

"I am heading home sooner than planned. As for Rachel...I haven't decided."

Heavy breathing rasped above his head and heat from the man's body loomed over him.

"You will forget her." The growl in the judge's voice knotted Clay's hands into fists.

"Right now I just want to get back to sleep. Good night, Judge." Clay slipped his feet under the covers and rolled to his side. The man found his way in, he could find his way out.

Rachel woke, dressed in the fancy dress she wore to the Fourth of July festivities the day before, and glanced out the window at Clay's cottage. Had he slept well? She'd tossed and turned all night. She didn't like disobeying her father, but she wouldn't let Clay slip out of her life. He was the first man to stir her heart and set her body on fire, and he wanted her to continue practicing medicine. She didn't care what her family thought. She'd be on the train with Clay when it left Salem.

The aromas from the morning meal drifted across the hall. Her stomach rumbled. Would Clay be eating breakfast? She checked her hair in the small mirror and hurried to the dining room.

Clay sat next to Donny, visiting and eating. He wore his usual work clothes. She stopped and watched him. He smiled more now than he had when he first arrived. He'd stopped fighting his blindness and had grasped the need to move forward. Her heart expanded with happiness. Part of his moving forward would be with her.

Rachel hurried into the kitchen and hastily added food to a plate. "Good morning, Mrs. Daniels."

"Mornin' to you, Doctor. I see you spent the night here. Any particular reason?" The woman's rheumy eyes scanned her rumpled dress.

"I didn't wish to go home." Rachel swished her skirts out the door and nearly bumped into Mrs. White.

The woman's eyes narrowed. "Dr. Tarkiel, isn't that the dress you wore yesterday?"

"It is. I spent the night in the infirmary if it's any of your business. Excuse me." Rachel walked over to Clay and leaned down to whisper. "Come to the infirmary when you're done.

A frown creased his brow, but he nodded. Whispering to the man wasn't going to keep the nosey women watching her from starting any number of rumors, but she had to talk to Clay before she gathered her belongings from home.

In the infirmary, she let out a breath and sat down to eat. She'd swallowed two bites of eggs when Clay walked through the door.

He stopped inside the door. "I heard Mrs. White. So you did spend the night here."

"Yes. I told you I wasn't going home. Though, I'm headed there shortly to gather my things. I'll stop by the train station and get tickets on the next train headed north."

Clay crossed the floor and stopped in front of her. "I want you to come with me, but I only want you to come because of me and not to torment your father."

His serious expression and flexed fist made her heart ache. His pride wouldn't allow him to be used for her retaliation on her father. She would never do that to anyone but especially not this man. He'd captured her heart and she'd do everything in her power to make him happy.

"You are the reason I'm going. I thought about it all night, barely sleeping. You're the man I want to spend my life with. If you asked me to marry you today, I would."

His face clouded over. "Is that what you want? To get married before we leave?"

Her stomach lurched at the unemotional delivery of his words. Did he plan to marry her, ever?

"No. I mean, not unless you do."

"You're the first woman I've ever considered marrying. But not until you've seen where we would live and determine if you like it. I don't want you bound to me and hate where I drag you off to." He frowned. "I've seen too many unhappy women who hitched themselves to a mining man and after years of primitive living, backbreaking work, and little to show for it, regretted they couldn't get out."

To allay her family's worries, she'd hoped to use the news they were getting married to soften the fact that she was leaving with Clay. It would have also made her father less likely to do something drastic.

"I'm fine with your reasoning." She was, after all, a forward thinking woman. She didn't need to be married to a man to travel with him.

He cupped her chin in his strong, warm palm. "You're sure you want to do this? Travel across the state with no guarantee of marriage?"

She swallowed the lump of disappointment in her throat. "Yes. I want to see where you grew up, what you have planned, and determine if the eastern part of the state is more open-minded to female doctors."

His thumb slid along her jaw line. A smile grew and soon the dimple on his left cheek came into view. "You're the most courageous woman I've ever met."

He removed his hand, and she nearly fell into him.

Clay slipped a hand into his trouser pocket. "Take this to purchase the train tickets. Get them for as soon as you can be ready to travel." He held out two five dollar gold pieces. "This should be enough for the first leg of the trip. I'll write a note at a bank in Portland for the remainder of the trip. I'd planned to telegraph Hank for funds when I was ready to leave."

Rachel took the money. "I can help. I've been saving. Besides, if I'm traveling as a friend, I might as well pay my own way."

"I'd rather—"

"No, I insist. This way it doesn't look like I'm a companion or mistress. Merely another passenger. Less chance of talk." She reddened thinking of what they could do away from prying eyes. They could behave like smitten newlyweds holding hands in public and talking intimately.

"I don't want you spending all your money on travel. You may need it to set up a practice." He captured her hand. "And I'd be proud if people thought you were my mistress, companion, or wife." The last slid off his tongue soft and low, making her heart pound and heat pool in her pelvic region.

"Clay, are you helpin' in class today?" Donny's voice broke into their conversation.

Rachel glanced beyond Clay's shoulder to the boy standing in the doorway. What would he think when they both left?

"Coming," Clay tossed over his shoulder.

When the boy spun out of the doorway and out of sight, Rachel put a hand on Clay's strong forearm. "You have to let Donny know what you're doing. He's going to be devastated when you leave."

Clay pulled her into a hug. "I've already figured it out. Jasper is going to bring the boy when he comes out to set-up our business. Donny can sell brooms out of our shop."

Her heart swelled to bursting. This was one of the reasons she loved him—his thoughtfulness of others' feelings. He had a caring nature that tugged at her own. He also knew when to be firm and take a stand. Like yesterday with her family and William.

Tremors of anticipation fluttered up her back. Wouldn't these qualities make a good lover?

"You are a wonderful man, Clay Halsey."

"Only because of you." His lips descended on hers. The kiss wasn't a see-you-later kiss. It was an open-mouthed, soul-deep connection of tangled tongues and heated tastes that left her dizzy and a bit wobbly when he pulled away. "Talk to you tonight."

"Yes," she forced through numb vocal cords and watched him—swagger? Yes, he had a definite swagger to his gait exiting the room.

Rachel giggled, pulled herself together, and set out for her house. If she was lucky, father would have left for work and she'd only have to deal with her mother.

"What do you mean you're moving out?"

Her mother's shrill voice bounced around Rachel's room as she packed suitable traveling clothes in a valise.

"I'm a woman with a career. I'll not live in a house where I am told who I can be friends with.

I'll move into a boarding house." Rachel buckled the bag shut. "May I ask Samuel for a ride back to the school?"

Her mother blocked her way to the door. "I thought you were staying in a boarding house?"

"I will when I find one. I'll leave my things at the school while I check out the possibilities." If the train left tomorrow, there'd be no need to get a room at a boardinghouse.

"Your father isn't going to like this." Her mother didn't step aside, just stood in front of the bedroom door, hands clenched in front of her.

"He should have thought about that before treating me like a child." Rachel nudged past her mother their shoulders brushing. "If he wants to see me, I'll send word where I'm staying, and he may call."

Celeste strolled out of her room, dressed in a pale blue outfit that highlighted her attributes and flattered her coloring. "I'm headed to a luncheon date. Can I give you a lift?"

"That would be wonderful! I also have some books in the library if you wouldn't mind packing them to the buggy for me." Rachel sent her younger sister an appreciative smile.

They stopped at the library and Celeste picked up the four rather large books.

"I still don't see why you have to leave," their mother wailed, following behind them. "Celeste, you shouldn't be helping her."

Celeste faced their mother. "If Rachel has finally found happiness, you should be happy for her, not issuing ultimatums."

Rachel gazed at her sister. Had her unhappiness been that visible to all those around her? She thought she'd hid her emotions as cleverly as her scar. Apparently not. At least her sister realized Clay made her happy and offered her help.

At the buggy, waiting for Samuel to stow the books and valise in the storage compartment, Rachel wrapped her arms around her sister.

"Thank you for understanding. I can't give up Clay. He makes me happy and a stronger person."

Tears burned at the back of her eyes. A lump crawled up her throat. She'd miss Celeste and Dr.Runkle. Before her father's demands, she would have missed him, too. Now, his accusations against Clay stung as vividly as a physical blow.

"Hey, you helped me connect with my true love, I'm not about to let mother and father ruin your chance." Celeste held her away and stared into her eyes. "Invite me to the wedding."

Rachel laughed as Samuel handed first Celeste, and then her, into the buggy. "How do you know there's going to be a wedding?"

Celeste's eyes grew wide, and her mouth twisted into a frown. "He hasn't asked you to marry him?"

"Not in so many words. He wants to make sure I can take the rural life before we make a commitment."

Rachel studied her hands as the buggy lurched forward. She wanted the long term commitment from Clay. Dreamed of being Mrs. Clay Halsey. Even if he didn't marry her, she would remain by his side if he continued to believe in her career as a doctor and make her feel like a beautiful, cherished woman.

Celeste touched her knee. "You're leaving Salem aren't you?"

"Don't tell Father, but we're taking the next train headed to Sumpter. Clay is ready to head home. I'll travel with him as his companion." Her stomach fluttered. They would spend countless hours together on the trip.

"Companion? If he doesn't ask you to marry him you won't be able to marry anyone if they find out you traveled as his companion," Celeste whispered and clutched her hand.

"If he doesn't ask me to marry him, I don't want anyone else, but I will have had time with him." Rachel patted her sister's hand. "He makes me feel strong and beautiful."

"You are." Celeste touched the scar. "Even with this you are one of the most beautiful women in Salem. And becoming a doctor against father's wishes and society— You are the strongest woman I know." Celeste hugged her. "I'm proud to be your sister."

Rachel swallowed the lump of emotion in her throat. "I'm proud to be your sister, too. You're beautiful and so politically smart. I know you will get us the vote one of these days."

Celeste laughed and released her. "I'll do my darnedest to make it happen in our lifetime." She squeezed Rachel's hand. "The school is in sight."

Rachel nodded, squaring her shoulders and stilling her nervous stomach. Why did she have to leave now, when she and Celeste were finally becoming true friends? Growing up, she'd loved Celeste as only a big sister could, but she also felt inferior to the beautiful girl who turned heads.

Now, hearing how her sister found her brave, looked up to her, and didn't find fault with her traveling across the state with a blind man, she wished she could remain a bit longer and savor the elation.

She stared at the school and shuddered. As much as she adored the students and most of the staff, she was ready to move on to being a real doctor. Clay would provide that. Whether he married her or not, she would always have her sister's love and admiration, Clay's belief in her doctoring abilities, and her own knowledge he was the only man she would follow anywhere.

Life sure held ironic twists.

Chapter 18

Clay sat on the bench behind the school. He'd made it a point not to seek Rachel. Mrs. White had ventured across him nearly every hour. He'd surmised after the third time, she hoped to catch him and Rachel together. Not that he cared a wit if the woman knew they were getting closer, but he wouldn't put it past the judge to have recruited the woman to spy. Donny informed him Rachel had returned near noon with a bag and books. After the midday meal, she left again. He hadn't heard her voice at dinner and presumed she hadn't returned. Either that or she planned to keep Mrs. White on her toes wondering what was happening.

The rustle of clothing and the faint whiff of citrus on the slight evening breeze brought a smile to his lips and lightness to his heart. The woman of his thoughts sought him.

She sat beside him on the bench. He didn't know if they were being watched, but he ached to touch her. Clay slipped his hand from his knee, moving across the space on the bench between them, and bumped into warm slender fingers. He covered them.

He faced her and wished for a millionth time he could see her expressions. "I heard you had a busy day."

"I packed some clothes in a valise and gathered the rest of my medical books. They're all packed in a small trunk in the infirmary. I have our tickets. The train leaves at eight tomorrow morning." She rotated her hand, placing her palm to his. "Do you want me to arrange for a cab to pick us up in the morning?"

His heart raced. He would head home tomorrow and take with him the desirable woman by his side.

"No. Jasper will take us. I'll write up a note for Mr. Griffin. Thank him for all I was taught and let him know I've headed home." He squeezed her hand. "You know what they're all going to think when we both are gone?"

"I don't care. Celeste says I'm doing the right thing."

He raised an eyebrow. "You've discussed our leaving with your sister? Don't you worry she'll tell your father and he'll try to stop us?

"She knows everything and won't tell. We actually understand one another better now. It's a shame I have to leave when we're finally getting along."

The regret ringing in her voice seized his heart. "You don't have to think of this as never seeing your family. If you don't like the area you can return. I won't keep you." Even though my life would be empty without you. "And if you do stay, you can visit your family as much as you want."

"I want to see where you grew up and meet your family." Her soft lips grazed his cheek. "I appreciate that you allow me independence and don't make me follow traditional rules."

"Are there people watching us?" He wanted to hold and kiss her to show her not only did he appreciate her independence, but he desired her as well.

"Most likely Mrs. White is peering from a window in the dorms." She snuggled under his arm. "But I don't care since we'll be gone tomorrow."

He drew her against his body, inhaling her unique scent of citrus, medicine, and Rachel. Clay settled his palm on her ribcage and fought the urge to caress her side and cup a breast. She wrapped her arms around his waist and hugged him.

"Are you spending the night in the infirmary again?" He tipped his head and kissed her hair.

"Yes, I didn't see any sense in getting a room somewhere for one night. Though my parents think I'm staying in a boarding house."

Her thoughtful tone piqued his senses. "I don't like you fooling your parents. It doesn't reflect well on our relationship." He'd bet before their attraction she'd never told her parents anything other than the truth and followed all their demands. Guilt plagued him and churned in his belly like sour milk.

"I'm not fooling them. When I told my mother I planned to move into a boarding house, that had been my course of action until I found out the train is leaving in the morning and I purchased tickets."

She snuggled and twined her fingers with his. "I haven't lied, just haven't kept them posted on my whereabouts." She sat up and twisted toward him. His hand slid to her back. "I'm twenty-six years old and a doctor. My parents don't need to know my every move. If I were a man they would have pushed me out on my own by now, if I hadn't left already."

Clay rubbed circles on her back. She leaned into his touch. "True. I just don't want them accusing me of tainting their daughter."

Her soft lips brushed his. "Let me worry about my reputation. After all, it's mine and no one else's." Her mouth pressed to his, her lips parted, and her wet, sweet tongue slipped between his lips. She'd proved a quick study in seducing his mouth.

The conversation and the world dissolved. Clay wrapped his arms around Rachel, drawing her body against his and savoring the feel of her soft breasts pressed against his chest. He hardened at the contact. She continued to entice him with her sensuous mouth. He needed to touch her soft skin. Trailing his hand up her back, he massaged her neck and traced his fingers around to the front. He slid his fingertips lightly over the satin texture and dipped under the neckline into the warmth between her breasts. She moaned and broke off the kiss, shuddering in his arms.

"It's still daylight. You all need to go inside."

Jasper's gruff voice shook Clay's haze of desire as soundly as if the man had rang a church bell beside him.

Rachel straightened, pulling away. "You're right, Mr. Smith."

Clay kept his arm around Rachel. What they'd done wasn't wrong, just in the wrong place.

"I got caught up in something. And shouldn't have." Clay stood and drew Rachel to her feet. "Jasper, we need you to take us to the train station in the morning. Doctor Tarkiel has a trunk and valise that you'll need to load at six-thirty?" he questioned Rachel.

"Yes, that would be fine. I'll have them sitting in the hall outside the infirmary." Her steady voice and arm looped in his settled the nerves he'd been fighting over taking her away from everything she knew. Even though he assured her she could come back any time, he hoped she loved Sumpter, his family, and him, enough to stay.

"I's thought you wasn't gonna leave until next month?" Jasper's accusing tone didn't surprise Clay.

"There's been a change of plans. I'll send the money for you and Donny to come to Sumpter. Plan on heading out on the original date." Clay took a step forward, his hand extended. "Nothing has changed in regard to our business."

Jasper took his hand and held tight. "This have anythin' to do with her pa bargin' into you all's room last night?"

Rachel gasped. "You didn't tell me Father was here. What did he do and say?"

Clay's gut clenched. He hadn't planned to tell her about her father's nocturnal visit. No sense in setting her more against the judge.

He jerked his hand out of Jasper's grasp and frowned at the man.

"He came by looking for you."

Her intake of breath told him more than any words she could've uttered. "He thought I was in your bed?" Her high pitch mimicked Celeste's irritating tone.

"He asked me if I knew where you were." Clay didn't want to rile her anymore. No telling what she might do, like dash off to give her father a dressing down.

"How dare you cover for him? He wouldn't barge into your room looking for me unless he planned to catch us together." The crunch of gravel fading and returning proved she paced. Her agitation whistled on the air with every breath she took.

She stopped. "What did he hope to prove by catching us? Did he think I'd stoop so low as to jump in your bed to spite him?"

Clay held his facial muscles in check.

She stopped in front of him.

He couldn't see her staring, but his face heated, and he knew she was.

"You aren't going to tell me are you?" She sucked in air, and her small hand grasped his. "Did he threaten you again?"

"No, he seemed appeased when I told him you were sleeping in the school." He ran a palm up her arm and cupped the side of her face. "Go inside, pack, and go to sleep early. We'll be headed out of here in the morning and no one can do anything about it. As you've said, you're a grown woman and can make up your own mind."

Her soft, warm lips touched his palm, igniting a fire. "I'll see you in the morning."

Heat seeped into his palm and radiated up his arm. Her retreating steps crackled the gravel and set his already tightly strung body to humming.

"You all better watch out if'n the judge don't like you messin' with his girl."

Jasper's voice yanked him away from the carnal thoughts bumping around in his head. "He can't do anything. She's a woman and a professional. No law that I know of says she can't travel where and with whom she chooses." Clay walked in the direction of the cottage.

Jasper's heavy steps followed. "Some daddies don't care how old their girls be, they still don't like 'em bein' dallied with."

"I'm not dallying with Dr. Tarkiel." He stopped. "I thought you were my friend?"

"I is, and I'm jus' sayin' travelin' with her and not marryin' her it looks like dallyin'."

"She's willing to wait until we arrive in Sumpter to decide if she wants to be tied to me."

Clay stomped after the man. What did he care what Jasper, a handyman, or anyone else thought? Only Rachel and he mattered.

Damn! Why had she suggested marriage?

He wasn't willing to bind her to him yet. She could change her mind about being tethered to a blind man after they traveled together.

For all he knew she'd get tired of his need for assistance and once they landed in Baker City, take the next train back here. He wasn't avoiding marriage to sully her reputation.

He wouldn't marry her until after the trip to spare her from a bondage she could grow to despise.

Clay stepped to the door of his room. "Wake me at five."

Jasper grunted and his door closed with a thud.

If they had enough time in Portland after getting money at a bank, he'd purchase a ring. That's the strongest commitment he could make until she was certain.

Chapter 19

A hand grasped Clay's shoulder and shook roughly.

"Wake up."

Jasper's deep voice ricocheted in Clay's head.

"I just went to sleep." He shoved the covers down and swung his legs over the edge of the bed.

"Then you's been up all night packin'. It's five. I'm goin' for Dr. Tarkiel's things. I'll come back for you when I's loaded 'em."

Clay waved the man away and scrubbed his hands over his face. He needed a shave. He might be blind, but he wasn't going to have people think Rachel traveled with him out of pity. His shaving soap, strap, and razor were laid out on the bureau.

He found the pitcher, poured water, and lathered up the shave soap. The one good thing about being blind, he could shave anywhere. No need for a mirror. A chuckle warmed his throat. Happiness swelled in his chest. Happiness was something he never thought would find him after the accident.

Now, he had something to look forward to besides hopefully one day regaining his sight—Rachel. This trip would be a test for both of them. To see how well he could function without his brothers' support and to find out if Rachel really had feelings for him. He had to know, and she had to discover if her feelings were due to her desire to help others and pity for him, or if she really loved him.

Clay picked up the razor and scraped at the whiskers. He'd learned the curves and planes of his face by feel. Running fingers over his skin, he found spots he missed. He scraped up the misses and washed.

He pulled on the britches he'd hung over the end of the bed, a clean white shirt, and his suit jacket. Sitting on the chair, he laced his boots.

"She's waitin' in the buggy, you 'bout done?"

Jasper's jovial tone tipped Clay's lips into a smile. "You saying I take longer to dress than a woman?" Clay dropped his shave gear into the valise and buckled it shut. "Did I get all my things?"

The scrape of wood on wood signaled Jasper checked through the bureau. "I's don't see nothin' in the drawers or hangin' on the wall."

"Then I'm packed. Let's not keep Doctor Tarkiel waiting." Clay picked up his valise and strode for the door.

Jasper fell into step beside him as they rounded the side of the building.

"Tell Donny I didn't have time to say goodbye. He knew I was leaving and shouldn't be too upset. I also told him you'd bring him out with you."

Harnesses jingled and a horse snorted. The

valise disappeared from his hand.

"How are you this morning, Clay?"

Rachel's cheerful voice set his heart thumping in his chest. He stretched a welcoming smile from ear to ear.

"Excited. I'm heading home with a beautiful escort." Clay found the side of the buggy and felt his way to the door. He climbed up. A tug on his sleeve plopped him down on the seat. Citrus invaded his senses.

The vehicle lurched forward. The crackle of gravel under the wheels filled the air around them with a lulling cadence.

He reached over and found her hand. "Are you truly happy to travel with me?"

He'd worried about it all night. Was he pushing her into something she didn't really want? Was she doing this only to irritate her father?

"I want to be where you are. You give me strength and friendship."

Her soft words hummed in his chest like a shot of good whiskey. "That's what I needed to know. Did you leave a note for your parents and Mr. Griffin?"

"Yes. Though, I doubt my words will sway any of them to think well of me." Her deep sigh tightened his gut. "I've decided the only people whose feelings matter are you and me."

Clay grasped her chin and kissed her lips. "I've come to the same conclusion."

Traffic sounds grew, along with shouts and the hiss of steam engines.

"I'll drop you's as close to the boardin' dock as I can," Jasper's voice hollered above the chaos.

"My word, there are a lot of people boarding this morning."

The surprise in Rachel's voice piqued Clay's curiosity. "Isn't it always busy when a train is boarding?"

"The last time we traveled to Portland, I don't remember this many people bustling about. There must be something going on." Her arm brushed against him, her body shifted at his side.

"Oh! It looks like there is some kind of a rally taking place. They have streamers on one of the cars."

Her body stiffened, and her hand clamped onto his arm. "Father is here. They have a podium set up, and he's standing to the side. How will we board without him seeing us?"

Resentment spiraled through Clay. "I thought you were an independent woman who wanted to go with me?"

"I-I am. I just—"

"If it's true, then we board the train, and if your father challenges, we tell him the truth. You wish to travel with me to my home." Clay stepped out of the buggy and held up his hand waiting for her. She clutched his fingers in a vise-like grip as she alighted from the vehicle.

"Here's your bags." Jasper put a bag in each of Clay's hands. "I'll follow with the trunk."

Rachel's small hand curved around his left elbow, and they proceeded through the crowd to the baggage car. A squeeze on his arm stopped Clay.

"Can I see your tickets?" a voice in front of them asked. Rachel's arm slipped out of his. "Goin' to Portland. Set the bags and trunk here. I'll get 'em loaded."

Clay set the bags down, and Rachel slid her arm back through his.

"May we board the train, now?" Rachel asked.

"You're gonna miss all the hoopla if ya do." The man laughed.

"We would rather get seated."

"Then suit yourself. Just go on down to the passenger car and find a seat. The conductor'll come along and take your ticket."

Clay nodded, and Rachel led him to the right. A hand grasped his shoulder stopping their progress.

"I'll jus' say bye here," Jasper said.

Clay stuck out his hand. "You're a good friend. I'll see you in a month in Sumpter." They shook.

"Mr. Smith, I look forward to seeing you again."

Rachel's sweet parting warmed Clay. She, too, had found a friend in the handyman.

"I's lookin' forward to it, ma'am."

Rachel resumed walking, and Clay fell into step beside her. Her arm tightened about his elbow and a sharp intake of air whistled at his shoulder. They'd been spotted by someone she knew.

"Your father?" he asked quietly.

"Worse. William."

The dread in her voice brought out his protective instincts. He squared his shoulders and prepared for whatever would come.

"Rachel, I can't believe my eyes, you with an escort to two political events in one week. You must be coming out from hiding."

Contempt rippled in the male voice, rankling

Clay's already rising ire.

"We aren't here for the rally. We're boarding the train. If you don't mind, we'd like to take our seats." Clay took a step forward, drawing Rachel with him.

"Does her father know she's leaving town with you?" The man's comment hovered behind them and above the clamor on the station platform.

Clay pivoted slowly. "I don't believe that's your business."

"Looking out for Rachel is my business." William's voice drew closer.

"When you broke off the betrothal you lost that privilege." Clay leaned forward, his fisted hands rising from his side. How dare this man who threw Rachel away like fool's gold now claim she was his business? His lip curled in distaste. "She's a grown woman. One who knows her own mind."

Clay turned to Rachel. "Where's our passenger car?" He strode away from the irritating man.

"Thank you," she whispered and squeezed his arm against her side.

"For what?" He flexed his fingers. He'd wanted a roaring good fight, but he guessed it wouldn't happen today. Ever since meeting the man, he'd been itching to pop him in the nose.

"For standing up for me and telling him I know what I'm doing."

"You don't have to thank me for telling the truth. I'll always be here for you." He pulled her hand to his lips and kissed her knuckles.

"Oh dear. Father straight ahead."

Her harsh whisper riled him. The man shouldn't instill fear in his daughter.

"Rachel—" Judge Tarkiel said, and her grip tightened on Clay's arm. "I didn't know you planned to attend the rally."

"Judge Tarkiel." Clay held out his hand. He didn't expect a firm handshake and wasn't sure how to proceed when the judge not only shook his hand, but clasped his arm in the process.

The man drew away. Clay pondered the cordial meeting until Rachel's fingers reluctantly let loose of his arm. Where was she going and why?

"Father."

"What are you doing with this man?"

The judge's whisper hissed not far from Clay's ear as the man's shoulder bumped his. The judge must have embraced his daughter. His friendly handshake only served as a political ruse.

Clay bristled at being used. "We didn't know there was a rally. We're actually boarding the train." He raised his voice making sure anyone standing nearby on the platform would hear his declaration.

Rachel grabbed onto his arm, running her hand down and lacing their fingers. "Father, I'm escorting Clay back to his family. If I like things there, you will receive a wedding invitation."

"You're doing no such thing!" Judge Tarkiel bellowed.

Footsteps and voices circled. Chaos clamored around them. Clay clutched Rachel's hand tighter. They couldn't be separated. She needed his strength and he needed her eyes. The press of bodies forced him to pull Rachel closer.

"What's happening?" he whispered in her ear.

"My father's friends are gathering around,

forming a wall."

"Does it look like I'll need to fight our way through?"

Rachel stared at Clay. He'd take on this mob to give her the freedom she craved. She kissed his cheek and took a step toward her father, keeping hold of Clay's hand.

"Father and anyone else here who seems to think my business is theirs. Mr. Halsey and I have tickets to Portland and we plan to be on the train."

She faced her father. His face had reddened since their first encounter. The anger in his usually loving eyes hurt, but she didn't let it stop what she had to say.

"I have wanted only two things since returning to Salem—to practice medicine, real medicine, and to be treated as an equal. Mr. Halsey has offered me both."

She tucked her hand through Clay's arm and drew him forward, peering at the men until they parted, allowing her and Clay to pass.

"What about your mother?" her father called.

"I left a note at the school." She grasped the handle on the side of the passenger car.

"There are three steps up," she warned Clay and climbed aboard the car with the help of the conductor. When Clay stood on the platform, she twined her fingers with his. They walked down the aisle between the wooden bench seats. She picked a shiny, slick well-used seat away from the platform and slid in.

Clay moved in beside her and sat. "You were wonderful." He placed a tender kiss on her cheek.

"Let's hope my note and explanation will appease my mother." She settled into the seat and scanned the people climbing on board the passenger car.

"If it doesn't, we'll handle whatever they try."

She smiled at his confidence in their bond. However, her father hadn't got where he was by giving up easily.

"Heavens! He doesn't know when to quit. My father... He's stomping up the aisle toward us."

"Rachel, child, what are you thinking?" Her father loomed over them, glaring at Clay.

Clay's body tensed and rose off the seat. Rachel held him down with their joined hands.

"That's the problem, Father, you think of me as a child. I want to be treated as an adult. For heaven's sake, I'm twenty-six years old. Stop treating me like I'm twelve."

"But these actions remind me of an impetuous child." He crossed his arms, stood in the aisle, and glared at her, not allowing anyone to pass.

"What I'm doing isn't impetuous. I've thought it out and wish to travel with Clay." She leaned forward. "Please, go back to the rally and let us continue in peace. I'll send a letter when I reach Sumpter."

"By then your reputation will have been sullied." His worry lines etched deeper. His tone grew more accusing.

"Her reputation is only being sullied by you arguing and causing a scene." Clay stood. "When I asked to court your daughter, you threatened me."

Rachel placed a palm on his forearm. It overwhelmed her to witness the way he came to her rescue even though he couldn't see his assailant.

"In Portland, I plan to purchase a ring to prove my commitment, and if by the end of this trip Rachel still wishes to spend her life with me, I'll marry her." He crossed his arms. "So, sir, you're the only person who's finding fault with your daughter's happiness."

Rachel stood beside the man she loved. A man who believed in her. "Father, please leave. We both know what we're doing."

Her father peered at her, at Clay, and back at her. "It appears there's nothing I can do to sway your decision."

"No." Rachel looped an arm through Clay's.

Her father's shoulders drooped. He stared at their locked arms and sighed. "I'll tell your mother."

Rachel nodded and drew Clay back down on the seat.

"Do you think he's giving up?" Clay asked.

"I hope so, but with father, you never know."

Chapter 20

Five hours and multiple stops later, the train pulled into the Portland station. Rachel stood and stretched her aching back from the bouncing of the train and her legs from sitting so long. She linked her hand with Clay's, leading him from the passenger car.

"What do we need to do first?" she asked, when they stood on the train station platform. The clatter of the wheels over the metal tracks still rang in her ears and her body wanted to sway like the motion of the train.

"Find out the cost of tickets to Baker City, have them hold our baggage, find a bank, and then a jewelry store."

Clay pulled her hand into the crook of his arm and waited. She leaned against his shoulder in a brief hug to show him she was still in this adventure whole-heartedly. Glancing at the flow of the crowd, she merged Clay into the stream and kept an eye out for the ticket office.

She stopped to the side of the ticket booth and read the signage. "It's eighteen dollars per person to Baker City. And it says two dollars more for a Pullman car." Her eyes skimmed all the information as Clay waited patiently. "The next train leaves at seven tonight and will arrive in Baker City at noon tomorrow." She faced Clay. "You need to telegraph your brother."

"Find the telegraph office here, and while I take care of that and get directions to a bank and jewelry store, you can have our baggage held to go on tonight's train."

His confident smile made her laugh. "You sound like a seasoned traveler." She spotted the sign above the telegraph office and set out in that direction.

His confident strides matched her own. He moved through the people milling about as though he saw each and every one. "The trip out here with Ethan and his family, I paid close attention believing I'd return alone."

She expanded her chest with pride at his stature and confidence. Other women gawked at him with wistful smiles. He cut a fine figure and he was all hers. Heat coiled in her center. The more time she spent with him the more her body craved his touch and kisses.

"The telegraph office." She placed his hands on the ledge of the window opening. "I'll hurry back."

Clay leaned on the casing, listening to the rapid tap of Rachel's heels departing. "I need to send a telegram to Hank Halsey, Sumpter, Oregon."

"I can help ya with that." The male voice had an aged warble to it. "Want to write it down?" A pad bumped his hand.

"No. You can write it down if you need to. Coming home. Train noon tomorrow. Brought a surprise. Clay."

"That's simple enough. It'll be two bits."

"Thanks. After you send that I have a couple questions for you." He twisted, leaning one elbow on the sill. Random footsteps tapped, thudded, and clicked, skirts swished, children whined, muffled men's and women's voices floated by in fluctuating waves. Scents familiar, sweet, harsh, and foul wafted on the air currents.

"I'm done. What did ya need?" the telegrapher asked.

"Directions to the closest bank and jewelry store. And if you don't mind, would you please write it down."

Graphite scratched against paper.

"Here ya go."

Air wafted toward Clay's face. He held a hand palm up, and the paper dropped into it. He folded the paper in half matching the corners.

"Is there a decent eating establishment near the bank and jewelry store?"

"Do ya want fancy or something to fill your stomach?"

"Fancy. I've a lady to impress."

The man chuckled. "Try the Hotel Perkins. They have a fine dining room."

Clay slid a half dollar across the sill. "Thank you for your help."

"Much obliged!"

Clay stepped away from the window and leaned against the building. Was Rachel having problems? He'd expected her back before he'd finished his tasks. He couldn't wander off searching for her. Who knew where he'd end up.

Frustration gnawed at his gut. This was why he needed an independent woman. And why he pushed her to continue with her doctoring. A clinging, dependent woman would be useless. He needed someone who would walk beside him through life and help make decisions. Luckily, he'd fallen in love with a very independent woman.

Rapid steps approached. He listened intently. They had a familiar cadence. Firm and quick.

"Finished?"

Rachel's sweet voice flowed to him as her arm slid around his.

"Yes." He handed her the folded paper. The paper rustled and she laughed.

"I should have known. It looks like these are only a few blocks away. Do you want to walk or take a cab?" She strode forward, and he fell in step beside her.

"After all the sitting on the train, I could use the walk."

"Me, too." She strolled at a leisurely pace. The hollow thud of each step indicated they sauntered on a board walkway. The bustling noise of the train station subsided. Footsteps and the waves of motion had slowed.

"I see the bank," Rachel said.

"Is it a large bank? What's the name?" He hoped it was a reputable bank and one that would honor his request.

"I've never seen a bank as large as this one. It looks like—yes, it's the First Bank of Portland."

"We need to speak with the manager." His funds in his Baker City account held more than he needed. Plus, during the four months he'd been gone, Hank should've added more.

Rachel's small hand placed his on a door handle. He pulled it open, allowing her to enter, and followed behind. She slid her arm through his once more.

Their steps rang out as they crossed a hard floor. Rachel stopped at the fifteenth step.

"Mr. Halsey would like to speak with the bank manager, please."

Rachel's congenial tone, tipped Clay's lips into a friendly smile.

"This way, please," a male voice replied.

Seventeen steps and they stopped.

A knock resounded. "Mr. Shepard, a Mr. Halsey would like a word with you." He liked the business clip of the man's words.

"Come in, Mr. and Mrs. Halsey," a voice boomed from the back of the room. Clay smiled at the misconception but didn't bother to correct him. The man would never see them again, and if he did, by then they would hopefully be married.

Clay caught the scent of rum-soaked cigars mixed with the subtle trace of leather. Ten steps into the room Rachel stopped. The edge of a desk pressed into his thighs. He extended his right arm.

Long, thin, smooth fingers grasped his hand.

"Mr. Shepard. We're passing through, and I would like to have you write up a bank draft. I have the funds in my account at Baker City National."

"Have a seat and tell me a little about yourself."

Clay smiled. He knew the man wouldn't hand over money without knowing some history. Rachel tugged on his sleeve, guiding him to a chair. He sat.

"My brothers and I have a stamp mill on Cracker Creek."

"Halsey... I believe one of your brothers was in here over a year ago. He procured some funds this way as well."

The man's genial voice and good memory boosted Clay's confidence. "That would be my oldest brother, Ethan. He was here arranging the delivery of our equipment."

The sound of a drawer opening and the rustle of paper was a good sign.

"How much did you and the missus need?" Mr. Shepard asked.

"Two hundred."

Rachel's intake of breath filled his chest with pride.

"That's a large sum, but since your brother wrote notes for more than that last time and there wasn't a problem, I'll write this up and get the money."

The scratch of a quill on paper relieved some of his worry. If the banker hadn't agreed to the transaction, he wasn't sure where he could have gone next.

"I need your signature."

Heat from the banker's presence hovered beside him. Clay ran a hand over the desktop searching for the paper. Rachel's small hand slid the quill into his fingers. She placed the finger of his left hand on the paper.

"Thank you." He grinned at her and wrote his name beside his finger.

"I'll get your money." The banker's heavy footsteps faded.

Rachel clutched his arm. "We don't need that much money." Her whisper puffed against his ear.

"We need train tickets, your ring, and dinner. I'd rather have too much than not enough." He patted her hand.

"But I don't need a ring, especially an expensive one."

The worry in her voice tugged at his heart. "Yes, you do. I want to prove to you and everyone else my intentions. I won't have you wearing some circle of tin when I can purchase something with meaning."

Footsteps approached and her hand slipped from his arm.

"Mr. Halsey. Here is your money."

Clay stood at Mr. Shepard's voice. "Please, hand the money to Rachel."

Paper rustled and Mr. Shepard said, "Since you're traveling I broke it into tens and twenties."

Clay preferred coins as they were easier for him to discern, but the sum in coins would have been unwieldy. Rachel would have to help take care of their finances during the trip.

Clay held out his hand. "Thank you, Mr. Shepard. It has been a pleasure doing business with you."

"You and the missus have a good rest of your trip."

Clay smiled as Rachel's arm slid around his. "We plan on it, sir. Thank you."

She maneuvered him out of the office and onto the bustling street.

"When we get to a place that's secluded, I want you to give me half of the money and separate the denominations."

Rachel's arm tightened and her steps faltered.

"It's not that I don't trust you, it's so no one sees that much money on you and tries to take it."

Rachel relaxed and chided herself for thinking he didn't trust her. Her heart fluttered at his protectiveness. "I understand. Why didn't you correct him when he called me missus?"

"I didn't hear you complaining and it was easier to let him think that than try to explain."

Rachel pulled him into the stoop of a closed establishment. She backed against the door, drawing Clay close in front of her.

"How do you want the money I give you?" she whispered.

"Give me half in a bundle of tens and a bundle of twenties."

She placed the folded money in his hand. "Three twenties."

He bent the upper left corners over.

She handed him the remainder. "Four tens."

He bent the upper right corner on them and put the twenties on top of the tens, slipping the folded money into his pocket. He kissed her cheek and backed away, motioning for her to return to the boardwalk. She looped her arm in his, relishing the feel of his strong arm and peering up at his powerful height.

"I see the jewelry store up ahead."

Giddiness bubbled in her throat like champagne. She, Rachel Tarkiel, would receive a ring. Her feet floated across the board walkway. Her practical side tripped her, and her feet dumped back on solid ground. There wasn't a valid reason to spend money on a ring.

"I don't need a ring." The words nearly choked her, but they were the truth. In all honesty, she didn't need a ring. Since their first meeting he'd shown his interest in her, and his attentiveness proved he cared.

"I want you to pick out something that you like, not something that's inexpensive."

"I don't know why you're making such a big deal out of a ring."

He stopped and fumbled, grasping her hands. "Because it means I'm pledging a commitment to you. Something I take very serious."

Her heart leapt into her throat, strangling her ability to say anything. She knew he cared for her and hoped they would have a future, but she hadn't realized, until this moment, the depth of his loyalty. He would never treat her like William had.

People stepped around them, gawking. Rachel wrapped her arm around his and walked down the boardwalk. "Okay, I see this is a symbol of your commitment. But I don't need a ring. You prove to me every day you care for me." Her heart skipped around in her chest. If all went well, he would prove it to her the rest of her life.

"Take my gift of the ring and wear it to remind you."

The sincerity ringing in his voice brought tears to her eyes. She blinked, trying to wipe them away and clear her sight during their last few steps to the shop.

"We're here." She placed his hand on the door handle, and he ushered her in.

"Can I help you?"

Rachel turned to the voice and found a stooped older woman sitting on a stool behind the counter, knitting.

"We're looking for a special ring," Clay said, crossing the room. Rachel grasped his hand and followed.

The woman's wrinkled face grinned. "You've come to the right place. My husband makes the most beautiful rings." She slowly stood and shuffled to a glass case to her right. Rachel drew Clay to the case. Glistening gems of every color twinkled on a bed of black velvet.

"They're gorgeous!" She couldn't hide her appreciation. Clay squeezed her hand, and she gazed at his beaming face.

"Pick the one you like the best."

If his eyes held emotion they'd have danced with glee in the delighted expression he wore. Happiness at his delight and the commitment he wanted fluttered in her chest like hummingbird wings.

"You have dainty hands. I'd go for one of the smaller stones."

The woman pulled out a tray of sparkling rings. Rachel picked up several, each one more stunning than the last, and studied them.

"I like this green one. It reminds me of spring and new things growing and blooming."

"That's a wonderful choice. Emeralds are a stone of love and contentment." The old woman held two rings. "Try them on. If they don't fit, my husband is in the back, and he can make it work."

Rachel held out her hand and slid the first sparkling gem on her finger. It fit perfectly. "This one will do."

"Let me see." Clay held his palm out. She placed her hand in his, and he fingered the ring, tugging slightly and feeling the stone. "You say this looks good on her finger?" he asked the woman.

The woman's face scrunched in anger as though she thought he disbelieved her. Rachel cleared her throat and nodded to her hand. The woman watched his fingers skim over every slant of the stone.

"Yes, sir, that stone looks right pretty on her finger."

Clay smiled and raised Rachel's hand to his lips and kissed her knuckles. "Then we'll take it."

"That one's sixty dollars. It's an excellent quality stone."

Rachel gasped at the price and studied the woman. Had she added to the price due to Clay's blindness? The woman met Rachel's gaze straight on, her gaze never wavering.

"Clay, you don't need to spend that much." She wasn't like her mother and sister. Expensive things didn't make her happy. All she wanted was him.

"You like it, the proprietor says it looks beautiful on your finger, we'll take it." He dug into his pocket and pulled out the money she'd given him.

Rachel held a snicker as the woman stared opened mouthed as Clay counted out two twenties and two tens and placed them on the counter.

"I'm starving. Let's celebrate with a nice dinner before we board the train." Clay held out his arm and she slipped her hand through the crook of his elbow.

"Thank you for all your help," he called to the woman as they exited the shop.

Chapter 21

Sitting in the dining room of the Hotel Perkins, Rachel stared at the crimson velvet drapes framing lace panels filtering the sun through the front windows. The bustling wait staff darted around carved pillars stoically holding aloft the tin ceiling design. She'd eaten in other fine restaurants in Portland over the years while traveling with her family, but this establishment left her speechless.

"Is the atmosphere right for our celebration?" Clay asked, his hand reaching toward hers across the intimate table.

"Yes, it's— I can't even explain how grand it is."

He smiled, and her heart tumbled even more for the man.

When they'd entered the restaurant he'd told the first person who approached they were celebrating. The man had led them to this wonderful little table and brought a bottle of champagne—a gift from the management. She'd only tasted the bubbly concoction once before.

"You didn't have to buy me a ring or do this." She waved her hand around the room. "But I'm enjoying every minute of it."

"As long as we're together, I promise to only make you happy."

He squeezed her fingers, drawing her hand across the table and to his lips, dropping light kisses on each knuckle. Her stomach fluttered. Heat flushed her body like a vat of hot water poured over her.

"Ahem—" The sound shook her out of the haze of desire she'd become veiled in. Rachel pulled her hand away from Clay's as the waiter placed their meal on the table.

"Roast three o-clock, potatoes with gravy six, and beans at nine," she said, before starting on her own meal. They ate in companionable silence until the waiter returned and offered a tray of decadent sweets.

She started to explain each fancy confection on the silver tray.

"You choose one and we'll share," Clay said.

"What if I pick something you don't like?"

"Then you'll get it all." Clay laughed and the waiter watched her with rapt attention.

"I'll take that one." She pointed to the chocolate cake topped with a swirl of creamy frosting.

"Excellent choice," the waiter said, placing the cake on the table between them.

Rachel picked up her fork and cut a small bite. "Open your mouth."

She smiled and slid the fork and bite between his parted lips. He closed his mouth around the cake and leaned back. The muscles in his lean face moved under his tanned skin. A dab of frosting remained on his lips. What would it taste like to lick it off? She refrained from making a spectacle and reached across the table, skimming her finger over his bottom lip. The softness sent a tremor of anticipation rippling through her body.

Clay's eyes widened at her touch. His lips parted slightly, and he leaned forward, drawing her finger into his mouth and licking.

His actions made the juncture between her legs throb. She moaned and he captured her wrist.

"Are you all right?" His voice was huskier than usual.

"Yes, no. I'm—" She leaned across the table and whispered, "Your actions are making a wanton woman of me."

A wide, smug smile deepened his dimple and softened the planes of his face.

She laughed. "Don't look so full of yourself. I don't care to be unraveled in a public place."

"Finish your dessert and we'll go to the train. We'll book a Pullman car which will give us a tiny bit of privacy and more comfort than a regular passenger car."

Her nerves buzzed. They would remain together through the night. In close quarters. She stared at the man sitting so straight and handsome. Her insides fluttered and heated. Whether they wound up married or not, he was the only man she would ever love. If she didn't take what moments in his arms she could, she would forever regret it.

She shoved the half-eaten cake to the middle of the table. "I'm finished."

Clay stood, walked around to her chair, and pulled it out for her. When she stood, he didn't step back. His lips nibbled on her ear, his warmth and nearness drugging her like a whiff of chloroform.

"Whatever you want tonight is yours. Sleep in separate beds or one."

Her body trembled at the thought of spending the night in his arms.

"Was the meal satisfactory?" the waiter asked, stepping in front of them.

Rachel inhaled, steadying her emotions.

"Yes." Clay held out his hand for the bill. Rachel's boldness during the meal had shown him a side to her he wished to explore in private. The waiter placed a paper in his palm. Clay slipped the paper to Rachel.

"Ten dollars!"

Her flabbergasted tone made him smile. "You're worth every penny." Clay pulled the folded tens from his pocket, handed one to the waiter, and then slid a silver dollar in the man's hand. "Thank you for a wonderful meal." He grasped Rachel's arm, and they strolled out of the restaurant.

"That was robbery! I've never eaten such high priced food in my life!" She fumed about the price of the meal all the way back to the train station.

His comments didn't appease her. Only one thing would quiet her. He pulled her into his arms and kissed her sputtering lips. He'd planned a brief kiss to get her thinking of something other than the price of the meal, but once his lips touched her petal soft mouth, he forgot everything but pleasing her and branding her as his. Her lips parted. He slid his tongue in and tasted sweet chocolate and tart champagne.

A rap on his knuckles shocked him. He jerked out of the kiss and pulled Rachel to his side.

"This is a public place. You two should keep such tomfoolery to your own home."

The shrill female voice rankled. But she was right. He'd forgotten they were in public.

"I'm sorry, you're right. I lost my head once my lips touched hers." He twined his fingers with Rachel's. "Let's get our tickets."

Rachel's soft laughter surprised as well as taunted him.

"What are you laughing at?"

"The look on your face when that woman chastised you." Rachel squeezed his arm and heat zinged through him.

"You looked like a little boy who was caught spying on girls bathing."

"I'm glad you find it funny. It was your repu-tation I tarnished." He would never understand this woman. Any other woman would have rep-rimanded him for his poor behavior in public. If someone hadn't stopped him, his hands could have started roaming over her body. The thought nearly stopped him in his tracks.

"Mr. Halsey, you can tarnish my reputation anytime you want." She laughed, and then inhaled a deep breath. "Besides, it was my fault, too. I should have pulled out of the kiss. I knew we were in the middle of a crowd, but when you kiss me... the world ceases to exist."

He groaned. "You keep talking like that, and I'll have to pull you in my arms and kiss you again and blast the old ladies who don't like it!"

Her melodious laughter chimed in his ears. He loved the sound of her voice and laughter. His chest filled with pride. His heart drank her in deeper.

She sobered and drew him to a halt beside her. "Two tickets to Baker City in a Pullman car," she said.

"Twenty each. You'll be on The Wallula," a male voice said.

Rachel rustled in her handbag.

"Have a good trip."

"We shall," Rachel replied, and Clay was once again favored with her arm around his as they strolled along.

"There it is, The Wallula. We have compartment number eight." She stopped. "Three steps."

Her hand wrapped his fingers around a railing. He used the hold to gauge the steepness of the steps. She trod on dull sounding wood stairs. He followed, and her fingers locked with his, drawing him forward.

"Heavens!" Her intake of breath released on a sigh. "This is the most beautiful coach I've ever seen."

Their footsteps were cushioned and muffled. The air smelled of wood and new upholstery. He tipped his head toward two muted voices. They weren't the first on the coach.

"The seats are velvet and padded."

The wonder in Rachel's words made Clay smile. "You haven't been in a Pullman car?"

"No. When I went back east to school, the route was mainly short hops on different trains, and when I came back, I was thrifty."

Clay shook his head. "From what I've encountered, I would say you're the only thrifty member of your family."

She laughed. "True. I could never fathom the money my mother and sister spent on clothing. A few nice dresses are all one needs. Not a whole wardrobe full of dresses only worn once or twice. Because, heaven forbid, someone should see you in the same dress twice at a political function."

Clay stepped toward her voice. "One of my favorite qualities about you is your practical attitude."

He wanted to wrap his arms around her, but had no clue how many people already filled the coach. There wouldn't be any privacy until the porter came through and made the beds. And then they'd only have a curtain between them and the rest of the occupants.

The incident on the station platform couldn't happen again.

"Have you found our seats?" He felt like they'd walked a mile through this coach.

"We're at the end..." Her voice trailed off.

"What's wrong? The end is good." He bumped into the back of her and caught her arms to keep her from toppling forward.

"I don't understand how we sleep? The benches are too short to accommodate your height."

"The compartment above comes down making a bunk, and they can make the seats into a bed." He grasped the back of the seat and settled down, patting beside him. Air and skirts rustled around him.

"But someone walking by could see..."

She sat next to him. He reached out, finding her hands clutched in her lap.

"There's a curtain that's pulled across. So while you aren't seen, you can be heard."

"Oh."

The uttered word tinged with disappointment warmed his body as if her hands roamed his bare skin.

He kissed her cheek. "I promise not to compromise you like I did at the station."

Noise echoed through the compartment as more people entered the coach.

"Is it nearing time to depart?"

He pulled out his watch, flipped up the cover, and fingered the hands. "It's six-thirty. Still half an hour until the train leaves." He listened to all the commotion behind them. "It sounds like the coach will be full."

"I can't believe this many people would pay the extra money to have a place to sleep. Do you think they're traveling farther than Baker City?" Rachel swiveled in her seat. Her hips bumped against his, ricocheting images in his mind best left untouched. "One woman has her valise. Should I have kept mine?"

Clay placed a hand on her arm stilling her movements. "You'll only be without your things for one night. I'm sure you'll be fine."

She jostled his shoulder, and her skirts rustled as she moved and looked about. "But if this one is let down and this one makes into a bed"—she inhaled—"how do we climb up into the bunk? I don't see any steps."

"Don't worry about any of that now. Sit back,

watch the people board, and soon we'll be moving."

She leaned against his side, snuggling close. Her action and nearness didn't surge blood to his loins but rather seeped warmth into his heart.

"We came through a sitting room on the other end." Rachel relaxed against Clay's wide body. Nothing had ever made her feel as safe as this man.

"This end must have the washrooms." Clay's fingers played with the curls at the side of her face. His hand roamed down to her neck. His warm palm against her skin sent tremors of excitement chasing through her extremities.

The coach jerked, a train whistle blasted twice, and the scene outside the window slowly rolled away. Ka-chunk, ka-chunk. The wheels of the coach spun along the track. The seat and floor vibrated. Rachel grasped Clay's hand. They were on their way to his home.

She hadn't said anything to Clay, but she'd secretly feared her father had telegraphed the authorities in Portland to try and stop them. Maybe this was one time when he hadn't used his high profile career to his advantage.

"Tickets." A man dressed in a dark blue conductor uniform stood beside their compartment, swaying with the motion of the train.

Rachel pulled the tickets out of her handbag. The man read the destination, punched a hole in each ticket, and handed them back.

"I'll be through in an hour to make the beds," the conductor said and moved to the compartment behind them.

"Would you like to use the washroom?" Clay whispered in her ear.

She shivered at the warm, moist air touching her sensitive lobe. "Why don't we go together?"

Her suggestion sounded most inappropriate, but she didn't care. She was a doctor, and his blindness offered a good reason she should escort him.

The smile deepening his dimple stopped her heart.

"You're being brazen, woman." He kissed her cheek and whispered, "But I like it."

<h1 style="text-align:center">Chapter 22</h1>

Rachel stopped at the doors. "Men or women's?"

"Men's." Clay smiled down at her. "A man would only think of us both being in there as a lark, a woman would get upset."

True. Men tolerated this type of brazenness far better than most women.

She shoved open the men's door, pulled Clay in, and slid the bar in place, locking others out. What now? She stood in the middle of the small room and scanned the interior. Beautifully carved wood accented the huge mirror. Twin washbasins sat in a polished wood counter. Brass faucets and spout hovered over the washbasins. Two small paneled doors on the end must be the toilets.

"D-do you need to use—"

Clay took a step and wrapped his arms around her, drawing her flush with his body. "You feel so good in my arms."

Her hat bumped his shoulder. He pulled the

pins from her bonnet and dropped the whole business on the floor.

"Now where was I?" Clay kissed her forehead and trailed kisses down her face.

Rachel sighed, entwining her arms around his neck and pressed into his chest. He slid his hands up her back and down to her backside, cupping her buttocks and drawing her lower body flush with his. His hardness pressed against her belly.

Her only thought—the wonder of his hands possessing her. Tremors of anticipation heated her body as he deepened the kiss, breaching her sighing lips. His tongue caressed hers, heating her blood and pulsing her pelvic region. How could his hands and tongue bring her body to such heights? It thrilled and scared her.

He ended the kiss, his forehead to hers. "I'm going too fast."

She shook her head, unable to form words. His smug smile tipped her quivering lips into a grin.

"Sit on the counter."

She pulled him along as she backed into the counter. He wrapped his hands around her waist and lifted her up, moving between her legs.

Her mother would apoplexy at the wanton position, but Rachel's body hummed with the desire to fulfill Clay's every wish. He grasped her legs, sliding her forward. His hands roamed up her legs, pushing her skirt to her waist and exposing her genitals at the opening of her drawers. He pressed his hardness to the juncture. She gasped as a jolt sparked through her body. She clung to his broad shoulders reveling in the sensation.

His hands roamed up her side, to her front,

and cupped her breasts. Air hissed from Rachel. She'd never known her breasts were so sensitive. Or was it just his touch? Clay continued massaging one breast as his other hand unfastened the buttons down the front of her dress.

She grabbed his head and drew his lips to hers. He'd taught her well. She slipped her tongue in and out, tasting and teasing as he'd tormented her at the train station.

His hand roamed over her bare skin, tingling, heating her even more. He spread the top of her dress open. She held out her arms, allowing him to push the garment down. His fingertips traced her breasts bulging above the whalebone corset, and she sucked in air. His velvety touch...heavenly.

Tipping his head, Clay kissed the swell of her breasts. Rachel moaned at the sensation of heat and moisture from his lips and tongue.

He slid the shoulders of her chemise down and pulled her breasts from the confines of the corset. Her eyelids flew open when he drew a nipple into his mouth and sucked.

"Heavens!"

Her exclamation brought a smile to the lips clasped around her nipple. He suckled and tugged. She had to touch him as he touched her. Rachel shoved his jacket down his arms. Her hands spread across his hard chest, kneading.

She unfastened buttons and splayed her fingers across his smooth skin, wiggling in the light dusting of dark curly hair.

"You're beautiful," he whispered before cradling her head in his hands and kissing her deep.

Rachel trembled. His strong hands were so

gentle, and they warmed her skin like hot summer sun. His mouth—warm, wet, and demanding—brought on the throbbing in her genital area. She squirmed, pressing against his hardness, but the ache wouldn't go away.

His hands roamed up her thighs. His fingers brushed her, and she nearly jumped off the counter.

"Shh, it's okay. I won't hurt you." He pulled his hand away.

She stopped his motion. "No! I'm not scared, it felt... Oh, heaven help me, it was like a bolt of lightning." His finger touched a spot that nearly crossed her eyes. She grasped his head and kissed him deep, delving her tongue into his mouth and savoring his taste. She squirmed under his ministrations and marveled over every excruciating jolt.

When her body writhed and jumped until she thought every nerve ending was ready to pop, his finger dipped into her. Slow, in-out, in-out, deeper with each insertion, wiggling and setting off a new set of sensations.

Rachel bit down on his shoulder as a wave of tremors rocked her body. His fingers stretched her cavity, filling and exciting her. Oh heavens! He rubbed that sensitive spot, again! She clung to his head as he captured a nipple in his teeth, tugging and suckling, until—sensations ripped through her. Blinding white lights and tremors left her limbs weak and lifeless.

She slumped against Clay's broad chest. His fingers slid from her wet center, and she registered his heavy breathing.

"Slip your undergarment and dress back up.

Someone's knocked on the door twice." He kissed her forehead and helped her into the top half of her dress.

Clay ran water into a basin and steadied his racing heart. If not for the man wanting in here, he would have taken her the first time in a washroom. He grimaced at his lack of control.

Rachel slid off the counter. Her clothing rustled, and when he deemed she was put back together, he handed her a wet cloth and buttoned his shirt.

"Thank you." She took the rag and kissed his cheek. "For the rag and the wonderful ride."

A knock sounded louder.

"I think we better head back to our seats."

Walking out of this room with him would be embarrassing for Rachel. He wouldn't see the looks and leers, but she would. Once again he'd let his body overrule his head. "I-I hope you don't get ridiculed for this."

She tucked her arm in his. "Let me worry about that.

They walked to the door, a wooden slat slid, and she pushed the door open.

"Excuse me, sir, could you step back. My husband is blind, and I don't want him tripping over you." Rachel tugged on his arm. "Thank you." They walked the fifteen steps to their compartment.

Her hat bumped against his shoulder. "See, nothing to it. Not a snide remark or over-calculating look."

Clay shook his head and smiled. After the way he'd ravaged her in the washroom, she should have been blushing and fumbling about, but his Rachel could handle any situation.

"Our beds have been made."

He caught the hint of disappointment in her voice. "Is something wrong?"

"They made two."

Her soft lips tickled his ear. He wrapped his arm around her waist hauling her against him.

Her voice whispered in his ear, "I thought you said we could sleep together?"

He turned his head and brushed his lips against hers. "We can sleep in the bottom one—together."

She slipped from his arms. "Watch your head." She grasped his hand and pulled him downward. "Lie down so I can close the curtains."

Clay stretched out on the bed. Her knees bumped his hips. Her scent wreathed his head as her body slid down his legs and back up, before her breasts skimmed his face, and then moved down his body. The air fluttered around him, followed by a feminine grunt.

"There." She lowered her body next to his, one arm resting across his chest, her breasts pressing against him. "We're all closed in for the night," she whispered in his ear. Her warm breath tickled his neck.

He ached to complete what they'd started in the washroom, but he planned to make love to her, and he couldn't do that in a crowded Pullman coach.

"Help me take this jacket off so I can get comfortable enough to sleep." He kept his voice to a low whisper.

He sat up, and her small hands helped him

removed his jacket and boots.

She placed his hands on her boots. He took the hint, unlacing the footwear and pulling them off her dainty feet.

Clay started to lie back down, when her lips touched his ear.

"I can't sleep in this corset," she whispered.

Blood rushed to his groin, and he muttered a curse. "Sleeping next to you is going to be hard enough without undressing you."

The whisper of cloth and his rapid breathing filled the compartment.

"Please," she breathed in his ear. Rachel's hands captured his and placed them on the lacings at the back of the corset. Her breasts pressed against him as he worked the knot loose. Once it was free, he loosened the laces and the stiff contraption slid down, freeing her breasts to mold to his chest as Rachel devoured him with a deep sensuous kiss. One the likes he'd never experienced before.

The whalebone garment poked him in the leg, and he drew out of the kiss, grasping the bottom of the corset and lifting it over her head. He tossed it to the corner. The thunk echoed in the small confines and no doubt was heard halfway down the car.

Rachel snickered. He held a laugh that burned in the back of his throat. He buried his head in the soft valley between her breasts and inhaled. Citrus, face powder, and the feminine scent of her that he'd learned on their exploration in the washroom welcomed him.

She tugged the tails of his shirt out of his

britches and roamed his back. Her dainty hands gliding across his skin pulsed his already inflamed shaft.

He lowered them to their sides, sliding one leg between hers. Skimming his hands over her chemise, he cupped her bottom and drew her tight against his leg. Her intake of breath and slow hiss indicated her willingness for more. If he could keep her quiet... He may not be fulfilled this night but he could bring her to heights. He rolled Rachel to her back and straddled her hips.

Starting at her neck, Clay kissed and ran his hands over her soft skin, moving down her body and slipping the chemise straps over her shoulders. Rachel obliged by pulling her arms out. He cupped her breasts, one in each hand, nipping and licking the nipples.

Her body wiggled under him, and when a moan started, he kissed her, drawing the sound into his mouth to muffle it. He pressed his face to her neck. "If you make noise, I have to stop."

"Don't stop. I'll be quiet," she whispered and kissed him.

Smiling, he worked her drawers down and off her legs, pushing the chemise up to her waist. He ran his hands up the inside of her legs, spreading them and enjoying the heat and softness of the tender skin. Her musky scent hovered inches from his face. He nearly moaned and bit down on his lip to wait for the throbbing in his shaft to abate.

Clay blew on her center.

"Oh!" Rachel's hips shot off the bed at the puff of air on her genitals. What was he doing? She opened her eyes. The dusky light outside the window revealed him perched between her thighs, smiling. What did he plan? Surely he wasn't...

"Heavens!" she whispered hoarsely as he sucked on the bud that shot fire through her body. His hands gripped her bottom and drew her off the bed to his mouth. He licked and suckled like a starving man. Her body responded in ripples of sensations that curled her toes. When she thought she could take no more, his finger slid into her while his tongue flicked her with vigor.

A fevered frenzy tore through her body. She grabbed her dress, shoving it in her mouth to bite down on and prevent her crying out. Just when that wave of sensations passed, he filled her with another finger, stretching, plunging. And his tongue—heavens, how could a tongue move so fast and so deliciously?

Her mouth was dry from the cloth, but she dared not remove it. Her body coursed higher, her hips moved to meet each thrust of his hand, and her body clenched his fingers, never wanting them to leave her. His tongue stopped, his hand increased speed— Her body shattered into pieces as lights flashed and everything went black.

Hazy feelings brought her back to the present. His fingers sliding out, a kiss on her genitals, and his warm breath against her cheek.

"That should hold you."

The smugness in his tone curved her lips into a smile.

She kissed his lips. "If you are this talented with your hand and tongue, I can hardly wait to see what happens when we do it the right way."

He moaned. "You are not making this easy. I

want to take you but don't dare."

Guilt assaulted Rachel. She'd received unequaled ecstasy from him and left him with an erection. Medical books had passages on how an enlarged penis was painful for a man.

"I'm sorry. Can I—" She placed her hand on the lump in his trousers and he inhaled.

He grabbed her wrists. "Don't touch me unless you plan to..."

Rachel eased from his grip, opened his fly, and pushed his drawers down, allowing his erection to spring into view.

"Heavens!" Other than cleaning an elderly patient in her schooling, she'd not had the privilege of fully examining or touching as fine a specimen as this.

She grasped the solid, velvety smooth shaft, loosely sliding her hand up and down the length. Clay moaned and wrapped a hand in her hair.

Fascinated by the round pink head, she caressed it with a fingertip.

"Rachel," Clay whispered hoarsely. "Either do something or leave me alone."

Rational thoughts left her. Her body, though sated from his attention, desired more. And she wanted to experience everything. She straddled his hips and lowered her body.

He growled and grasped her hips.

"Shh..." She leaned forward, placing a hand over his mouth. "Do you want my dress? I bit down on it to not make noise."

He shook his head, pulled her lips to his, and raised his hips off the bed, plunging deep. A brief spasm of pain ripped through her, confusing and crashing her back to her senses. Her body went still. What was she doing? This could cause a child.

Clay drugged her with a tongue tangling kiss. Her body responded, and ecstasy swirled in delicious ripples. He slid in and out, heightening the sensations where they were joined, and tumbled her into a darkness filled with shooting stars and limb numbing lethargy.

His breathing intensified, his motions drove deeper, and he groaned into her mouth, his arms clutching her tighter. His body stilled but for the pulsing inside her.

She lay atop his chest, gradually hearing the clack of the train, the murmur of others in the car, and realizing she'd let her emotions take over when she should have been using her head. Even as her body relished the languid, fulfilled sensation, her mind raced with the horror she could become with child. She would never want Clay to marry her because of that. And she didn't have time for a child, not with starting a medical practice.

Rachel shoved off Clay, flopping onto her side. Stickiness between her thighs caused her to groan.

Clay reached out, his hand connecting with her shoulder. "What's wrong?"

"Nothing. I- I." She stared at the substance tinged with pink smeared on her thigh. She stared at the small drop on Clay's abdomen.

She couldn't get pregnant. It would hinder her career as a doctor. She'd listened avidly to all the stories from the women doctors at the university. Many waited to have children until they'd become instructors or settled into a practice of just birthing.

The bewildered expression on Clay's face sent her heart thudding. What would he think when he discovered her fear of pregnancy?

Rachel leaned down next to his head and whispered, "I'll get this cleaned up." She yanked up a bottom corner of the sheets and wiped the aftermath of their lovemaking from her thighs and his stomach. The crimson stain didn't bring guilt, only concern. She was now truly a woman. Clay's woman.

He tucked himself back into his clothing and closed the fly. His mouth set in a straight line and a frown marred his forehead.

Sitting beside this man and watching him put himself back together felt like the most natural thing in the world.

She pulled her drawers on and her chemise down.

Stars blinked in the dark sky outside the window. She snuggled up to Clay's side, relishing the closeness but fearing what her actions may have caused.

His arm slowly circled her shoulders, and his lips tickled her ear. "Are you all right? I didn't... I didn't hurt you did I?"

His whispered concern tightened her throat. "No. You didn't hurt me. It was a wonderful experience." She kissed his cheek.

"Why did you...roll off so fast if it didn't hurt?" His fingers played with her hair, keeping her head next to his lips.

"I—" She swallowed the lump of anxiety clogging her throat. "I realized..."

"What?" His thumb moved back and forth

across her jaw, the soft gentle strokes lulling her.

"I could get with child."

His thumb stopped, and his arm went rigid around her. "You don't want to have my child?"

She pushed her body up to lean with her forearms on his chest. "No. I want your children, some day, after I've been a doctor for a while."

"When will that be?"

The skepticism in his voice and his stiff body constricted her chest and pierced her heart. "I'm not sure. After I've established myself in the area. Three years, maybe longer."

He didn't say anything. She slid back to his side, but didn't snuggle close. His arm remained under her, but he didn't draw her near.

A tear slid down her cheek. She'd just experienced the most wonderful event in her twenty-six years, but she'd tarnished it by her selfish actions. Would Clay forgive her? Could she forgive herself if she became pregnant?

Chapter 23

The clack, clack, clack of the train permeated Rachel's slumber. She opened her eyes. Sun blinded her with a blaze of yellow light before tall pine trees flashed by the window dulling the glare. An arm pulled her tight against a hard body.

Did Clay forgive her? Sleep had eluded her as she worried he wouldn't understand her fear of having a child. She knew of ways to prevent pregnancy and would use them from now on. But first she had to find out Clay's feelings.

His solid body pressing against her brought responses she'd never dreamed of. And the sensations igniting her body last night... Her lips curved into a smile and happiness fluttered in her chest. Sleeping in Clay's arms all night was close to the heaven he'd given her before they fell asleep.

Rachel snuggled her bottom into his groin. His hardness pressed back. Anticipation of things to come swirled in her mind. Remembering the texture and heat of Clay, she came alive and quivered.

She couldn't follow through on those urges, not until she was prepared.

She rolled, keeping space between them, and faced him.

"Good morning," she whispered and kissed his lips chastely.

"It is."

His hand snuck into her chemise and captured a breast. The touch skittered vibrations and caused her body to throb. She bit her tongue to keep her mind off the pleasurable feelings.

"Hour 'til Meacham!" the conductor hollered from somewhere down the coach.

"Where or what's Meacham?" She drew his hand from her clothing and listened to the other occupants moving around.

"It's in the Blue Mountains. They stop there for the passengers to get breakfast and to stretch their legs."

Rachel's stomach growled.

"Sounds like we need to get dressed and be ready to leave the train. They don't allow much time." Clay grasped her arms, lifting her to a sitting position. "Find your corset, and I'll help you into it."

Rachel didn't want to leave their cozy compartment. They had things to discuss. But they couldn't hide behind this curtain forever, ignoring the world.

She pulled the corset over her head and presented her back to Clay. "Lace me up."

His fingers slid down her neck to her back, and the garment tightened around her.

"That's good." She settled her bosoms, slid her

petticoats over her head, tied them at her waist, and leaned forward for her dress and Clay's jacket.

"Oomph..." Something struck her in the back. She glanced over her shoulder. Clay sat up, groping about, panic etched on his face.

"Are you all right? I'm sorry. I was tucking my shirt in and my foot slid, striking you..."

The anguish and recrimination in his voice, tugged at her heart. "I'm fine." She grasped his arms, stopping his flailing.

"I'm sorry, I never..."

"I know." She leaned her forehead against his. "Stop apologizing. You didn't do it on purpose."

His body went rigid. "If I could see I would've known where you were." He ran a hand over his face.

The scratching sound of his hand across the day's growth of whiskers sent a quiver of excitement through her. What would it be like to have his whiskered face in the places he'd been last night? She shook her head. Where had all these wanton thoughts come from? Until Clay, she'd never dreamed a man could be anything other than a necessity to build a family. Something she hadn't planned on doing. Now, her mind spun around ways to experience the sensations he opened her to last night.

His down-turned lips and sullen expression tugged her back to the present. She wouldn't let him dwell on what he couldn't do. Not when he was capable of so much. "Here's your jacket. Let me get my dress on and we can get out of this tiny compartment

He took the jacket, but set it on his lap, his

hands crossed over the top.

She donned her dress and buttoned it. Rachel ruffled her skirts around her and slid a leg over Clay, straddling his lap.

"I'm going to slip out, open the curtains, then use the washroom." She cupped his face and kissed his firm set lips. She ignored his non-response. "Get your jacket on, and we can walk to the washrooms together."

She slipped over him and peered out the curtains. Several compartments had transformed back into seats. Sleepy heads popped out between drapes along the aisle. Rachel grasped their curtains, drawing them open and tying them back with the maroon braided cording.

Clay sat hunched over and dressed. His rumpled shirt bagged out between the jacket lapels. She twined her fingers with his and pulled him to a sitting position at the edge of the bed. He held up a hand, gauging the upper bunk and keeping his head from hitting it as he stood.

"Don't you get tired of taking care of me like I'm a child?"

The disgust in his voice rolled off her like rain on oilcloth. "No, I enjoy helping you because I l—" She slapped a hand over her mouth. Was he ready to hear she loved him? Would that only make him feel obligated to marry her after last night? She didn't want him out of obligation. She wanted him because he loved her. "I like being around you." Rachel smoothed his shirt over his chest, tucking it tighter into his trousers.

He grabbed her hands. "We're standing in public."

"No one can see what I'm doing inside your jacket."

He released her. She hooked his elbow, and they strolled to the washrooms. She stopped and faced him toward the men's washroom, placing his hand on the latch.

"I'll be across the hall," she said and stepped into the women's. Two women stood in front of the mirror washing their faces and combing their hair.

Rachel entered a closet resembling an out-house, only finer. The rich, finely carved wood reminded her of a table her mother had in the parlor. She raised the smooth wooden lid with embellished edges and peered down into a pure white porcelain bowl. She finished her necessity, pulled the lever, and slipped back into the washroom.

One woman remained and stared unabashedly. Rachel faced the washbasin and mirror. Her makeup had smeared during the night; parts of her scar shone shiny pink through clumps of flesh-colored lard. Panic tightened her throat. Her makeup compound was in her valise in the baggage car, and her hat lay in the hammock in the sleeping berth. How was she to face the others in the coach, let alone meet Clay's brother, looking like this?

Her hands shook as she tried to smooth the remaining makeup and cover her pink raised skin.

The woman finally left. Rachel grasped the edge of the counter inhaling, forcing air into her lungs, and slowing her frantically beating heart.

The streaked and blotchy makeup remnants looked worse than the scar. Scrubbing with a cloth, soap, and water, she removed all the makeup from her face. The shiny pink scar, running the length of her face, stared back at her. What she wouldn't give to wake up one morning and not see this hideous sight.

She unpinned her hair and dragged her fingers through the disheveled mass.

A knock on the door echoed above the clacking of the train wheels rolling over the tracks.

"Rachel? Are you all right?"

She didn't answer. Wasn't ready to face anyone, even Clay.

The door opened. "Rachel?" Clay stood in the threshold, his brow creased.

"I'll be out in a moment." She couldn't hold back the slight tremor in her voice.

"What's wrong? Are you alone?" He stepped into the small area. His presence bolstered her courage.

"I'm alone. I-I'm…My makeup smeared last night, and I had to take it off. I need my bonnet, but that won't hide it completely. I don't want my hideous face to be my first impression on your brother." She sounded so shallow, so like her sister. Ugh! That was it. She'd leave her hair down and be damned what others thought.

"Hank will like you because I do." He held out a hand. "Are you finished? If so, come on. Others would like to use this room without me standing in it."

"Go back to our seats. I'll be there in a moment." Rachel walked over to him. "Thank you." She stood on her toes and kissed his cheek. A wave of desire rippled through her at the rough texture of his unshaven face.

"For what?"

His husky tone and hand cupping the back of her head, holding her on her toes spurred her emotions into a frenzy. "For checking on me," she said on a breathy sigh.

Clay had decided to keep his hands off her and convince her to go back to Salem after he kicked her in the compartment. He didn't want to cause her any pain or be a burden to her. But the vulnerability over her scar and the way she melted in his hands, he couldn't let her go, even knowing it would be the best for her. He brushed his lips across hers and captured them in a searing kiss. This morning he'd awakened wanting her. After tasting her the night before, he would want her every single day. She'd become his elixir for life.

"Ahem."

"Sorry." Clay slipped Rachel's hand over his arm, and they walked out of the washroom and the fifteen steps to their seats. If not for his hold on Rachel, the sway of the train would've thrown his stride off. He'd noted the train swerved into more curves since they awoke.

"Oh, they already put the beds away." Rachel's hand slid down his arm, grasping his fingers and tugging him down. He reached out, feeling for the seat, and sat on the velvet surface.

Her arm bumped his shoulder. She fidgeted with her hair.

"If you weren't done you could've stayed in the washroom longer." He stilled her hand and realized it was the side of her face with the scar.

"I'm just—"

"Trying to hide the scar." He placed a finger

alongside her face and ran the pad down her raised skin. "It's your heart that matters, not what you look like." He kissed the scar and drew his fingers through her silky loose hair.

"I try to remember that, then someone stares at me, and I grow conscious of my scar again."

"Hold your head high and no one will say a word." He settled back on the seat and placed his arm around her shoulders.

Rachel leaned against him. "The scenery outside the window is beautiful."

"It's a lot like Sumpter. Same mountain range." He fiddled with the hair hanging over her shoulder. "I hope you like the mountains. I'm pretty sure we'll stay in the office at the stamp mill. The cabin is one room and not a good place for a woman to stay, though Darcy spent the night there once."

He snorted, remembering the night Gil brought home the snip of a woman and her brother. Gil and Darcy had slept in the same bed right there in the middle of all the rest of them. At the time he'd been jealous his little brother had found a woman who loved him in spite of his having run away from his family and being sour on mankind.

Clay kissed the top of Rachel's head. He'd found his woman. Now, he needed to prove to himself and everyone else he could take care of her. Especially if she'd become with child last night. Her fear of that happening constricted his chest. What made a doctor so fearful of having a baby? Her explanation was poor. Did she really believe he was incapable of taking care of her and a child? Is that why she was so adamant to get her practice established? His head throbbed and his chest tightened to think she didn't have faith in him.

"I'll need to stay in town if I'm going to set up a medical practice."

The slight waver in her voice perked his senses. The skeptical tone said she still didn't believe he wouldn't stand in her way to be a doctor.

"I'm not going to hide you away at the mill. We'll stay there a couple days. I'll get caught up on what's happening, find out what houses are available, and find a shop for Donny, Jasper, and me. If the house we get won't work for your doctoring, we'll figure something out." Clay slid his hand under her hair, settling his palm around the base of her skull. He turned her to face him. "I'll keep my promise. You can be a doctor."

Her small fingers scratched across his whiskers. "That is one of the things I love most about you. Your promises."

The clatter of the wheels on iron slowed, as did the motion of the train.

"We must be nearing Meacham." He kissed her palm and wished he could show her how he really felt about her, but that would have to wait until they were alone.

Chapter 24

Clay waited until the other passengers left the train. From his trip to Salem, he knew they had barely twenty minutes to get food. The other travelers would've already filled the railroad stop restaurant. He didn't plan to eat here, only stretch his legs.

Rachel tugged on his arm. "Shouldn't we hurry to the restaurant?"

"No. While they're known for their good food, it's expensive, and we'll have to hurry. We'll go to the buffet car after a walk. They'll have sandwiches and sweet breads." Clay turned. "Let's walk down a street and back, my legs need stretched."

The board platform of the station gave way under his feet to the hard packed ground of a street. The noise and bustle of the station faded. In the distance, the whirl of saw blades and the hollow thunk of wood hitting wood grew. The tang of freshly sawn lumber wafted across the cool air. He'd visited here a couple times with Ethan when they negotiated lumber for the stamp mill. Meacham was noted for its excellent railroad stop and lumber.

"This town has few business establishments. I only see the railroad hotel, which is magnificent, a general store, and several wood yards."

Rachel's hesitant steps roused his curiosity. "Do small towns bother you?" He stopped. If this town with the bustling railroad bothered her how would she feel in more rural Sumpter? "We can go back to the train if you're uncomfortable."

"It isn't the town so much as..." She pulled him closer and spoke low. "There's a man watching us."

"What does he look like?" They were close enough to Sumpter that it could be someone he knew.

"About my height, long scraggly brown hair and beard, small pointy nose, and he limps prominently on his right leg." She shuddered. "There's just something about the way he's staring that..."

Clay didn't know who the man was, but he didn't like the fear in Rachel's voice. "Let's go back to the train, I've stretched enough."

The twist of her body every five steps told him she still watched the man.

"Is he following?"

"Yes, sort of. He could just be going the same direction." Her uncertainty ignited his protective instincts.

"Let me confront him." He stopped and pivoted, releasing her arm.

"He's gone now. See, I was being fearful when there was no need." Her relief rushed out on a sigh.

Clay wasn't so sure. But who would follow

them unless it was someone who realized he was blind and planned to rob them? He ground his teeth. He'd not let anyone harm Rachel.

"Here's our coach. I'll leave you and find that buffet car you mentioned." Rachel's voice drifted above him as she climbed the steps.

He grasped the handrail. "I'll go with you." Clay climbed the stairs and settled a hand on the middle of her back.

"There's no need—"

"There is. We'll stop a porter or conductor and ask where to find the buffet car." He kept his hand on her back as they walked down the aisle and stopped.

"Sir, where might we find the buffet car?" Rachel asked.

"Go back through this car and keep going, you'll find it between the first and second class cars."

"Thank you." Rachel twined her fingers with his and walked back the way they'd come.

She stopped. Air puffed across his face and the squeak of metal on metal pierced the air.

"Watch your step, there's a gap between the platforms as we step from one coach to the other."

He followed Rachel's voice and the tug of her hand, stepping wide. The fresh air was replaced by the stale air of confinement. They'd entered another coach.

"Everyone must be either walking or eating in town," Rachel said. Their steps clunked on the wood floor. "This is what I remember riding in when I went to school, the leather padded seats. Not the plush velvet and beds of the palace car."

A squeak. Fresh air. Wind ruffled his hair again.

"Another gap. Careful."

He again stepped wide.

The aroma of bread, coffee, and apples wrapped around Clay. They'd reached the buffet car.

"Oh, this is more than I'd thought. They have tables and... Oh, look, sweet rolls." Rachel pulled him to a stop. "We'll have two coffees. Do you also want milk or water?"

Clay shook his head, enjoying letting her make the decisions.

"And two of those, two of those, and two of those."

He chuckled. "Who all are we feeding?"

"Just us. I want to make sure I get something you like."

"Fifty cents," said a male voice.

She released his hand. The muffled jingle of coins and the sound of pottery sliding emerged over the low conversations of others in the car.

"Here." Rachel grasped his hands, turning them palm up.

A plate weighed down each hand, and he wrapped a thumb around the edges. Rachel hooked his elbow, and they walked several steps before she stopped.

A clunk of two cups placed on wood resonated in front of him. She took the plates. Pottery thunked on wood.

"There's a bench seat to your right."

He grasped the table and sat. Something tapped his feet. He reached out with a foot and met the soft resistance of fabric. Rachel sat across from him.

A plate bumped his hand resting on the table.

"At three o'clock is a ham sandwich, six is a sweet roll, and nine is an apple," Rachel said as a cloth fluttered over his hand. "And here is a napkin."

Clay caught her hand. "You take good care of me." He raised her knuckles to his lips. "Tell me now if you feel you'll tire of helping me. I don't want you waking one day and resenting me."

Her fingers squeezed his. "I don't see that happening. You give me freedom to be a doctor, you give me your respect and admiration, and you care for me. That's more than many women have." She sighed. "I feel blessed to have you."

His heart opened even more to her. He bit his tongue to hold back his proclamation of love for her. He'd wait. A month—for her to see if she could live a rural life. If she still felt the same about him and doctoring miners, he'd tell her and marry her. But not before he was certain she had no misgivings about them.

He kissed her knuckles, again, hoping she liked Sumpter and his family.

Her intake of air jerked his attention to the present.

"What?"

"That man from the street. He just stuck his head in and looked right at us."

Damn! Who was this man and why was he following them into the train? Clay shot out of his seat.

"No!" Rachel's hands clutched his arm. "You

can't go after him."

Clay sat as frustration seethed through him. He couldn't go after a man he couldn't see. He'd not let Rachel out of his reach until they connected with Hank in Baker City.

"Eat." He shook off the tension, relaxing his muscles, and picked up his sandwich. "We'll go back to the coach as soon as we finish. If you see the man again, try to get me close. I have a couple questions I'd like to ask him."

Rachel could barely swallow her sweet roll. Clay wanted to confront the man. There was no way she'd take him knowingly to the man. He'd looked shifty and angry. A combination she knew meant trouble. If the man appeared again, she'd try not to reveal it to Clay through her actions. If the man followed them to Baker City she'd point him out to Hank.

Clay finished his meal and sat quietly. She didn't like the fact he was so quiet. What was he thinking about? How to confront the man? After the sweet way he'd treated her when they first sat down and his fear she would grow tired of him, she wasn't about to put him in danger. She would prove to him she could stick it out and that she loved him.

"I'm finished." She slipped her apple in her handbag. It would make a hard weapon to swing if need be.

Clay stood, holding his hand out to her. She rose, rubbing her body against his. Let his mind wander to thoughts other than the stranger.

He grasped her upper arms and drew her body flush with his.

"I'll do everything I can to keep you from harm." His warm breath scented with coffee fluttered the curls around her face before his mouth descended. His lips parted in a wet, hot, deep kiss. Cinnamon, sweetness, and coffee lingered on his tongue as it caressed hers. The sensation weakened her limbs and left her hazy.

She clutched his jacket to remain standing when he drew back. "You kiss me like that and you'll be mopping me up off the floor."

He hugged her tight. "Sorry, when I think of losing you..."

"You won't, at least not if I have anything to say about it. Come on. Let's go back to the coach." She twined her fingers with his. Several of the women in the buffet car glared. She didn't care. When Clay wanted to kiss her, she'd allow it.

Rachel kept an eye out for the man on their way through the cars. She didn't see him and hoped he'd decided against whatever he'd had in mind when following them. At their compartment, she sat, drawing Clay down beside her and snuggling against his side.

"How much longer until we reach Baker City?" Her stomach churned worse than when she'd taken the doctor's exam. Would Clay's family accept her? The churning slowed and her anxiety turned to excitement. She couldn't wait to see the world Clay grew up in. It would show her so much about him.

Her breasts tingled as his arm pressed against them. Sweet memories of last night whisked through her head. They also needed privacy to talk about last night.

"We'll be there around noon." He wrapped his arm around her. "I hope he brought a horse for me to ride. I've missed riding while at the school." His fingers ran up and down her ribs. He always found a way to touch her, and she enjoyed every second his fingers traced her body.

"Did you do a lot of riding after the accident?"

"Horseback is about the only way other than walking to get around in the Cracker Creek area. That's where the cabin and the mill are located."

"How do you get supplies to the mill?" She'd never been into any remote areas other than a picnic or two outside of Salem as a child.

"There's a road to the mill, but if you're traveling between mines you have to go through the woods, into and out of canyons, and over hills and mountains." He leaned his head on hers. "We'll find you a place in Sumpter so you don't feel so isolated."

"All aboard!" the conductor hollered.

The train's deep blasts of air, summoned the travelers. Activity outside the window caught Rachel's attention. Passengers bustled out of the railroad hotel hurrying toward the train.

"I'm glad we walked and ate in the buffet car." Rachel pressed her body tighter against Clay as the train rocked from people climbing on board and hurrying to their seats.

"I remember the hassle of feeding Ethan, Aileen, the kids, and me when we rode the train to Portland." He chuckled. "I found the buffet car when I wandered off by myself. Ethan wasn't too happy with me."

Rachel stared at him. The man didn't let his blindness stop him from anything he set his mind to. With this determination he shouldn't have any doubts about his abilities, yet he did. She'd help him see he had no limitations.

"I imagine you scared them all wandering off like that."

"Scared isn't the word I'd use for Ethan's reaction."

The whistle blew again in longer bursts and the train started forward.

"What is Hank like? Will I get to meet any of your other brothers?"

"Hank is quiet. You think he'll never get anything done he's so laidback, yet he does more work than two men in a day. I know you won't meet Ethan for a while. He and Aileen and the kids were headed to England to see about some land in Aileen's first husband's family. Zeke and Maeve, it depends on where their working. They're both Pinkerton detectives."

Rachel stared at Clay. Pinkerton detectives. "My, your family is interesting."

"And Gil, Darcy, Jeremy, and baby Sadie will most likely be there when the train pulls in. I swear that snip of a woman has more energy than ten."

She laughed. "I'm looking forward to meeting all of your family. They all sound wonderful."

Her breath caught as the pointy-nosed man stepped into the coach, peered directly at them for a moment then ducked back out.

"You saw him. Is he in this car?" Clay's body stiffened and his arm squeezed around her.

"No, an animal was nearly struck by the train. It just startled me." The lie, her pounding heart, and Clay's hold squeezed breath from her lungs. Why was the man following them? What were his intentions? And how could she protect Clay when she had no idea what the man wanted?

Chapter 25

Rachel stepped off the train at the Baker City depot and waited for Clay to descend the steps. The area rivaled the Salem station in activity and size. Wagons surrounded the two-story lapped-sided building with a wrap-around balcony. Her gaze drifted up to the ornate cornices in the peak.

Passengers and freight crowded the narrow board platform. Rachel wrapped her arm around Clay's, hugging him close as she scanned the people for either a man who resembled Clay or the pointy-nosed man she believed to be following them.

They stepped off the platform and stood in the dirt between two sets of tracks. A large, three-story hotel sat to the left of the street dead ending at the railroad depot.

Rachel craned her neck, to see through the people and wagons leaving the station, for anyone still standing or walking their direction. "I don't see anyone who looks like you."

"Maybe he didn't get the telegram." Clay cupped her elbow. "Take me to the baggage claim. We'll have our bags delivered to the Crabill Hotel."

"What about Hank?" She didn't mind spending more time with Clay alone, but she didn't want to miss their escort to Sumpter.

"If he doesn't show by noon tomorrow, we'll set out for Sumpter."

Rachel stopped. "How will we get to Sumpter? You can't see and I don't know the way."

"There's a road from here to Sumpter. When we rent a buggy they can direct you to the road. Then we'll get someone in Sumpter to take us to the stamp mill."

Clay tugged on her arm. She resumed walking. Nothing daunted this man. One of the reasons he'd become special to her.

Two valises and her trunk sat on the dock by the baggage car. She smiled at the attendant dressed in the same uniform as the porters on the train.

"Would you please have these delivered to the Crabill Hotel for Mr. Clay Halsey?"

Clay pulled a coin out of his pocket. He held it up and the attendant took it.

"Yes, ma'am." The attendant smiled, pocketed the coin, and whistled to a boy leaning against the station on the shady side of the building.

Rachel tucked her hand in the crook of Clay's elbow and they walked toward the buildings. She scanned the street, taking in the well-dressed people and neatly presented store fronts. The atmosphere resembled home. The variety of shops

and large buildings rivaled those she grew up fre-
quenting.

"I didn't realize Baker City was—a city."

"It's the largest town on this side of the Blue
Mountains. It started as a stop for the emigrants
traveling to Oregon City and grew after gold was
discovered in Auburn."

The impressive hotel was only a short stroll
from the train depot.

"We're here", she said, stepping under the roof
extending the length of the building.

Clay pulled her to the side. "Before we go in,
I'd like to find out your feeling so I don't make an
idiot of myself."

Her heart raced. Would he get one room to
share? It wasn't proper, but she wanted to explore
what he'd opened up to her last night. And this
time, having her doctor bag available, she'd be
prepared.

"Do you want to share a room or do you want
separate rooms?"

The uncertainty ringing in his voice settled her
jumbled nerves. "I want to spend the night in your
arms."

The wrinkles in his brow flattened and a smile
deepened his dimple. "I don't think I could have
slept knowing you were in a room down the hall."

She stepped away from the wall, drawing Clay
with her, and stopped at the threshold of the hotel.

"We're here."

Clay reached out, captured the door handle,
and moved her forward with a hand at her back.
She entered an elongated lobby. She skirted a long

table covered in newspapers spanning the middle of the area and they made their way to the registration desk in the back of the room. A tall thin man sporting a bushy mustache stood behind the desk.

"May I help you?" His deep warm voice was followed by a smile.

Clay stepped up to the counter, keeping one arm around Rachel's waist. "My wife and I would like a room for the night. One not too far from a water closet and bath."

"We have just a room." The clerk swung the large ledger toward Clay. Rachel dipped the quill in the ink and signed them in as Mr. and Mrs. Clay Halsey. Flutters of excitement rippled her skin. How long before she could sign everything in this manner?

The clerk glanced from her to Clay and down at the ledger. "Welcome Mr. and Mrs. Halsey." He plucked a key from a small cubicle behind him. "You'll be in room two-twenty."

"Thank you. Our baggage should be arriving from the station soon. Please send it up." Clay twined his fingers with hers and she led him to the wide staircase along the wall on the right side of the lobby. The scent of food rumbled her stomach.

"We'll wait for our luggage to arrive, and you can freshen up. Then we'll come back down and enjoy a leisurely meal."

"Stairs," she said quietly.

Clay put out his hand, grasped the railing, and walked up the stairs beside her, smooth as a sighted person.

"Last one," she said at the top and led him down the hall to their room. She twisted the glass cut knob and entered a cozy room.

Rachel led Clay to an upholstered arm chair, one of two beside a small side table. The bed boasted a colorful quilt and plump pillows. A small washstand with a pitcher and bowl stood in one corner, a gilded mirror hung on the wall above.

"The room is lovely." She took off her hat and poured water in the basin.

Clay rubbed his two day stubble. "Would you rather bathe in a tub?"

"That would be heavenly." She sighed. She wasn't priggish, yet, wearing and sleeping in the same clothes for two days left her feeling unkempt.

A knock on the door startled her.

"That should be our bags." Clay said, standing. "I'll get it." He walked to the door and opened it.

Rachel kept her scarred face averted from the door. The boy from the station entered. He set the valises on the floor by the end of the bed and pulled in the trunk.

Clay drew a coin from his pocket and handed it to the youth. "Thank you. Please ask at the desk to send up hot water for a bath."

The boy tipped his hat and departed. Closing the door, Clay faced her. "Find the clean things you want to put on and we'll find that washroom."

Rachel placed her valise on the bed and began rummaging through it for clean clothes. Clay crossed the room, fumbled with the handle of his bag, and did the same.

Commotion in the hallway stilled her hands.

She listened.

"They're packing the water to the washroom. Ready?" he asked, his hand poised on the door-knob.

"Yes." Her heart raced. Would he sit in the room as she bathed? The thought of his presence even though he couldn't see raised the heat in her body.

She took his arm and Clay escorted her out of the room.

They walked to an open door. A Chinese man walked out carrying two buckets. He bowed his head and continued on. She stepped into the room. A tin tub in the middle took up most of the floor space. One chair sat in a corner and a shelf held folded towels.

Clay bumped into her back. "Is there something wrong?"

"There isn't much room." She stepped to the hooks on the wall and hung her garments on one hook.

"In the tub?" He stepped in the room, closed the door, and ran his hand over the frame, slipping the hook in the eyelet to fasten the door shut.

"No, the tub is large. The room—"

He stepped toward her, grinning. "If the tub is large, then we shouldn't have any problems."

Their bodies brushed as his fingers sought the hooks and he hung his clothes. He leaned into her.

Her breathing accelerated. Her heart thrummed against her ribs. His nearness heightened her senses. He slipped the jacket down his arms, releasing his musky scent into the air. His heat penetrated her clothing.

"Are you bathing in your clothes?" He unbuttoned his shirt. The dark curly hair scattered across his chest beckoned to be touched. She raised a hand, sifting her fingers through the silky curls. Her palm tingled.

Rachel helped him remove his shirt and began unbuttoning the fly on his trousers. He didn't stop her as she pushed his trousers and drawers down his body. He was already hard and quivering.

She gently pushed Clay down onto the chair and unlaced his boots. His hands wound in her hair. She removed his boots, socks, and garments. He leaned back in the chair, a dimpled smile lighting his face. What a glorious sight!

Rachel reached out to take him in her hands. At the first caress, he stopped her.

"Your turn."

He stood and his hands worked at unbuttoning her dress. His lips trailed wet kisses down her neck to the top of her chemise and corset. He nudged the dress down her arms and into a pool around her feet. Her petticoats followed. The corset loosened and soon dropped to her feet as well. He untied the ribbon on her chemise. She shivered as his fingers glided over the tops of her breasts as he slowly maneuvered the garment down her body.

"Sit."

She stepped out of the ring of garments and sat on the chair. Clay knelt at her feet and removed her shoes and stockings. He reached for her hand and drew her to her feet. Pressing his body to hers, he slid his hands down her sides, waist, hips, thighs, and legs, removing her drawers. She stood before him completely naked, not feeling the least bit intimidated or dirty.

"Let's get in the water before it goes cold."

Rachel led him to the side of the tub. He stepped in, sat down, and leaned back, opening his arms in invitation.

A giggle escaped as she stepped into the tub and settled her backside between the vee of his legs.

Clay wrapped his arms around Rachel, drawing her against his chest. He'd told himself they would only bathe. His control slowly unraveled as he held her and experienced her boldness. He wanted her. Only a fire in the building could keep him from taking her before they made it back to the room.

"Where's the soap?" His hoarse voice didn't sound like him.

A slippery bar slid into his hand.

"Slide forward. I'll wash your hair." Her body slid down his. Her head settled in his cupped hand. Wetting her hair, he lathered the tresses, massaged her scalp, and memorized the contours of her small skull. He rinsed the soap from her hair and drew her to sit in front of him.

Clay lathered his hands and spread the soap down her neck, over her small shoulders, around to her handful breasts, and down her flat stomach. With each inch of her smooth flesh he touched, his desire for her grew tenfold. Her head tipped back and rested on his shoulder. He kissed her cheek, and her lips sought his.

She slipped her tongue between his lips and seduced him. His pulsing shaft ached as it pushed against her backside. She spun, circled her arms around his neck, and pressed the full length of her body to his.

He groaned. "Don't. This isn't the place…"

Rachel rubbed up and down his length, her breath coming in shallow pants.

Pounding on the door echoed through the room. "Clay? Clay, you in there?"

"Damn." He held Rachel tight. "Yeah, Hank."

"Get dressed. I'll meet you in the restaurant."

Rachel shook, and lilting giggles erupted from her.

"Shh… You want him to hear you?" Clay grinned at the absurdity of the situation.

"If he knew you were in here, he knows we signed in as Mr. and Mrs. He has to be curious where I am." She pushed against his chest and knelt between his legs. "Want me to wash you up quick?"

"Just my hair." He leaned forward. She poured water over his head and massaged his scalp. The passion of the moment dissolved, but he'd rekindle it later tonight in bed.

She rinsed his hair, and the water lowered around him as she stepped from the tub. He stood and stepped out onto a braided rug. Before he asked for a towel, one moved down his body, starting at his hair, lingering in his groin area, and moving on down his legs.

"I can return the favor," he said reaching out and grasping the towel.

"I've already dried."

Her smug tone brought a smile to his lips, and he grabbed her. "You might have missed a spot." He started at her head and worked his way down, kissing her soft skin.

She sighed and wound her arms around his neck, dragging his lips to hers. He liked this passionate take charge woman. He couldn't wait to discover more of her in a real bed.

He gently nudged her away. "We need to get dressed, or Hank'll come back up here."

Chapter 26

Rachel tugged on the veil of her hat two steps into the restaurant. Clay didn't give her time to apply her makeup. His insistence her scar didn't matter irked her. He didn't witness the stares and expressions of pity and horror.

A man at a far table stood. He had curlier hair, a more pronounced chin, and a straight nose. Otherwise, he could have been Clay's twin.

He stared at her before his eyes narrowed. What had she done to deserve a scowl? She'd yet to meet him.

She led Clay to his brother.

"You're a sight for sore eyes, Clay." Hank stepped forward and hugged his brother. She knew they were close, but hadn't expected this show of affection in public.

"Hank, I'd like you to meet Dr. Rachel Tarkiel. She escorted me home and is thinking of hanging around and seeing what kind of a medical practice she can start here."

Clay's infectious grin curved her lips into a smile. She held out her hand to Hank. "It's a pleasure to finally meet one of the infamous Halsey brothers."

Hank's brow rose, and Clay laughed.

"Infamous?" Hank peered at her. He was close enough his gaze scanned her face, settled briefly on her scar, and returned to her eyes.

"You and your brothers are all he talks about." She resisted the urge to fiddle with the curls at the side of her face. Clay placed a hand over hers on his crooked elbow. Did he sense her agitation?

"I don't see how you could miss us with this pretty doctor taking care of you." Hank's gaze traveled the length of her, and he scrutinized his brother as well.

"Heck, I didn't miss you." Clay squeezed her hand. "I wanted to persuade Rachel to come with me. I had to paint you as civilized."

Her stomach rumbled. Clay and Hank both moved at once. Hank held out a chair, and Clay stepped forward.

She placed Clay's hand on the back of the chair. Hank stepped aside, and Clay seated her before moving to the chair beside her.

Hank took a seat across the table, watching them closely. "I already ordered."

Rachel took a sip of water.

"Good, we're starving. We only had something from the buffet car this morning." Clay leaned back in his chair.

Hank glanced from her to Clay and back to her. "So you going to tell me what's going on here?"

Rachel shrugged, not sure what Clay wanted to tell his brother.

"The register said Mr. and Mrs. Clay Halsey, yet you just introduced her as Dr. Tarkiel."

"We aren't married. We're still working out the details." Clay squeezed her hand again.

"Are you really a doctor?" Hank narrowed his eyes and darted his gaze between her and Clay.

"Yes, I have my diploma and the results of my boards if you would like to see them."

"Rachel was the doctor for the Blind School. She wanted something more challenging, and I offered her a chance to come out here and be the doctor for the Sumpter area." Clay stared determinedly toward his brother.

"Where's she staying?" Hank leaned back as the waiter delivered plates piled high with roast beef, potatoes, and boiled carrots.

"At the office until we find a house in Sumpter that will work."

Rachel spun Clay's plate. "Meat at six, potatoes and gravy at eight, and carrots at three."

Clay released her hand, ran his fingers along the edge of the table, found his knife and fork, and started on his food. She smiled at his resourcefulness and raised a bite to her mouth, thankful the short veil stopped at her nose.

"You two seem awfully friendly."

Hank's accusing tone shot ice shards to her abdomen. Why was he so untrusting? From all Clay had told her, she'd expected a much warmer greeting.

Clay smiled in her direction. "We've spent a good amount of time together while I was at the school."

"Like bathing together?"

Heat burned her chest and raced up her neck to her face. What they'd done was improper, but not when she considered they would soon be married. At least if she had anything to do about it.

"I told you, we're thinking about getting married, and what we do isn't any of your damn business." Clay's jaw twitched and his hands fisted around his utensils. "We're both grown people and know what we're doing."

"You think Ethan would condone this kind of behavior?" Hank's voice rose, and people at nearby tables stared at them.

"Shh…" Rachel hissed. "This is a matter to be taken up in privacy." She glared at Hank. "You aren't acting anything like Clay described you."

"Has carrying the burden of the stamp mill soured you?" Clay pointed at her. "Eat."

Rachel smirked inwardly at the surprise on Hank's face. He didn't realize his brother's acuity of his surroundings.

"How did you know she wasn't eating?"

"I hadn't heard her utensil scrape the plate in a while." Clay took a bite.

"She could have been eating with her fingers."

Clay laughed. "Rachel's too civilized. That's why we aren't married. I didn't want to tie her here if she doesn't like it."

Rachel stared at Hank. "Has he always thought for other people?"

Hank laughed and clamped a hand on Clay's shoulder. "I do believe you've met your match in this one."

"She is rather feisty." Clay grinned. "So did you bring horses or a wagon?"

"Wagon, I had supplies to pick up." Hank flipped open his watch. "If we don't hurry we'll be hard pressed to get home before dark."

"Are you through, Rachel?" Clay slid his chair back and stood.

"I'm ready." She stood as he pulled her chair out for her. She looped her arm around his, and they followed Hank to the lobby.

"I'll get your things." Hank started toward the stairs.

"You'll need help." Clay slipped from her arm. "Wait here, we'll be right back." The two ascended the stairs, and she shifted her attention to the wide front windows.

The pedestrian traffic was slow, but wagons, horses, and coaches constantly passed the window. Scuffling at the top of the staircase caught her attention. Clay and Hank struggled over who would go down the stairs first. She glanced back to the window.

Her heart stopped.

It was him.

The pointy-nosed man from Meacham stared at her through the window. His wild-eyed gaze lifted to the men descending the stairs. He grinned wickedly and limped away.

She wanted to point the man out to Hank without revealing her discovery to Clay. He would make it a point to find the man. Her stomach churned, souring her meal. The man had looked dangerous. She didn't want Clay to engage him in a fight.

The brothers dropped the trunk at the bottom of the stairs.

"You can't tell me some scrawny kid hauled that up the stairs by himself." Hank bent over, his hands on his knees sucking air. "What's in there?"

"Medical books." Rachel calmed her nerves and smiled at the men. She needed to get Hank alone and tell him about the man following them.

"The horses and wagon are down at the livery. You two stay. I'll bring them around." Hank headed to the door.

Rachel took a step to follow and talk to him outside.

"Rachel?" Clay put his hand out. She walked to him and twined their fingers. She'd have to find another time to get Hank alone and tell him they were being followed.

Chapter 27

Dusk settled over the canyon. Rachel stared at the huge building emitting the loudest pounding noise she'd ever heard. Clay's explanation matched the evenly spaced hits resounding in a continuous rhythm.

"I assume the noisy building is the stamp mill," she said loud enough to be heard over the din.

"Yes." Clay pulled her tighter against his side. His breath heated her neck and ear. "It runs around the clock to keep up with the demand."

"How will we sleep with that racket?" Her body ached from sitting on the hard wood bench and the jostle of the rutted road they'd followed.

"You'll find the sound lulls you to sleep." His hand slipped to her hip and he squeezed. "A little activity before sleeping helps, too." His voice, barely perceptible in her ear, made her glance at Hank.

The wagon stopped in front of a smaller building. Clay climbed down and extended his hands to her. She slid to the edge of the seat and placed her hands on his shoulders, dropping into his arms. He held her tight, and she breathed in the scent of shave soap and Clay. His head tipped down and his lips closed in on hers.

"Help me get your things inside," Hank said, his irritated voice interrupting the spell.

Clay growled and released her.

"Are you going to the cabin tonight?" Clay asked, moving along the wagon box to the back.

"I've been staying here since everyone left. Made more sense."

The sly grin on Hank's face should have aggravated Rachel, but she giggled. He was having fun keeping them apart.

"Then the sooner we find a place in town the better." Clay grabbed one end of the trunk and Hank the other.

"If you're planning to live here and not marry this woman—"

"Please, call me Rachel."

"Rachel, then you better be ready to take the wrath of Myrle."

Rachel's abdomen tightened. Who was Myrle? A woman Clay romanced before he arrived at the Blind School? Jealousy gurgled in her stomach. The unpleasant taste and the pounding of the mill prickled her skin. She didn't like the sensations.

Clay cringed as if in pain. "I forgot about her."

"W-who is Myrle?" She hated asking and sounding like the jealous sort, but she had to know if he'd given another the same affection he'd bestowed on her.

"She's a woman who helped us through tough times when our parents were killed," Hank said, nodding to the closed door.

She trotted to the door and opened it for them, relief making her feet fly across the ground.

"She can get ornery when she thinks one of us isn't on the straight and narrow path," Clay said.

His furrowed brow and pensive expression was endearing. He cared what the woman thought.

They set her trunk near a wall in the kitchen and returned to the wagon. She scanned the room. A smooth wood table with six chairs sat in the middle of the floor. A drain board and hand pump ran along one wall. Reigning supreme on the inside wall beside a door stood a large shiny cook stove. The set up was well thought out and homey. But a far cry from the large kitchen Matilda managed at her parents' home.

Crossing the plank floor, she pushed on the inside door and walked into what must be the parlor. A barrel stove stood in one corner. A braided rug covered the open center and several wooden chairs and rockers ringed the rug. Kerosene lamps rested on sconces on the walls. She compared the sparse furniture and crude lighting to the gaslights, velvet furniture, and objects of art in her mother's parlor.

Two other doors led out of the room. One had a line of pegs on the wall where a coat and hat hung. The other stood open, revealing a hall.

Hank and Clay banged through the kitchen door, carrying the valises.

"Which room are you in?" Clay asked as she stepped out of the hallway threshold.

"I'm in Colin's. Didn't want to sleep in that big bed of Ethan and Aileen's by myself." Hank carried her bag into the last room on the left.

Clay followed.

"What do you think you're doing?" Hank pushed Clay out of the room backward. "Rachel stays in here, she's the guest. You stay across the hall in Shayla's room."

Clay dropped the bag and knocked his brother's hands off his chest. "Don't push me and don't tell me where I'm sleeping."

They'd lived together before, but he'd grown up in many ways while at the school. He no longer needed a big brother to look out for him, and he wanted Rachel to see him as a whole man. He damn sure didn't want his brother telling him what to do. Especially in front of her.

He caught Rachel's citrus scent. Air fluttered passed him.

"I can take the smaller bed."

The waver in her voice bothered him. "No. You and I will sleep in Ethan and Aileen's room."

"Is that the arrangements you had at the school?"

Hank's preacher attitude was getting old fast. "No, we didn't. But we aren't at the school." He picked up his bag and pushed passed Hank, stepping into the room. Clay dropped the bag with a loud thud and pivoted.

"Rachel?" Clay stood in the hallway and held his hand out.

She twined her fingers with his. He led her eight steps down the hall to the washroom.

"In here is a tub and running water." He opened the door. "If you want a bath you have to heat the water in the kitchen and haul it in here. Cold water is always available, and there's a drain so you don't have to scoop the water from the tub."

"I don't see a water closet." Her hat brim bumped his shoulder.

"There's a privy outside. There hasn't been a need to add a water closet. Aileen was tickled with the water pump."

Her fingers loosened and tried to slip from his grip. He hadn't had an opportunity to visit her home, but he was pretty sure it made this one look shabby. Did seeing how primitive they lived give her second thoughts?

"Go get ready for bed. I'm going to catch up on things with Hank." He cupped the side of her face and kissed her lips. She didn't respond. Damn. He shouldn't have brought her here, or gotten closer to her. She would rip his heart out.

She slipped from his hand. "Good night, Hank."

Her steps faded in the direction of Ethan and Aileen's room. Would she even welcome him in the bed tonight? If Hank hadn't been so pushy he wouldn't have pushed back and would have slept in Shayla's small bed for propriety.

But dammit, he'd learned while he was gone that he could be his own man and make decisions. Something his older brothers had failed to let him do.

Hank yanked on his sleeve, and he followed the sound of his brother's footsteps down the hall, through the sitting room, and into the kitchen.

A metal lid clanked on the stove. The whoosh of the pump priming, the rattle of cups, his brother's heavy steps—he'd missed these sounds tucked away in the cottage by himself. He'd always had the chatter and activity of his brothers around him.

Some nights at the school, he'd been so lonely he thought he'd go crazy. Then Rachel started warming to him, and he'd thought of her night after night and what it would feel like to fall asleep and wake with her in his arms.

A chair scraped the floor. "Sit."

He walked to the table, pulled out a chair, and sat.

"Are you sure this woman is a doctor?" Hank lowered his voice.

"Why are you so untrusting?" Clay slapped a hand on the table. The sound rang through the room like a gun shot.

Hank cleared his throat, and the chair under him squeaked. "Sh-she's got a nasty looking scar. Only prostitutes are that beat up."

Clay surged to his feet and yanked Hank out of his chair. "She's not a whore," he said through clenched teeth, the pounding in his head overriding all other sounds. "She's a doctor, her father is a judge, and that scar came from saving her sister from a runaway wagon." He shook Hank. "And if you imply anything different again, I'll forget you're my brother."

"Clay, don't do this."

Rachel's soft voice seeped into his haze of rage. A small hand rubbed his back.

He unclenched his hands. The chair behind Hank scraped across the floor as his brother gained his footing. Rachel slid her arms around his waist.

"We're all tired. We'll talk in the morning."

Her citrus scent filled his nostrils. He wrapped an arm around her shoulders. "You shouldn't have come out here?"."

"I need..." She rose on her toes. "I need to use the privy and haven't the faintest idea where to find it in the dark," she whispered.

He slipped his hand down to hers and headed for the door. The fresh air would do him good. Outside, he turned right and followed along the lean-to. At the corner he counted fifty steps.

"Oh, I see it. Lucky there's a moon tonight." She squeezed his hand. "I can find my way back."

"Do what you need. I'm going to be here enjoying the mountain air." He released her hand. The snap of twigs and crunch of dried pine needles as she made her way to the outhouse were sharp over the dull thud of the stamp mill muffled by the trees.

Nothing about Rachel should've given Hank cause to think she was a whore. He cringed. Other than his bathing with her, and now he planned to spend the night with her in his arms. But to come to that conclusion because of her scar? Now, he understood why she adamantly covered it up. People thought the worst before they gave her a chance to prove otherwise.

The door smacked shut. Footsteps approached.

He walked toward her. "Ready to go to bed?"

"Yes. I'm so tired I think I dozed off in the privy." She giggled.

"You weren't in there that long." He wrapped an arm around her shoulders.

"It was so dark, I imagined what it must be like for you, and I thought I heard someone mumbling behind the building. So I must have dozed off and been dreaming."

Clay didn't want to scare her, but he wanted her back in the house. No one should've been behind the outhouse. The building sat behind the office at the edge of the forest.

He ushered her back inside.

"The lights are on, should we turn them out?"

"Yes." He motioned her to do so, and he locked the door.

"Ready?" Rachel asked from across the room, near the inside door.

He crossed to her and followed her through the sitting room and down the hall. She turned into the room on the left.

He hesitated at the door. "Good night."

"You're not sleeping in here?" Disappointment laced each word.

"I thought about what Hank said. Proprieties..."

"I don't care about that. I'm in a strange place, and I don't want to sleep in this bed alone."

The conviction in her voice sped up his heart. Clay stepped in the room and closed the door.

"You're sure about this? If you do stay in Sumpter"—Lord, he hoped she would—"this could hurt your reputation if someone finds out."

"What do you think people are going to say tomorrow morning when they find out I spent the night in this house with both you and Hank?" The bed creaked as she climbed in. "As I see it, my reputation is already a mess, so why punish myself by sleeping alone?"

He liked her logic. Clay found a chair, sat down, and removed his boots and socks. Did she watch him? The knowledge Hank slept on the other side of the wall kept his desires in check. They would sleep in one another's arms tonight and nothing more. Not until they had the house to themselves.

He left his drawers on and slid under the covers. She snuggled against him. Soft flannel rubbed against his side. Her arm draped across his chest.

She'd set her boundaries tonight as well. He kissed her head.

"Don't let Hank's initial response to me come between you." Her soft words whispered the hair on his chest.

"Now, I see why you're so adamant about covering your scar." He hugged her. "I'm sorry."

She rose up, drawing her body from his. "Why?"

"Having to endure people's prejudgment."

She kissed his cheek. "It's the same for you. Look at my father's behavior toward you. He never took the time to get to know you. Only judged you because you can't see."

"I won't ask you to take your makeup off any more."

She snuggled back down beside him.

"Good night, Rachel."

"Night."

Her body relaxed, and her breathing settled into an even rhythm. He'd keep her safe in his arms tonight.

Clay mulled over the night's events. His brother's prejudice seemed out of character. Give him time. He'd see Rachel for all her wonderful qualities.

Her comment about someone mumbling behind the outhouse kept him awake. Who could it have been? The man she said followed them onto the train? Did he get off in Baker City as well?

Who was he?

What did he want?

Chapter 28

Rachel awoke and smiled. Clay faced her, his arm wrapped protectively around her waist. She stared at his face only inches from hers. To wake up every morning and gaze upon his face would be a dream come true.

She trailed her fingers down the muscled ridges of his arm. His grip tightened. In one fluid movement she was on her back, and he hovered over her. His hardness pushed against her lower body.

"Good morning," he said in a raspy first of the day voice.

"Yes, it is." She ran a finger along his whiskered jawline.

Clay collapsed on top of her. His weight startled and excited her. She wrapped her arms around his neck and savored his weight and hard body. Her body came to life, heating, aching to be closer. She pressed against him, seeking more contact.

He dipped his head and seduced her with a

long, wet kiss.

Her body longed for more, but her head screamed, "No." Rachel turned her face from his advances to catch a breath and clear her head. His hands slid under her, cupping her buttocks and pressing her against his hardened length. Her genitals throbbed. Her heart raced in anticipation of the wonders he could show her body.

"Stop." She shoved her hands between them, trying to pry their bodies apart.

Clay froze, his hands pulled out from under her, and he rolled off. "Sorry, I've never woke next to a woman before. Guess I got carried away."

Clay's disappointment drew his features into a boyish pout. His contriteness tugged at her heart.

"It's not that I don't want your attention. I haven't unpacked my doctor's bag from my trunk."

His brow furrowed. "What's that have to do with fooling around?"

"I have items in my bag that will keep me from becoming with child." She caressed his cheek and felt his jaw clench. How did she explain her feelings to him about becoming pregnant? "I crave your touch, but a child right now would sabotage my livelihood as a doctor."

"I see." He rolled off the side of the bed and sat.

He didn't "see". His actions spoke louder than his lack of words.

Rachel slipped behind him, pressing against his back and nibbling his neck. "I desire you more than I thought possible to crave another."

His body remained tense, unresponsive. "But your practical mind can't see you could have both.

A child and be a doctor."

"I told you, I can't do both yet. A child would require time away from my practice, which isn't good when I'm starting out. I could also bring home a disease." She grasped his hand when he started to stand. "I don't want to endanger a child."

Clay ran a hand over his face. "Or you don't think I would make a good father."

"No." She slid onto his lap, straddling him. "You would be a loving, protective father. It's me, not you."

Rachel skimmed her hands over his shoulders and through the hair on his chest. His body jerked.

"I would adore a child with you. Just not now." She wanted to be a wife and mother. But that was a dream she'd shoved out of her mind to concentrate on being a doctor. She wasn't going to waste the years of schooling now. Not when she was so close to proving to everyone she could be a doctor. A good one.

"Then don't touch me like you're doing now. I can't promise I won't get other ideas." Clay captured her hands with one hand and ran the other up her leg and under her nightdress. An eyebrow arched when his calloused hand cupped her naked hip.

"No drawers?"

"No."

He growled and stood, sliding her to her feet in front of him. "You aren't making this easy."

"I'm sorry. But I don't see why we can't enjoy one another." Her face heated. "Like in the train."

"You two getting up today?" Hank called.

"Yeah." Clay brushed by her, groping for the chair and his clothes. "That's why. Until Hank is back at the cabin, we're only sleeping in this bed."

She grabbed the shirt he'd slid his arms in, stopping his actions. "What else is bothering you?"

"Nothing." Clay tugged the shirt from her hands and continued dressing.

Something bothered him. His dismissive tone, clenching jaw, and drawn features gave him away. Did he still think she didn't believe he'd make a good father?

Rachel stepped around him and dressed. Fine. She'd tell Hank about the man following them, and then borrow the wagon to return to Sumpter and inquire about a house. Clay stalked out of the room before she'd finished dressing. She entered the kitchen and found Hank standing at the stove cooking eggs.

"Let me help you." She grabbed the apron on a hook by the stove and ducked her head into the neck strap. She tied the strings behind her back and set about putting plates on the table.

"Where's Clay?" Rachel poured coffee in the cups on the table.

"Said he needed to go for a walk."

She stopped and faced him. "Is that a good idea?" Fear knotted her insides.

"He knows his way around these woods."

"But you don't know." She grasped his arm and sat, drawing him into a chair beside her.

Hank's eyes, the same brown as Clay's, peered into hers. "Don't know what?"

"In Meacham, we left the train and took a

walk. A man stared at us and followed us back to the train. While we were eating in the buffet car, he poked his head in. His expression." She shuddered. "Then I saw him in Baker City. When you and Clay went after the baggage. He peered in the window and laughed. He's unstable and he's following us. Clay, I think. The man stared at Clay like he knew him."

Fear for Clay constricted her chest. "He shouldn't be left alone until we find this man."

Hank stared at her. "How do you know he isn't following you?"

"No one is following me. There's no reason." Unless her father had someone following her to make sure she was safe? She shook her head. The man had shown unstable actions. She shivered at the memory of his beady eyes and deranged laugh.

"What does he look like?" Hank sat back, assessing her.

"He's my height, shaggy brown hair and beard, skinny, and he limps on his right leg."

The door opened and Clay walked in. Relief shot her to her feet and across the floor. She wrapped her arms around him. He smelled of fresh air and musky male.

"What's this?" He returned the hug. "I wasn't gone that long."

"Breakfast is ready," Hank said.

Rachel walked back to the table and took her seat.

Clay crossed the room and sat down next to her.

"Eggs at six and biscuits at twelve," she said,

picking up her cup for a sip of coffee.

"Rachel tells me there's a man following you."

She spit the coffee onto her plate and glared at Hank. She'd told him in confidence.

"Yeah, she described him to me at Meacham." Clay patted her back. "Are you all right?"

"She saw him in Baker City."

Clay stopped patting her and slid his hand to the back of her neck. His cool fingers massaged her tense muscles.

"Why didn't you tell me you saw him?"

The disappointment in his voice cooled the heat his hand caused. "I didn't want you charging off to find him."

He cupped her cheek. "But I can't protect you if I don't know what I'm up against."

She wanted to revel in Clay's touch and forget about the mystery man, but they had to find out who he was and what he wanted.

"I'm not worried about me. You're the one he glares at and watches intently." She shivered, remembering the way the man had stared at Clay in the buffet car. Pure hatred had burned in the man's small eyes.

"If he's around here the men will see him and tell us." Hank's easy dismissal angered her.

"There are acres and acres of forest he can hide in." She scowled at Hank and stared at Clay.

"And that's why you don't go outside this house without Hank or me with you." Clay dropped his hand to her shoulder and squeezed.

"I didn't come here to be a prisoner." She shrugged his hand off. "I was that in Salem." Here she planned to start a fresh new life. One with a challenging career.

"You won't be a prisoner. You can come and go as you like, just not alone." Clay reached out to her, but she moved from his touch.

"Now you sound like my father, telling me what I can and can't do. I'm a grown woman, in case you haven't noticed, with a degree to practice medicine. I believe if I can make decisions about other people's health I can make decisions about my own well-being."

Clay ran a hand over his face. Tarnation, she was being difficult.

"I'm not saying you can't take care of yourself, but you're in a strange place. When you know your surroundings, then I'll feel better about you going out alone. People who aren't used to these woods get lost easy."

"Eat," Hank said. "Food's getting cold, and I have work to do."

The edge of irritation in Hank's voice and the sharp scrape of a chair vibrating the floor spoke volumes. His brother was not happy with the discourse brought by their arrival.

Clay fumbled on the table for his fork. His walk had done little to clear his mind. He wanted Rachel to stay and become his wife more than anything he'd ever wanted, but her assertion this was just another prison lingered. That and her adamant stand on not getting with child worried him. Perhaps she wasn't ready to marry and settle down—especially with him.

Utensils scraped plates and dishes clanked as

they ate in silence. The dismal atmosphere seeped into his skin. He'd come home, but so far the elation he'd hoped for had yet to surface. Waking with Rachel in his arms had brought joy. He wished he could have shown her how deep his affections ran for her. But her insistence to have her doctor bag had dampened his desire. He still wanted her, but now worried she may already be with child from their passionate night on the train. What would she do if that had happened?

"I'd like to borrow the wagon and go to Sumpter to look for a place to set up my practice."

Rachel's comment thrown into the awkward silence stunned him. Why did she need to go to town already? Did she already regretting traveling here? It hurt to think she hadn't asked him to take her.

Hank cleared his throat. "I have to unload the supplies, and then we need the wagon to haul lumber for repairs."

"Then I'll take a buggy."

The finality of her words brought a smile to Clay's lips.

The chair across the table from him scraped the floor. "We don't have a buggy," Hank said.

"Oh."

Rachel's breathy despair tugged at Clay. He shoved his plate to the middle of the table. "We can ride horses to Sumpter." He couldn't wait to get on a horse.

"That's a bad idea," Hank said as dishes clattered on the drain board.

Clay stood. He wouldn't be a prisoner any

more than Rachel. "We'll be fine. We know there's someone watching. Rachel will keep an eye out, and I'll be alert."

Rachel placed her hand on his arm. "I've never ridden a horse," she said so soft he almost didn't catch her words.

A city girl. They walked or rode a buggy where they wanted to go.

"We still have that old black nag?" he asked Hank.

"Yes, but she'd never be able to outrun anything on that old mare."

"She won't have to outrun anything, just feel comfortable." Clay walked to the door. "Is the mare here or at the cabin?"

"The cabin."

The disbelief in Hank's voice didn't dampen Clay's excitement at riding. Dishes clanked. He heard Rachel's small feet scurrying around the room.

"I'll go get the horse. You clean up the meal and be dressed to ride in an hour." Clay grabbed the door latch.

"You aren't going by yourself?"

Rachel's reprimand tickled him. It proved she cared more than she let on.

He swung toward the sound of her voice. "I'll see if there's a spare man at the mill."

"I'd appreciate that." Her tone had softened.

Hank's rough hand grabbed his and pulled the door open. "I have work to do." His body brushed Clay's as he walked out the door.

Rachel's arms wrapped around Clay. "Be careful."

Clay drew her into an embrace and kissed the top of her head. "I'll take someone with me and be back in an hour. Put on whatever will work to straddle a horse. We don't have any side saddles."

"It wouldn't matter, I don't know how to ride that way either."

Her nervous giggle pierced his heart deeper and he hugged her close. "I know this is different than what you're used to. I wouldn't blame you if you ordered me to take you back to the train."

She pulled back. "I've faced worse challenges than living in a rural community. And if you think this is all it would take to make me leave you..." She wound her fingers in his hair and tugged his head down. "Then you aren't paying attention."

She pressed her velvety soft lips to his. He didn't need any more invitation. He took over the kiss, possessing her lips and delving into her heat. His hands skimmed up and down her body, melding her to him, pressing her soft breasts against his chest and cupping her backside.

A sharp whistle pierced the air. He jerked. Why did it sound familiar and surge anger?

"What's wrong?"

Rachel's dreamy voice slipped him back into the haze of need.

"Nothing. I better go, or we won't get to Sumpter today." He kissed her quickly on the lips and backed away, feeling the door jamb with one hand.

Outside, the cool morning air calmed his heated body and shot his thoughts to the whistle. He knew of only one person who gave that whistle. A man he'd hoped to run into for the last ten months.

Chapter 29

Rachel hurried through straightening the kitchen. In the bedroom, she found a split skirt that must have belonged to Aileen. Though loose around the waist and too long, it would be more suited to riding than anything she owned. She rolled the skirt's waistband and tied a cloth belt around her waist to hold the garment up and make it short enough she didn't step on it when she walked.

Dressed, she set to work applying makeup. She wanted to make a good impression on the people in Sumpter. It could mean the difference between her practice growing or floundering. She mixed the powder and the lard and noted her supplies getting low. At the mill she wouldn't need to conceal the scar if she wore her bonnet whenever she went outside. If they made many trips to town, she'd need to order more powder and purchase more lard. At home, the drug store owner knew the reason for her purchase and kept a supply on hand. What would the store clerk here think when she ordered powdered makeup that prostitutes and actresses used?

"Are you ready?" Clay called.

Rachel patted the makeup on the side of her face and stepped to the hallway. "Almost. Have a cup of coffee."

Clay stood in the doorway to the hall. "Need any help?" His eyebrow arched.

"No. I just have to put my hair up." She pivoted back into the washroom, applied one more layer of powder and brushed out her hair, pulling it up on the sides with bone combs and twisting her hair into a bun at the back of her head. She nodded at her reflection and crossed to the bedroom to retrieve her hat and gloves.

Clay sat in the kitchen sipping a cup of coffee, a dusty battered hat on his knee.

"I'm ready to go to town but not so sure I'm ready to ride a horse." As a girl she'd dreamed of owning a horse, but after the accident her mother wouldn't hear of it.

He stood and grinned, placing the ugly hat on his head. "The horse I'm putting you on couldn't toss you on the ground if her life depended on it. Just sit in the saddle and let her follow me."

"And how do you know if your horse is going the right way?" She walked to the door and he followed.

"Because he's traveled the route a time or two." Clay caught her arm, drawing her near. He sniffed and put a hand on her chin. "You ready to impress the good people of Sumpter?"

"Other than the riding skirt I borrowed of Aileen's which is too big, yes, I believe I'm ready."

Clay put his hands around her waist, running his fingers over the rolled up material and down the length of the ties. "We'll have to see if the store has any ready-made riding skirts." His hands roamed up her sides. "You know, Myrle might have one, too. She's a little shorter than you, but closer to your waist size."

Before she could protest, his face descended and their brims banged together. Her hair pulled from the hatpins. His hat tipped back on his head.

"We'll have to figure out how to avoid that." He shoved his hat back in place and tugged on her hand, heading out the door.

She fought a bubble of laughter at the sight of the sad looking black horse standing beside a powerfully built sorrel gelding.

"Are you sure she won't die with me on her back? She can barely hold herself up." Rachel walked up to the horse and petted her nose. The mare raised her head and Rachel caught a spark in the animal's eye. "Does she have a name?"

Clay stood beside her. "Our mother called her Beauty."

No wonder the men kept a horse no longer of use to them. She'd been their mother's. Her throat became scratchy with emotion. She cleared it and asked, "That would make her how old?"

Clay ran a hand down the old mare's neck and remembered the day his father brought the mare home for his mother. Now, Beauty didn't hold her feed well in the winter but was still in pretty sound shape. No one had cared to ride her after their mother died, but no one had the heart to sell her either.

"She was in her prime when... She's over twenty."

"And been well taken care of." Rachel squeezed his arm. "Tell me what to do to mount. I know my foot goes..."

Clay placed his hands on Rachel's waist and lifted her onto the horse.

"Thank you, but that doesn't teach me how to get on by myself."

Rachel pried his hands from her waist. Before he could discern what she was up to, her body fell into his arms.

"Now," she said, her breath coming in shallow pants as she pushed out of his arms and stood on her own, "show me the correct way to mount."

He grinned and shook his head. Independent. The quality he loved most about her.

"Place your left foot in the stirrup." He held out the stirrup and helped guide her foot in. "Grab the horn with your left hand and put your right hand on the back of the saddle." He moved behind her and grasped her waist again. "Use the foot on the ground to push off, and pull your body up so you're standing in the stirrup." He held her as she pushed off. "Move the right hand to the horn and swing your right leg over the horse's rump."

"I did it!"

Her childlike exclamation expanded his chest with pride that he'd given her the experience. He adored her enthusiasm and didn't doubt her face beamed.

"Yep, you now know how to get on your horse." He squeezed her thigh and handed her the reins. "Keep these loose enough you aren't pulling on her mouth."

"Do I need to hold them any particular way?"

"Whatever's comfortable and works."

Clay walked to his horse. The gelding had remembered him, walking up to him when he called. They'd been together since he turned fifteen. He mounted and breathed in piney mountain air and the dusty muted scent of horse. He'd missed the smells, the people, and the sense of belonging the past four months. He hoped the woman next to him learned to love the area as much as he did.

"Ready?" He reined the horse toward the jingle of sleigh bells barely audible above the pounding of the stamps.

"Yes. Do I hear bells?"

The hollow clomp of her horse followed beside him. "After the accident, Aileen strung bells off the walking bridge over the creek so I could find the bridge when I went out by myself." He walked his horse through the creek beside the jingling sound. The splashing of the horses and the growing thud of the stamps drowned out the bells.

"Aileen sounds like an intelligent woman. I'm anxious to meet her."

"That'll be a while. She and Ethan won't be back for at least six months." He missed his older brother, but was glad Ethan had found happiness.

The pounding of the stamps directed him to the road leading toward town.

"Do we follow this all the way?" Rachel called to him. "I have to admit I was busy staring at the scenery last night and didn't notice if we took different roads."

The old mare kept up a good pace. He waited until the pounding was muted before replying.

"There are a couple of side roads to other claims, but this is the main road. It's only been here a year, just since we started building the stamp mill. We needed a way to haul in all the equipment and materials. Now the workers use it to come to work and the miners along this route use it to go to town."

"Your family should be proud of what you've accomplished in a short time."

Pleasure surged through him. He had the respect of the desirable woman next to him. Something he'd worked to gain from his brothers.

Rachel stared at the dirt and grass street separating less than a dozen buildings. On the way to the stamp mill yesterday, they'd skirted the town. Her first sight of the ragtag village had crumbled her high hopes of a fulfilling medical practice.

One lone tree stood at the far end of the street symbolizing her despair. She was adrift in a world she was unaccustomed to and wanted desperately to make it work.

"There isn't much here in the way of accommodations." She stopped her horse and took a deep breath. Rural. Primitive. Her chest squeezed with apprehension. Could she function here as a doctor?

Did she want to try?

"I know it wasn't very much before I left, but I'd hoped it had grown because of the stamp mill." Clay stopped his horse and twisted in the saddle.

"If it's grown since you left, then it couldn't have been more than a building or two." Rachel urged her horse forward and stopped beside him. "I can't... There's no way I could survive as a doctor in this town." If she couldn't be a doctor, how could she stay? Becoming his wife without giving doctoring a chance, she'd never be fulfilled. Never be able to give him all the love he deserved.

Clay waved an arm. "There are lots of miners up in the hills that would rather stop here to be doctored than go all the way to Baker City." He stared ahead. "At least talk to some people." His horse moved forward and she followed.

Talk to people. What people? There wasn't a soul on the street or lounging in front of the General Merchandise store. She doubted they carried the powder she needed or even a riding skirt as Clay had suggested.

Clay's horse stopped in front of a two story house. "Is this a two story house with a sign that says food?"

"Yes." How did he know that?

He patted his horse on the neck and dismounted, catching her horse by the headstall.

"We'll go in here for something to drink and the latest gossip." He stepped to the side of her horse, raised his hands, grasping her around the waist, and pulled her off the saddle, placing her feet on the ground.

"Oh...my legs." She clutched his arms, marveling at the strength he possessed holding her upright. Her wobbly legs refused to cooperate after the long ride.

Clay's arms circled her waist and drew her closer. "Your legs will get used to this in no time. Until then, you can lean on me all you want."

The intent expression on his face and hand creeping up her back shot heat through her body. His desire to hold her matched her need to be held.

"Why, bless my soul, if it isn't Clay Halsey."

Rachel jerked her head to the female voice. Clay loosened his hold but didn't remove the arm circling her waist. He drew her to his side.

"Myrle, bet you thought you'd seen the last of me." He held out a hand to the older woman, embracing her to his other side. Her head came to Rachel's shoulder. The woman's rheumy faded blue eyes studied Rachel.

"I knew I'd see you again. Hank comes in regular telling me what you're up to. But he didn't say anything about a wife." Myrle stepped away from him and walked up the three steps to the front porch.

Clay followed, his arm still tucked around Rachel. Was he going to tell the woman they weren't married? She'd find out soon enough.

He navigated the steps, drawing her along. The woman's backside disappeared through the front door.

They crossed the porch, and Clay held the door. Cooking aromas assailed her as her gaze roamed the small room hosting six cloth-covered tables and four chairs each.

"Over here." Myrle held a coffee pot in one hand and three cups in the other. Clay stepped into the room, dragging the old hat from his head.

Rachel tucked her arm though Clay's and navigated through the tables to the one the woman indicated.

Clay held a chair for her and sat to her left.

"Hank didn't say anything about you getting married," Myrle said again, assessing her.

"That's because we aren't married, yet." Clay picked up his cup and took a sip.

Rachel's stomach quivered with uncertainty. Did the yet mean he still planned to marry her? Did she want to be stuck in this place with little to do? She peered at his relaxed face and easy smile. Her heart flipped. Would it be bad to have little to do if she could wake every morning in his arms?

Myrle studied her harder, squinting. "Well, you were being pretty darn familiar for not being married."

"Mrs.—"

"Myrle. If you're a friend of Clay's you're a friend of mine, until I determine otherwise." The old woman continued to watch her.

"Myrle, this is Doctor Rachel Tarkiel," Clay said.

Rachel scowled at him. Did he fear she'd say something wrong?

Myrle's eyes widened and the straight line of her lips softened.

"A doctor?" The woman switched her critical stare to Clay. "I thought you were just blind. Do you have some other ailing?"

Clay laughed. "No. Rachel was the doctor at the Blind School. We got along well, and I asked her to come visit and see if this might be a place she'd like to practice medicine."

"I see..." Myrle shot her gaze back to Rachel.

"I'm wondering, though, after seeing the size of your town, if I could stay busy here." Rachel picked up her coffee cup and watched the woman over the rim. "And there doesn't seem to be a lot of housing."

"So the two of you would live in Sumpter?"

"If we can determine Rachel would have work, and I can find a place for a business venture I've started." Clay nodded. "I don't want to live in Baker City. I need to be close to the mill in case I'm needed."

Myrle's shrewd eyes studied her. "And what about you? Would you be able to live here? We aren't too worldly around here."

Rachel agreed. The town held little appeal. Of course, the first few months and possibly the first year would be slim until people trusted her. But could she live day in and day out in this primitive area?

Clay twined his fingers with hers. She stared into his eyes. The sharp brown had faded a little more each time she gazed in his eyes. But she still sought solace in their unseeing depths. Would loving him be enough to sustain her?

"I-I guess we won't know until I try it awhile." Clay's face changed subtly at her words. He'd been willing her to wholeheartedly love his town, but she couldn't, not yet.

"That's why we aren't married. If she decides to stay, then we'll discuss wedding plans."

His stiff formal voice made her chest ache. She'd hurt him by not embracing his life.

Myrle clanked her cup on the table, breaking Rachel's gaze on Clay.

"We have one empty building next to the post office. It might work for your business, Clay, but it would be a poor place for a doctor. Now, the Leonard's place that sits back near the trees, it's empty. You could use the parlor as your doctoring room and live in the rest, but it needs some work. Been a while since anyone set foot in it."

Clay stood and pulled Rachel to her feet. "Come on, let's take a look at both places, then come back here and have some lunch before we head back to the mill."

Chapter 30

Clay sensed Rachel's hesitation as they walked hand in hand down the street. Sumpter was more secluded and primitive than the city where she'd grown up. Between the differences and helping him, he was asking a lot of her. He'd go through the motions today, see if she showed any interest. If she couldn't make this work, he'd have to dig deep and decide what to do. He wished Ethan were here. His older brother always had a way of figuring things out.

His gut churned from the thought of her leaving. If she left and he didn't follow, his heart would suffer for a long time. But if life here became agony for her, he'd suffer as well. Best to hurt now and let her go than have her grow to hate him.

"This building looks kind of small for two businesses," Rachel said.

"Take me to a corner so I can step it off."

He stopped when she did.

"This is the—" She twisted and stretched. "I

think the north corner. Which way do you want to go—across the front or to the back?"

"Both."

"Let's go across the front first."

She tugged, and he counted his steps until she stopped. "About twenty feet across. Okay, how long?"

She pivoted him, and they started along the side. The sun's rays bounced off the building, adding heat to the already warm summer day.

"Thirty long. You're right. It would be a tight fit for both Donny's broom making and the writing tablets." This wasn't good news. He needed room for Jasper and Donny when they arrived in a month.

"What's on either side and behind the building?" If there was enough space they could add on.

"Behind, there's nothing until the trees. One side is the post office about twenty feet away. The other side is open."

Her soft steps shuffled along the dirt. What was she thinking? Did he dare ask?

"I'll come back tomorrow and walk through the layout so I can decide the best way to enlarge this building." He'd need to spend the afternoon and evening whittling sticks he could construct into the shape of the rooms.

"We could take the time today."

Her faint words suggested she had walked a distance away. Clay faced that direction. "I have to gather the items I need to manufacture the building so I can visualize it."

"I didn't— Well, then, I guess we should take a

look at the Leonard house."

Her soft voice, almost a whisper, made his heart plummet hard into his gut. This subdued, uncertain attitude gave rise to the notion she didn't care enough for him, and he was right in holding off marrying her.

He knew his feelings for her. He was in love. Any day, no matter where, would be good with her in it. But he wouldn't make her suffer.

"You don't have to look at the house." His words barked harsher than he'd planned. His sense of loss already overwhelmed him.

Her steps approached, her small hand captured his. "What's wrong? Are you upset you'll have so little time to get the building ready before Mr. Smith and Donny arrive?"

He traced her knuckles with his thumb. Everything about this woman made him happy. Why couldn't she feel the same?

"Yeah, just preoccupied."

"Which side of town is the Leonard place? Myrle didn't really say."

Her happier tone raised his spirits. "It should be... I have to think. I believe it's on the slope behind the mercantile."

Rachel led him across what the residents called a street. His feet stubbed the vegetation sticking up sporadically.

"Morning, Clay, Miss," Mr. Duckworth's voice bellowed.

Rachel stopped, and Clay faced the direction of the voice.

"Mr. Duckworth, how's the family?" he asked,

figuring they stood near the mercantile porch.

"They're all doing fine. I heard you were coming home. Things improved any?"

Clay shook his head. He'd known the Duckworth family most of his life. Everyone in Sumpter knew the life history of each other. "Nope, still walking around in the dark."

"Then you don't know there's a right fine looking woman leading you around. If I was you, I'd hang on and not let go." The man chuckled.

Rachel's fingers squeezed his, and Clay laughed.

"Thank you for the observation. I'll recollect on it." Clay waved. "Let's go look at that house." He clasped Rachel's elbow and started forward. She fell into step, drawing him to the left.

"It's the largest house I've seen here."

Her voice rose on a lilting note and shot hope to his heart. Maybe, just maybe...

Rachel stared at the house as they approached. By far it proved to be the best built house in town. It needed repairs and a whitewash, but she could see the possibilities.

The stairs creaked under her feet and a missing board needed replaced on the porch.

"How long has this been empty?" She wiped at the dust on the windows and peeked in. The trees shading the sides and the porch roof made it hard to see into the dark interior.

"I think they'd been gone about a year when I left." A board squawked under his weight. "They had a good carpenter build the house, but they weren't much on keeping things up."

"Can we get a key and look inside?" She peered back toward town, the view wasn't unpleasant. She could stand here and see who came to town and gaze upon the majestic trees on the far slope.

"I'm pretty sure the door isn't locked." Clay ran a hand along the wall and grasped the brass doorknob. The door swung open with a creak.

"Oh!" She stepped across the threshold. The large entry could easily accommodate chairs for her patients. The left opened into a parlor, the right a dining area. Stairs led to the upper floor. She followed the short hall to a primitive kitchen. The stove looked useable, though dated. Two enamel basins sat on a drain board. She didn't see a hand pump.

"Is this the kitchen?"

Clay's voice behind her made her jump.

"Yes. The cook stove would do. It looks like water comes from a well outside." She couldn't keep the disappointment from her voice.

"That's easy to fix."

"Really?" Availability of water in an emergency would be helpful.

"I can order what we need from Baker City and have Hank help me."

His confidence bolstered her enthusiasm. "It's a cute kitchen, or could be with the right curtains and tablecloth." She opened the pantry door. Plenty of room for food and medical supplies.

She headed to the hallway. "Let's check out the upstairs."

Clay caught her arm as she walked by. "What

about the other rooms down here? Will they work?"

The anxiety drawing the corners of his mouth down and hiding his dimple twisted her heart. He wanted her to like this house.

"They would work perfectly." She placed her hand on his cheek. "I'm a little disappointed in the size of the town—"

He turned his face away. She moved with him, stepping close, molding her body to his. "But I'm not going anywhere. Not without you."

To prove her point, she knocked his hat off, captured his head in her hands, and kissed him. She drew out of the kiss slowly, brushing her lips across his. The sensation sent wild thoughts buzzing through her head.

Clay crushed her to him and returned the kiss. He took command, his tongue tangling with hers and creating feelings so intense her body ached for more. She tugged his shirt from his pants and ran her palms over the hard muscles of his back. The heat and texture of his skin aroused her even more. Her blood surged, making her lightheaded.

She drew back only enough to say, "Clay, upstairs." If they were lucky the past residents had left a bed.

Clay scooped her up in his arms.

Rachel giggled. "I'm sorry, but you're not carrying me up these stairs." She slipped out of his arms and led him to the stairway. They ascended into a short hallway. Three doors graced the bare walls.

She opened the first door. A delightful room

swathed in rose covered wallpaper overlooked the town. The second door revealed a smaller room with one window shaded by a tree.

Rachel opened the last door and stopped.

The room ran the length of the back of the house. A large bookcase covered one wall. Between two windows looking out at the trees beyond the house sat a hulking bed frame.

"Was Mr. Leonard a large man?" She walked to the foot of the bed. The square posts came to her shoulders, and the flat edges were longer than her hands laid fingertip to heel.

"He was tall, but the missus—she could take up a whole wagon seat by herself." Clay followed her into the room. He traced the bedpost. "Is there a mattress?"

"Yes, but it's fairly dusty." Rachel ran a gloved finger across the fabric covering. The wide line reminded her of drawing in the dirt as a child.

"So we won't finish what we started down-stairs?"

The wistfulness in his voice caused her to laugh. "Will this satisfy you?" She hugged his waist and placed her head on his chest. "I love this house. I think it would be perfect."

He embraced her, leaning his head on her hat. "I was—" He cleared his throat. "I was ready to put you on the train back to Salem."

She leaned away to peer into his face. "Why? Have I given you the impression I don't want to be here with you?" How could he so easily send her away? Didn't he care about her? His kisses and caresses were more than desire. She was sure of it. He had to love her, didn't he? Her stomach clenched.

"You seemed disappointed. That maybe you couldn't deal with me, my blindness, and living here."

He took her head in his hands, his face inches from hers. She stared into his eyes, his warm breath wafted across her face.

"I don't want you to go." He tilted his head and kissed her softly, tenderly.

Tears pooled in her eyes, blurring her vision.

"But if this place or I can't make you happy—I don't want you to stay out of a perceived duty." He kissed her again. "I want you happy. And if that means leaving, I-I'll agree even if it would kill me."

Her heart leaped about inside her chest. He cared. The emotion in his words proved more than his kisses. Rachel sniffed back the tears of happiness and kissed him.

Clay tasted salty tears on her lips and pulled back. "You're crying."

"They're happy tears. I promise." Rachel ran her hands under his shirt again.

Her caress fanned the fire she'd lit in the kitchen. His body exploded in flames of need. Feeling the crown of her hat, he released the hatpins and sent the bonnet sailing through the air. Her soft hair caught on his rough hands as he caressed her. Rachel's head lolled back. He dropped kisses the length of her velvety soft neck.

"Clay."

The one breathy word sent his heart soaring. He scooped her up and found the bed with his knees. They descended onto the mattress. He used his arms to cradle her from the fall and his crushing body.

Clay sneezed as dust tickled his nose. Rachel coughed, laughed, and coughed again. The powder settled on his skin, making him itch.

"Bad idea," Rachel said, squirming under him and causing more filth to enter his nose.

Clay turned his head and sneezed. Rachel's body shook as she coughed. He pushed off her, caught her leg, and pulled her to the edge of the bed, drawing her up to her feet.

"You warned me." He patted between her shoulder blades. Tonight. He'd show her how much she meant to him tonight. Somehow he'd figure out a way to get her alone.

"Oh, we both look like we climbed out of a hole!" Her coughing evolved into fits of laughter. "Let's find the well and see if we can clean up before we go to lunch and find out how to purchase this house."

"You mean it? You want to stay and live here, with me?" Elation pulsed in his chest, hindering his breathing.

"Only if you marry me in no more than two months. I'll not wait any longer than that."

Clay heard her toe tapping on the floor. He visualized her hands on her trim hips, a scowl on her face. He loved this woman!

He stuck out his hand. "It's a deal." Her slim fingers touched his palm, and he tugged her against his chest, kissing her until he had to come up for air.

"Don't start that again." Her palms rested on his chest, pushing her out of reach of his mouth. "I'll not be thrown on that dusty, no doubt, flea-infested bed again. At least not until we have a new mattress."

He released her. Her footsteps moved a few paces, stopped, then moved again.

"What are you doing?"

"Retrieving my bonnet and pins. You tossed them opposite directions."

"I don't like you wearing hats. It gets in the way." His knuckles bumped the end bedpost. He walked straight out from it, recollecting the door should be ahead of him.

"I'm not too crazy about that ugly hat you wore today either." Rachel touched his arm, and he caught her hand.

"That hat and I go way back."

"It looks it."

Their steps were muted by covering on the hall floor.

"Stairs."

He grasped the railing and started down, Rachel tucked by his side.

This would be their home. He could already smell bread baking, hear children's voices.

He stopped. How long would it really be before Rachel was ready for children? After a while would she decide not to have any at all?

He wanted children.

Chapter 31

"What's wrong?" Rachel asked, tugging on Clay's sleeve. He'd stopped in the middle of the stairway a grim set to his mouth.

"I-I just... Nothing." He half turned from her and slightly bowed his head.

She studied the side of his face. Whatever he wasn't willing to talk about meant a good deal to him. His furrowed brow and downturned lips constricted her chest.

"Are you sure there's nothing wrong? You look like you have something you want to say." She turned down the hall to the kitchen. They'd need plenty of water to clean this place up, and she wanted to see if the well was in good condition.

When he didn't respond, she continued as if nothing were amiss.

"The well would be out the back kitchen door wouldn't it?" she asked, continuing through the kitchen.

"Yes. It should be." He followed, his brow

wrinkled in a frown and a hand rubbing his face.

The backyard was overgrown. A space to the side sprouted weeds and a vegetable here and there, proving at one time a garden had flourished. Beyond the garden she spotted a rock well.

"There it is." Rachel walked to the circular formation and placed her hands on the edge. She peered into the dark hole. Cool air fluttered the curls around her face. Picking up a pebble, she dropped it into the darkness.

"Plink."

"There's still water. Now...to find a bucket and rope." She scanned the area. "Why didn't they leave the rope and bucket by the well?"

"They probably did."

Clay leaned his backside against the well and crossed his arms. The male stance fluttered her heart.

"If we can't get water, we can at least brush the dust off one another." She took a step closer and brushed at the dust coating his sleeves. Her back had to be coated like his forearms.

"Okay, I'll turn my back to you. I'm guessing you'll have to start at the top and brush me off all the way to my hem." She backed toward Clay until his hand stopped her.

His hands scraped the fabric as he swept them from her neck all the way down her riding skirt. He coughed and slapped his hands together, creating a cloud.

"I can't see if it's gone, but I think I breathed it all in." He coughed again.

Rachel spun around. A thin coat of dust covered the front of him. She laughed and brushed her hands over his shirt. "I think the only way to get rid of this dust is to take a bath and wash our clothes."

"I could suggest a spot in Cracker Creek that's an excellent swimming hole." Clay's eyebrow arched and a dimple graced his cheek.

"I'm sure you could, but you promised me lunch, and my stomach is ready." She looped her arm in his and began the walk to the main street and Myrle's. "Maybe Myrle would let us use a bucket of water at the back door."

A small entourage entered the far end of the street. The man on the lead horse bore a striking resemblance to Clay. Sunlight glinted off something on the man's vest. He was followed by a woman and child astride an eye-catching palomino and a dark horse carrying a young man tying knots in a small piece of cording.

"I think you're about to see some family," Rachel said, stopping in the street and waiting for the group to approach.

The woman swung off the horse, child and all, and threw an arm around Clay. "Clay, you're a sight for sore eyes. I couldn't believe it when Hank sent a telegram saying you were coming back."

Clay wrapped an arm around the small woman and smiled. Rachel shifted her attention to the man still sitting on his horse. He didn't attempt to dismount. His full lips tipped into a smile.

"About time you came back so Darcy'd quit wearing my ears off about how you can't possibly be happy in a school." He swung his leg over the front of his horse and slid to the ground. In three strides he clasped Clay's shoulder. "Good to have you back."

The woman turned her attention to Rachel. Her gaze roved from her disheveled hair and dirty face to the rolled waistband of her riding skirt.

"That looks like Aileen's skirt," she said, shifting the child to her other hip.

"It is. I borrowed it when Clay said we were riding to town." Rachel ruffled the curls by her scar. She skimmed a finger over her scar. Dust coated the makeup. All the better to hide her disfigurement. She didn't want the same response from these two she'd received from Hank.

Clay reached out to her. She twined her fingers with his. "Gil, Darcy, Sadie- is Jeremy here?"

"Over here, Clay." The young man slid to the ground in the same fashion as Gil and walked nonchalantly over to the group.

"Family, this is Doctor Rachel Tarkiel."

She smiled at the group, not missing the thorough stares. "Soon to be Doctor Rachel Halsey."

"Oh, a doctor in the family. That's wonderful." Darcy grabbed her free hand. "I can have you help with the next baby. I didn't care for the doctor that helped with Sadie. He wouldn't let me out of bed for days."

"You mean he didn't want you out of bed. You were fixing my breakfast the next morning." Gil wrapped an arm around his tiny wife and tickled this daughter's leg.

"It's all in what the patient is able to handle." Rachel watched the silent signals between the two and the way their gazes and bodies connected. She glanced at Clay. Would they have that kind of connection after they married?

"Then why did you make me stay in bed for six weeks when I broke my leg? I was ready to get out after two?" Clay tugged her closer, his arm encircling her waist.

"Because you would have climbed on a roof again had I let you out of my sight."

Gil, Darcy, and Jeremy laughed. Little Sadie guffawed a fake laugh and made them all laugh more.

Rachel's stomach growled.

"We were heading to Myrle's for lunch. Then we have to find the owners of the Leonard place." Clay patted her hip. "We're going to buy it."

"Blazes, you two move fast!" Darcy handed Sadie to Gil and looped her arm though Rachel's. "So tell me all about the plans you have for the house. I might be able to talk my husband into letting me stay a while and help."

Rachel found herself propelled away from Clay, their fingers slipping apart.

"I thought we were cleaning up?"

Clay voiced the frustration she felt at being dragged away from him. "Darcy, we'll tell you all about it at lunch. First, we need to go to the back of Myrle's and beg a bucket of water. That house was dusty." Heat crept up her neck, suffusing her cheeks from the knowing expressions on Gil and Darcy's faces.

"We'll get a table." Gil spun his wife away. Jeremy followed behind, leading the horses.

"Nice family," Rachel said as she and Clay walked to the rear of the building.

"Yeah, Gil found a woman that's feisty enough to make him mind and has a strong sense of family."

Family. Clay wondered again if he and Rachel would have a family. His fists clenched thinking of her foolish reasoning earlier. He wanted more of an answer from her about not wanting to get with child. Did her reluctance have anything to do with his blindness? Did she believe him incapable of helping raise children? The thought drained all the fight out of him.

"What's bothering you? You look like you lost your best friend." Rachel smoothed her palm over his cheek.

Her gentle touch didn't rush heat through his body. It conjured up images of her tenderly holding a child, their child.

"Do you really want kids or is your reluctance genuine?" he blurted out, hoping her words would quell the fear rumbling in his gut.

"If we have children I'll be happy, but I don't need children to be happy."

Her offhand comment smacked as smart as a slap.

"Are you afraid to have children because I can't see? Can't protect them?" His fists clenched at his side. This was a matter he'd shoved to the back of his mind every time it surfaced. But it had to be addressed now, before they were married. "Because if you want kids but are afraid I won't be a good father, we best not get married."

Rachel's feet stomped up the two porch steps, and her scent invaded his senses. She grabbed him by the face as an exasperated breath rushed over his face.

"First off, you can do everything short of whipping me and I'm not leaving you. I'll not let you toss what we have away just because you're feeling sorry for yourself."

Clay wanted to deny her accusation. Wanted to say he was self-assured enough to not take her dismissal of a child as a slap at him. But he couldn't. Self pity was something he fought every day in this darkness.

She continued, "Because Mister, I don't feel sorry for you. I think you are the most courageous man I've ever met and the most thoughtful and gentle. You will make a wonderful father."

Her assessment lodged a lump the size of a fist in his throat.

She drew a breath, her thumbs caressed his cheeks. "Like I said before, as a doctor, I come in contact with illnesses and diseases I wouldn't want to bring home to a fragile child, or expose them to through patients coming into our home. To bring a child into this world then watch it die because of me..." She gulped loudly. "That would nearly kill me. I would like children, but not until I have fulfilled my dream of being a doctor and helping others."

The soft yearning in her voice said she wanted children. He covered her hands with his, drawing one to his lips. If she needed to wait, so could he, as long as she wanted his children.

"I want to have your children. They would be beautiful. They'd be intelligent and loving... I just don't want to have them until I decide what direction to take with my career."

He wanted to tell her he understood, but she interrupted.

"And when that time comes, we'll determine the best way to take care of them, together."

She leaned forward, her lips meeting his, drugging him in a lingering seduction.

The door banged open. "Gil says you two need a bucket of water. Looks like I should throw it on you to cool you down." Myrle laughed and the door slammed shut.

Rachel drew out of the kiss. He wasn't ready to let her go and hugged her against his chest, reveling in her strength and delicious curves.

"So you want to have children, with me, just not right away, and you could tolerate living here?" Clay's heart cavorted with happiness.

"Yes. I'm not leaving here unless you do."

A smile curved his lips, and he kissed her. "Then we have two months to get the house ready for a wedding."

Rachel's heart hammered in her chest. Elation fluttered in her abdomen. "We can have the wedding in our home? Heavens! That would be— Oh!" She jumped and wrapped her arms around Clay's neck, kissing him.

He laughed. "I take that for a yes."

Rachel pushed out of his arms. "Quick clean up. We have to eat, fill Darcy in, and then buy the house, so I can start planning." She spotted a broom sitting by the back door.

"Stand still, I'll broom you off. Then you do the back of me." The dust drifted away on the slight afternoon breeze.

She put the bucket of water on the edge of the porch and splashed her face. Water in her eyes, she realized she'd forgotten to ask for a towel. The door opened. She blinked and glanced up at a blurry Gil. He held out a towel.

"Myrle sent me because she thought you two would need to be pried apart."

The gleam in his eyes made her laugh. "Maybe a moment ago, but we're getting cleaned up now." She stepped back, and Clay dunked his hands in the bucket.

Rachel dried her hands and lightly patted her face, trying to keep the makeup in place. Clay bobbed up from washing his face, and she slipped the towel in his hands, and then stood on her tip-toes to whisper in his ear.

"Dry your hands, then see if my makeup is smeared." She held still as his fingers gently probed the right side of her face.

"Perfect." He placed a kiss on her temple.

Rachel glanced at Gil still holding the door, his brow furrowed.

"Come through the kitchen. It's faster. The food's been on the table a while." Gill held the door open.

Rachel looped her arm through Clay's and stepped into a kitchen filled with mouth-watering aromas of baked bread, roasting meat, and spicy gingerbread. Her stomach rumbled loud, and Myrle swung away from the stove.

"Best get in there and quiet that belly of yours." She grinned and winked as they continued to follow Gil through a door and into the eating area.

Jeremy had cleaned his plate and was stealing bites from Sadie.

"Jeremy, how many times do I have to tell you to quit stealing Sadie's food?" Gil snatched the young man's fork away from the toddler's plate.

"She isn't going to eat it all, are you, Sadie?" Jeremy cooed to the child who smiled at him as if he'd just handed her a piece of candy.

"No. Jemy have mine, Papa." The child's sweet face and big eyes beseeched her father.

"Only if you're done." Gil sat down beside his wife and dug into the food on his plate.

Clay pulled out an empty chair, and Rachel sat. He moved to her left, found the empty chair, and sat, pulling it closer to her.

"Chicken at three, mashed potatoes at six, and carrots at nine." She moved his water cup to the middle above his plate. "Water at twelve."

Rachel inhaled the mouth-watering aroma of the roast. She couldn't remember when she'd been this hungry.

"So what were you two discussing in the back so long?" Darcy flashed a peek at Clay, and then studied Rachel.

"Our wedding." Clay picked up his glass.

Rachel's excitement about having the wedding in the dusty old house they were going to buy gave him hope they could make a marriage work. His mind wandered to the tongue lashing she'd given him. He'd deserved it.

Darcy clapped her hands. "When?"

"Two months. That should give us time to get the house ready and Rachel's family to be contacted and arrange a trip." Clay halted the bite going to his mouth. He also had to get the building ready for Jasper and Donny.

"Jeremy, how'd you like to work for me for a couple months?"

"Really?" His adolescent voice squeaked. "Me, work with you?"

"With getting the house ready and a building for my new business, I'll need someone to make sure my orders are being followed." Clay faced the direction of Jeremy's voice. "Someone I can trust."

"Gil, Darcy, can I stay here and help Clay? I'm not really needed in Galena right now anyway." Jeremy's voice lost the squeak as he justified his question.

"Gil, that will leave you all alone, because I plan to stay here and help Rachel," Darcy chimed in.

"I'll miss you all, especially my two girls, but these two could use the help."

Clay nodded to his brother. "Thanks. We're going to have our hands full." Clay told them about Donny and his broom-making business and the writing tablets he and Jasper would make and sell. Rachel jumped in now and then. The conversation lasted past the disappearance of the food and several cups of coffee and Myrle's famous huckleberry pie.

Myrle sat down to visit after the other customers had left.

"Who owns the Leonard house? Rachel and I would like to buy it." Clay held his breath, hoping it was someone in the area.

"You're looking at the owner," Myrle said. "I bought the building from Milton Leonard when he left. I thought about moving the business over there, then decided it was out of the way and I didn't want to renovate to make room for the ladies who live with me now."

Clay couldn't contain the smile curving the corners of his mouth. Rachel clutched his hand.

"Well, it's sold. Tell us a price, and I'll ride to Baker City. No, my new foreman will ride to Baker City tomorrow and make the transaction."

"Hot dang! I'm a foreman!" Jeremy's hand slapped down onto the table, rattling the dishes. "Did you hear that, Darce?"

"Yes, Jeremy. And you do realize this is an important job Clay's giving you?" Darcy said in a tone Clay'd heard his mother and Myrle use a time or two.

He held back the snicker and turned to Myrle. "So what's your price?"

Chapter 32

Clay held the old mare as Rachel dismounted. At the sound of her feet hitting the ground, he circled her waist with an arm, snugging her up against his body.

"You realize with Gil's family staying at the cabin and Hank going to visit, we'll have the place to ourselves?" He'd thought of nothing else after Gil announced he'd settle Darcy, Sadie, and Jeremy into the cabin for their extended stay.

"I do. How about we take a bath and discuss what we can do while he's gone?"

Rachel's playful tone sent heat to his muscles and infused him with energy. "You check the water reservoir in the cookstove and round up buckets while I put the horses away." He kissed her neck and led the horses to the shed and corral Ethan built after he and Aileen moved into the house.

Finally, they would be alone for the evening in a real bed without having to be discreet. They should wait until after the wedding, but their feel-

326

ings ran hotter than any he'd ever experienced. In his heart, they were already married.

He unsaddled and fed the horses. His gelding nickered when Clay led him to the corral. A nickering reply echoed through the trees behind the outhouse.

There wasn't a road or any reason someone should be in that area. Clay closed the corral gate and stared in the direction of the sound. He didn't like the idea of someone hanging around. His fists clenched. Didn't like that he couldn't see anyone standing next to him. Not knowing and standing here felt like cowardice. He might be blind but he wasn't a coward.

Clay broke off a limb and moved it back and forth in front of his feet, checking for any objects that might trip him. He stopped and listened. It was unusually quiet. The thud of the stamps didn't fill the air. Hank said the mill was shut down due to maintenance. The impatient stomp of a horse's hoof directed him more to his right. His movement was slow and precise. He didn't want whoever he was sneaking up on to hear him. The stick thunked something hollow. He stretched out a hand. His palm met a rough wood surface. The outhouse.

He started into the trees behind the building, his ears keyed to every sound. A horse stomped and blew air. The slight evening breeze brought the dank, dirty scent of a hard-ridden horse.

The animal's heat and dampness touched his outstretched palm. He stroked the sweaty lather on the horse's neck. His other hand skimmed over the saddle, empty gun scabbard, the stirrups hung about average. Who and where was the rider?

Rachel hummed as she set all the buckets she could find by the water reservoir. She entered the bedroom, laid out her night clothes, and scrubbed the makeup from her face, dabbing on the citrus oil she used to clear away the lard in the makeup base.

A bath would be heavenly after their dusty frolic on the bed at their soon-to-be home. Her head buzzed with happiness. They would pay Myrle the moment Jeremy returned from Baker City with the money, and the house would be theirs. She pinched herself. She saw so many possibilities with the house and the building Clay planned to use for his business.

Rachel hummed, rummaging through her doctor's bag. She pulled out a small sponge and thread and tied one end of the thread around the sponge. She raised her skirt to her waist, placed one foot on the chair, and inserted the sponge in her vagina, leaving the string dangling from her body. With the house to themselves, she planned on showing Clay how deep her love for him ran.

The kitchen door banged open. "Rachel? Rachel?"

Clay's deep frantic call chilled her blood.

"I'm here." She hurried to the kitchen, meeting him at the threshold between the kitchen and parlor.

He wrapped his arms around her, embracing her to his chest. "There's a horse out behind the privy. I don't know who it belongs to and I-I thought something might have happened to you."

"I'm fine. But who could it be?" A vision of the bearded man laughing at the hotel twisted her stomach in knots.

"I don't know. I can't believe a worker would leave his horse saddled behind the outhouse. It has to be the man you saw following us." Clay released her and stepped to the door, placing the bar across.

The idea that someone lurked about dampened Rachel's earlier elation at having the place to themselves. Could the horse belong to the man following them? If so what did he want?

"We'll have to keep an ear out for Hank when he returns."

Clay kicked a bucket, bent over and picked up two, and walked to the reservoir.

"Do you think it's wise to take a bath if someone is lurking outside?" She stood back watching him place the buckets under the reservoir spout.

"The doors are barred. Whoever it is can't get in without us hearing him." He shot her a devilish grin that ignited the slow burn of desire heating her body. "We might as well clean up and enjoy our alone time." He turned the tap and held a finger into the bucket. When the water touched his finger he turned off the tap and put another bucket under it.

"You carry those into the tub, and I'll start filling another one." No matter how many times she watched him carry out a feat, she still found herself amazed at his abilities.

He headed to the washroom, and she filled the last bucket in the kitchen. Clay returned, she filled buckets, and he hauled them until the reservoir was empty.

"I'll refill the reservoir while you get into the tub." He cupped her chin, raising her lips to his. "I'll be quick."

"You better." She kissed him and set off to the washroom. She was undressed and relaxing in the tub when he came quietly through the door in stocking feet.

Rachel watched him methodically slip from his dirty clothes and stand in all his glorious maleness beside the tub.

"If you're clean are you sure you want me to get in with you?" He gripped the side of the tub and swung a leg over.

"It would be easier to wash you if I get out of the tub." Rachel stood as Clay stepped in.

"But not nearly as much fun." His arms circled her, drawing her flush against his body. His hardness pressed into her abdomen. Desire flushed her skin and throbbed the juncture of her legs.

"I agree." She wound her arms around his neck and kissed him with passion.

He growled. "Help me clean up so we can take this where it belongs—to the bed."

He lowered into the water, and she straddled his lap. His enlarged penis caressed her genitals and lower abdomen as she rubbed against him and washed his hair, face, torso, and arms. The sensations brought both pleasure and torture. She swiveled around and the appendage stroked her backside while she washed his feet and legs. His hands stole around her body, cupping her breasts and teasing her nipples.

By the time Clay was clean, passion and desire burned in her hotter than if she'd been lounging in the cookstove. She stood, drawing him up with her.

Clay stepped out of the tub and scooped her into his arms, carrying her out the door and into the bedroom.

"We're wet," she said when he placed her on the bed.

"We'll dry off."

His body covered hers, and indeed, the heat between them dried the beads of water. His lips drugged her with a long, wet, tongue-tangling kiss. She pushed her heels into the bed and rubbed the aching juncture of her legs against him. Her body cried out to be sated.

"Take me," she whispered against his lips and spread her knees.

He slipped a hand between their bodies. His fingers discovering her folds, she arched her body when he touched a sensitive spot. His smug smile turned his handsome face even more deadly.

"You are a passionate woman who I plan to keep happy a long time." His finger slid in and he stopped. She felt a tug on the sponge she'd inserted.

"What's this?" he asked, tugging again.

"Stop." She stilled his hand with her own. "That's to keep me from getting with child. It's—it's not supposed to interfere with what we're doing."

Clay loosened his grip on the string. His gut clenched at the uncertainty of what she'd done to herself. His emotions teetered between accepting her practical side and aggravation that she was so set on keeping his seed from joining with her. If she were a woman he didn't love, he'd be interested in the process, but he loved her and wanted to have children with her. Many children.

Her body shifted under him, arousing his shaft with her subtle gyrations.

"Is whatever you did foolproof?"

Her motions stopped. "Why?"

"Just wondering why I can't pull out of you before my seed spills rather than you… Not sure I like you shoving things into your body to keep me out."

Her small hands grasped his face. "I'm not keeping you out. I'm barricading my womb to keep from getting with child. I want you in me. I want to feel all of you. I need to feel you." Her upper body rose and she pressed her lips to his. She kissed him open mouthed, tangling tongues, and her hands fisted in his hair. The deep kiss and her body moving against him excited and nearly broke his concentration. Which was what she wanted.

She hadn't answered his original question. He pulled out of her kiss, straightening his arms and levering his body off hers. "Will this barricade keep you from getting with child?"

Rachel squirmed under him. Not in a "tantalizing touch my skin way" but uncomfortably.

"It's not completely effective. But reports are it works most of the time."

Clay lowered his body onto hers, pinning her under him, feeling her soft mounds and sleek skin. He wanted her. Now and forever. One day they would make a child, if by mistake or by her time-table it didn't matter, as long as they were together.

He ran his hands down under her backside, drew her up, and entered. Whether she wanted a child or not, he needed her in every way.

She arched, driving him deep. He sunk into her, savoring the thought her barrier was no protection from his ardor, and drove her over the edge multiple times before releasing.

Pounding woke Clay. He scrambled out of the bed and groped around the room for his britches.

"What's going on?" Rachel asked in a sleepy voice.

"Hank must be back. Stay put. I'll let him in."

Clay pulled his britches on and hurried to the kitchen door.

"What's the big idea locking me out?" Hank fumed, shoving past him into the house.

Clay placed the board back in the brackets. "I found a riderless horse tied behind the outhouse earlier and thought it best to keep the doors barred, considering I couldn't go looking for whoever it was."

Hank stopped pumping water. "Is the horse still there?"

"I don't know." Clay sat down at the table and ran a hand over his face. "I didn't want to drag Rachel outside with me to look around."

Hank's footsteps vibrated the floor as he walked to the door. "I'm going to take a look. Wait for me to come back."

Clay nodded. Wood scraped wood and cool

night air washed across his bare torso. He should close the door, but the fresh air felt and smelled good. Hank's heavy steps grew near and the door shut out the cool air.

"There's no horse now, but I could see where it was tied." A chair scraped next to him. "What could you tell about the horse?"

"When I found it the animal was still lathered up from being ridden hard. The stirrups were set for an average sized man, and the rifle scabbard was empty." He leaned back in the chair. "That's why I came in and barred the door. I can't see someone holding a gun on me."

Hank placed a hand on his shoulder. "Sorry I yelled. I thought you'd barred the door to keep me out because..."

Clay smiled. "That too."

Hank punched him in the arm.

"Hey! If that's how you're going to treat me, I'm going back where I'm treated nice." Clay stood.

"I bet. You two should live apart until the wedding." Hank stood, too.

"Once we get the house livable, Rachel will move in." Clay walked to the door.

"What if your fooling around makes her with child?"

Clay smiled. "Then you'll be an uncle again." He walked down the hall to the bedroom. He wanted Rachel to fulfill her dream of being a doctor, but he wouldn't mind if her "barricade" didn't work. He was ready to be a father.

Chapter 33

Rachel rose out of bed. Lights swirled in her head. Her stomach churned and the sharp tang of bile rose up her esophagus. She reached for the chamber pot. Clutching the porcelain bowl, she groaned and retched again.

This was the second day she'd woken to an upset stomach, two weeks past the time her menses should have started, and a little over a month since she and Clay made love on the train.

She groaned. A child grew within her. Tears trickled down her cheeks and she wiped them away. Clay had left for Baker City the day before with Mr. Smith and Donny to purchase equipment for their businesses. She missed him but was glad he wasn't here. The time alone would help her decide how to proceed.

Early morning light filtered in the bedroom windows on either side of the huge bed. She ran her hand over the mattress and smiled, remembering the first night they slept on it. The memory played in her head like a wedding night of her dreams. Clay had reverently led her up the stairs and thoroughly loved her. A tear trickled down her cheek.

Another sign of her condition. She didn't generally cry easily.

Darcy would show up in an hour. She had to get herself presentable and somehow make it through the morning without the perceptive woman figuring out what ailed her.

Her heart should be light and excited at the prospect of carrying Clay's child, but her mind wasn't ready to relinquish the hope of a thriving medical practice. Two patients had arrived the first day she moved into the house. Both had needed stitches. She loved starting her new practice and being a doctor. A real one, not just a nurse to the students at the Blind School.

Her stomach churned, and she retched what little was left into the pot. Rachel walked slowly to the washstand, poured water on a cloth, and wiped her face, placing the cool cloth on the back of her neck.

How could she be a doctor and take care of a baby? Take care of herself?

Rachel rubbed a hand over her abdomen and looked at the medical books in the bookcase. She wanted both. Until she knew what she was going to do, she wouldn't tell Clay. She knew what his answer would be no matter how he promised she could be a doctor. All men wanted their wives and mothers of their children to be at home doing laundry and cooking meals.

She dressed, stopping when the urge to vomit struck, and waited patiently with her eyes closed for the nausea to pass. The thought of applying makeup to her clammy face reduced her arms to wet noodles. Better to get some dry bread and tea in her stomach before she tackled that chore.

Rachel descended the stairs slowly. She smiled at the improvements she, Darcy, and Myrle had made to the house. The walls and ceilings were free of dust and cobwebs. New rugs scattered over the polished wood floor, and scrubbed walls awaited artwork. Eventually, they would need to replace the wallpaper in the dining room, but for now, it served as parlor and dining room. Her medical equipment and a surgery table Mr. Smith built to Clay's specifications took up most of the parlor.

In the kitchen, cheery yellow gingham curtains and tablecloth greeted her, all sewn with Darcy while sitting under the shade tree out back. She now considered herself having two sisters. Celeste and Darcy. Her soon to be sister-in-law was a bundle of energy and so easy to talk with. She had poured out nearly her whole life story the afternoon they sat under the tree sewing.

Rachel stirred the coals in the cookstove, added kindling, and filled the teapot from the newly installed hand pump. Clay had been true to his word. He and Hank installed the hand pump in the kitchen the first week and made a washroom off the pantry adding a wonderful large brass tub and hand pump. The man spoiled her. She smiled, and her stomach fluttered. He would never let her be without anything she wished or desired.

Her thoughts sobered, and she settled on her current problem. How could she manage a career and a family? She wanted both. Would a marriage withstand the strain?

The tea kettle whistled. She cut a slice of bread and plopped it on the top of the stove. At the pantry she gathered a tin of tea leaves and jar of preserves. Her gaze traveled to the small store of medicines and herbs she'd ordered through the mercantile.

On the shelf sat a solution to her problem. Her hand hovered above the tincture. A few drops in her tea...

She clutched the tea and preserves, hurrying out of the pantry.

If Clay ever found out where her mind had wandered, she'd be alone forever.

Rachel turned the bread on the stove, spooned tea into the tea pot, and poured boiling water in. The steam scented with the sweet tea leaves settled her nerves and her stomach. Tea steeping, she plucked the toast from the stove and spread the huckleberry preserves Myrle had made.

She and Darcy could pick berries, and Myrle could teach her how to make preserves. Her mother had planned a life as politician's wives for her daughters and hadn't bothered teaching them many cooking skills. Rachel had learned to cook from hanging out in the kitchen with Matilda.

The prospect of picking berries today and the tea and toast enlivened her spirits and appeased her stomach for the time being. Darcy knew of her scar, so she'd only wear a bonnet while picking berries. Rachel entered the parlor, set a second cup of tea on the table, and opened a box of supplies Dr. Runkle had sent with Mr. Smith.

The old doctor had sent along instruments he would no longer be using. Tears burned in her eyes. It was highly unlikely the man would still be alive when she made a trip back to Salem. She wiped at the tears and continued unwrapping the instruments, placing them on the table.

The patter of small feet skipped down the hall. "Ra'l. Ra'l," Sadie called.

Rachel smiled at the child's pronunciation of her name. "I'm in here, Sadie," she called, finishing her unpacking.

"There you are." Darcy followed her daughter into the room. "What chores are we tackling today?"

"I would like to pick huckleberries and learn how to make preserves." Rachel faced Darcy and the child.

Darcy's eyes opened wider, and Sadie's cheerful face fell into sadness. The child walked to her.

"Ra'l hurt," Sadie said, her small hand reaching up.

"No, I'm not hurt." Rachel stared at the two.

"Are you feeling well?" Darcy asked.

Surely her earlier bout of nausea wasn't apparent? "I'm fine, why?"

"You look a little pale, and you didn't apply your makeup."

Rachel's hand shot to her scar. She hadn't thought what their first reaction to her scar would be. Heat flushed her face. "I'm sorry. If it bothers you I'll go put my makeup on."

"No. If you didn't feel like covering it that's fine. I've just never seen you—you know, like this. I thought maybe something was wrong."

"No, you don't need to stare at the hideous scar. I'll cover it."

Darcy caught her hand when she started out of the room. "It isn't hideous. I just wasn't prepared even though you told me how long it was. I didn't—I didn't realize what I'd see."

Rachel wanted to jerk out of the smaller woman's grasp and hide in her bedroom. But her mother's training on handling any situation snapped her spine straight and had her sniffing back the tears that wanted to fall.

Sadie tugged on her skirt. "Me kiss it."

Rachel scooped the child up in her arms.

Sadie carefully kissed the scar and traced her tiny finger down the line. "All better," she said and squirmed to get down as if the scar had magically disappeared.

"I agree." Darcy looped her arm with Rachel's leading her to the kitchen. "Let's have tea and go pick berries."

They didn't have to bother Myrle. Darcy knew how to make preserves. After lunch, they cleaned the three buckets of huckleberries they'd picked and started cooking the fruit. Darcy had gone upstairs to check on Sadie napping, leaving Rachel to take in the emotion overwhelming her. It was stupid to be this excited over a daily chore. Her life had been easy and unfettered with chores of survival, unlike Darcy's.

Rachel pushed the curls clinging to the side of her face back and stared at the dozen small jars sitting on her drain board. Elation and pride welled in her chest. Tears burned in her eyes. Heavens. She'd made preserves. It wasn't an emotional triumph. Being with child would be a trial if she cried over everything. She blinked back the tears and stared at the jars. The proof she'd been domestic sat in front of her. The mess and warm kitchen, as well.

Pounding on the front door jerked her out of her thoughts. She swiped the apron across her eyes, hurried into the hall and to the door. She swung it open to a man raising his fist to bang on it again.

"You the new lady doc?" he asked, his gaze fastening on her scar. He wasn't as large as Clay. The dirt in his graying brown hair told her he'd been in a mine.

"Yes, I'm Dr. Tarkiel. What can I do for you?"

Darcy's hurried steps came up beside her.

"My son is stuck in the mine. A rock rolled, and I'm scared to move him."

The hope shining in the man's eyes pushed her into motion. Adrenaline surged, jittering her motions.

"I'll get my bag. Do you have a buggy?"

The man shook his head.

"I'll get my horse saddled, you can use her." Darcy pushed past the man and down the front steps.

"Wait here." If she had to ride a horse she

needed to change into a riding skirt. She ascended the stairs quickly, stripped off her dress, stepped into a riding skirt, and pulled on a cotton blouse. She buttoned it quickly, hurried down the stairs, and grabbed her bonnet from the hook by the back door and her doctor's bag from her office.

"Ready." She pulled the front door shut behind her as Darcy arrived with her saddled horse.

"Where are you taking her so I can let Clay know when he gets back?" Darcy asked.

Rachel continued to mount the horse and mentally slapped herself for not thinking about asking. Clay would be worried if he returned and had no clue where she'd gone.

"Tell him it's James Tupper's mine. He'll know the one." The man mounted his horse and headed up the road the Halseys had built to put in their stamp mill.

They traveled at a trot. Rachel had questions she wanted to ask but she still had trouble staying on a horse doing any gait other than a walk. The jarring also didn't sit well with her stomach, but she couldn't tell the man to slow down. Not when another's life could be at risk.

They veered off the road about halfway to the stamp mill. Once on the narrow trail, they slowed to a walk for which she was grateful. Now she could ask questions.

She urged her horse to get as close to the tail of the one leading her as possible to hear and be heard. "Are you Mr. Tupper?"

"Yes."

"What's your boy's name?" She shifted in the

saddle easing the soreness starting to set in from the bouncing trot.

"Harvey."

She inhaled. "How old is he?"

"Fifteen."

That would make the boy close to Jeremy's age. How could this man remain so calm when his son was hurt and lodged under a rock?

"I'm—I hope I can help him." She fell silent and let her horse lag behind slightly. Would Clay be this calm if his son were trapped under a rock? She didn't think so. He would have worked his hardest to get the boy out and then brought him to the doctor.

"The going gets tougher here." The man turned his horse into a narrower trail cut in the rock.

She stared ahead. They were scaling the side of the mountain. Farther up she saw the opening of a cave or mine. When the boy was loose and stabilized, how would the two of them carry him to safety?

Chapter 34

Clay walked out of the newly constructed shop. Donny and Jasper remained inside tidying up their work stations and arranging the new equipment. He'd expected Rachel to show up at the shop by now. She couldn't have missed their arrival. He untied his horse from the hitching post and mounted. The horse knew the way to the house.

The horse stopped, and the front door banged open. A smile spread across his face, and he patted his pocket. He couldn't wait to give Rachel the gift he had hidden there.

"Clay, might as well stay seated," Darcy said, her quick footsteps tapped across the porch.

"Where's Rachel?" Apprehension knotted in his guts. No one had spotted the man who followed them to Sumpter. The thought he was still out there somewhere niggled at Clay every waking moment he wasn't in Rachel's arms.

"James Tupper's mine. A man came and got her. Said there was an accident." Darcy placed a hand on his leg. "Soon as Jeremy gets back from the mill he can take you."

"I'll head that direction, it'll take less time." He pulled his horse's head around and pointed it toward the road to the mill.

"You shouldn't set out by yourself."

Darcy's words went unheeded. He tapped his heels to his horse's side and the animal set off at a slow lope toward the mill. If he met Jeremy on the road it would save time. If he made it all the way to the mill, he'd grab Jeremy or Hank to take him to the mine. Either way was better than sitting around waiting.

Rachel followed Mr. Tupper into the mine. He held a lantern that illuminated an area eight feet around them, revealing dirt walls and rock littered floor.

"How did the rock fall on your son?" The cloaked silence of being underground raised goose flesh on her skin.

"We dug into a soft spot, and before we could brace it half the wall fell, catching Harvey." The man kept moving, his steps steadily increasing in length and carrying him faster and faster until Rachel stumbled, jogging to keep up with him.

"Mr. Tupper, I know you're anxious but you're going too fast." Rachel caught a toe on a rock and grabbed at the dirt wall to keep from falling.

"Sorry, ma'am. I just..."

"I understand, you're getting closer to your boy and want to do something." She caught up to him. "But it will take me longer to get to him if I have a sprained ankle."

He nodded and walked slower. She saw the glow of another lantern. They approached the illuminated area, and she spotted a young man half buried in dirt and rock.

Rachel hurried forward. "Get him uncovered. I can't help him if I can't see what's wrong." She knelt at the boy's head.

"Harvey, do you hear me? I'm Dr. Tarkiel."

She felt for the pulse in his free wrist. His chest rose and fell in labored breaths. He didn't respond to her voice.

She raised one of his eyelids. The eye was rolled back. With gentle fingers she probed the back of his head and found a knot and sticky blood. She'd be surprised if he didn't have a concussion.

"We have to get him free of the debris. Until the dirt is removed I won't be able to see if there are any broken bones." She leaned forward, scooping the dirt from his chest. With every two scoops more dirt slid down. She saw why the man hadn't attempted to free the boy by himself. It took the two of them working in tandem to keep the boy from being completely engulfed in the dirt.

Rachel stepped away from the light of the lantern and slipped out of a petticoat. She returned to the unconscious boy and tucked one side of her petticoat under his shoulder. Holding the other end up, she shielded the debris from falling on the young man's face.

Mr. Tupper continued to scoop dirt tirelessly.

Clay heard the steady clomp of a horse approaching and the lilt of Jeremy whistling.

"Jeremy!" he called out, stopping his horse and waiting.

The hoof beats picked up pace and stopped a few feet from him.

"What're you doin' out here?" Jeremy asked.

"Rachel went to the Tupper mine to help someone. I need you to take me there."

"I'm not sure where it is."

Jeremy's frustrated declaration sunk in Clay's gut like a rock in a well. The layout of the mines in the area flashed in Clay's head. "How far are we from the mill?"

"About a mile an'-a-half."

"Then if we head back to town, the next trail to the west should be the one to the Tupper mine." Clay reined his horse around and started out at a trot. A nagging sensation ate at his gut like the stamps crushing rock. He had to get to Rachel.

"You're comin' to a trail," Jeremy said from beside him. "Hold on. I'll go first so your horse follows." His horse trotted by. Clay followed the sound of hollow hoofed steps and brush scratching leather.

They traveled a half a mile with the brush tugging at his boots before he heard the clatter of shale rock under foot. The mine should be only a short distance now.

"Do you see the mine or any horses yet?" Nervous sweat beaded his forehead. He wouldn't be able to calm his nerves until he saw Rachel and knew she hadn't come to any harm. This was foolish. As a doctor she would have to go out to mines and other dangerous places to take care of people, but he'd planned to be along when she did. A lone woman could be lured into any number of traps. He knew Tupper to be an honest man with a nearly grown son, but the hair on the back of his neck kept tingling—a sure sign something was up.

"There, I see the opening and Darcy's horse and another one."

Clay made a mental note to get Rachel a sound horse. His horse quivered and surged, leaning him back as they made the final climb to the mouth of the mine.

His horse stopped, and he heard the clatter of shale from Jeremy's dismount. Clay dismounted and grabbed the stirrup as his feet slid in the loose rock.

"Over here," Jeremy called.

Clay found solid footing and walked the direction he heard Jeremy's crunching footsteps.

"I don't see a lantern near the entrance."

"They probably have them all in the mine. Hang on to me and follow."

Clay ran a hand along the cave entrance and started in keeping one hand along the wall. Jeremy grabbed a fist full of Clay's shirt. The boy breathed fast beside him.

"H-how far back do you think they are?"

The tremor in Jeremy's voice reminded Clay the boy hadn't grown up in mines like he had.

"I'd say, as long as the mine has been here, probably fifty yards or better." He kept a steady pace, kicking a rock here and there. After about ten minutes he heard the buzz of voices and scraping. In the dark silence sound carried well.

"Do you see any light yet?"

"Yes. There's a glow deeper in the tunnel."

Clay stretched out his steps. He'd soon hold Rachel in his arms.

"His breathing is getting shallower. We have to get him out of here soon." Rachel wished for the tenth time they had help. She couldn't clear the debris and keep it from falling on Harvey's face. One person couldn't keep up with what continued to fall.

A commotion in the mine caught her attention. She peered into the darkness outside the lantern light. Her heart caught in her throat at the sight of Clay walking into the circle of light. Her eyes drank in the wonderful sight of him. A mild curse behind him drew her attention to Jeremy.

"Need some help?" Clay asked as Jeremy guided him around the lantern sitting on the ground.

"Yes." Relief and happiness flooded her voice. "We can't get Harvey unburied to get him out of the mine."

Clay knelt next to Mr. Tupper and moved his hands all over the dirt and the boy.

"James, do you have some timbers in here?" Clay asked.

"Yes, back a few yards."

"Take Jeremy and bring as many as you two can carry. We need to brace this dirt so it doesn't keep falling down."

The man stood, taking Clay's orders without

even a blink of his eyes. He snatched up one of the lanterns and Jeremy followed him.

Clay held his hand out. Rachel placed her hand in his and leaned toward him, wanting a kiss and to feel his strong arms.

"I prayed you'd come and help," she whispered before her lips touched his.

He drew away from her lips. "You're not leaving with anyone again unless I'm with you. It's dangerous to be traipsing around alone."

"I can't wait around for you if someone is hurt."

He cupped the back of her head in his palm and lowered his head into the brim of her bonnet. "Then I guess I'll have to never leave your side." His lips crushed against hers, searing, demanding, and controlling.

Her body shivered from the heat of his lips and the affirmation he would never allow anything to happen to her.

"Is this enough?" Mr. Tupper and Jeremy dropped half a dozen boards on the ground.

"Jeremy, roll a couple large rocks over. One beyond Harvey's feet and one beyond his head." Clay started scooping dirt out beyond the young man's feet and pointed for Jeremy to roll the first rock there.

Rachel continued to hold the petticoat to keep dirt from falling on Harvey's face. Clay and Mr. Tupper wedged the boards, one on top of the other, behind the rocks and in front of the dirt, forming a barrier to keep the dirt from running down. The three men scooped the dirt free from the unconscious Harvey.

Rachel evaluated him for other injuries after the dirt was removed. A rock had landed on his ribs. She feared they were either cracked or broken. Moving him could do further injury, but they had no choice.

"I'm worried he may have cracked ribs due to the rock. His limbs don't appear to be broken. We should move him from this precarious spot to a safer one and use two boards to carry him out of here. I don't want his ribs getting twisted. They could puncture a lung."

She instructed Jeremy and Mr. Tupper how to slide Harvey along the ground to get him out of the way of the cave in. Rachel grabbed the top board and tried to pry it loose.

"Rachel, no!" Jeremy yelled.

The board popped out from behind the rock. The end struck her in the middle. She doubled from the impact and the ripping pain. The earth rumbled as strong arms scooped her up and everything went black.

"Move! Pick him up and start moving!" Clay hollered hurrying through the mine toward the entrance. His heart hammered against his ribs. Fear clogged his throat making it hard to breath. He didn't have a clue what had happened to Rachel. The sound of a board hitting a body and the air hissing out of her had driven him toward her. He'd picked her up and started out of the mine at the sound of the crumbling walls.

Rock hitting rock, the thunder of earth moving, and the snap and creak of boards giving brought back the day he'd lost his sight. He froze. Would he end up trapped in the mine this time with no one to find him?

Rachel moaned, and he heard James and Jeremy struggling through the dark with the boy. These people needed him. Rachel needed him. He breathed deep the musty air and wrestled with his self-doubts. He was the only one who could navigate the darkness and not become disoriented. Anger propelled him through the mine. He may have lost his sight but he damn sure wasn't helpless.

"Anyone have time to pick up a lantern?" he asked, letting the others know they weren't alone. He knew the isolation of being alone in the dark. He'd suffered through it many times.

"No," Jeremy squeaked in a quivery voice.

"Shuffle your feet along the ground, Jeremy. That way you know if there's anything in the way."

Clay clutched Rachel to his chest, keeping her head up so he didn't bang it into a wall, and hurried forward. Was she still alive? Her limp body sent icy spears of fear shooting into his heart. What would he do if she didn't make it? How could he live with himself? He could carry her out of this mine, but what then? Who would know what to do for her? He couldn't even see what her injuries were. Frustration swirled in his gut like a raging storm.

"It's not so dark now," Jeremy said.

"We must be getting near the entrance. Keep steady." Clay encouraged. "Wake up, Rachel," he whispered to the woman in his arms. "Come on, Doc, there's a boy that needs you, and I need you."

Clay sniffed. Fresh, warm air floated past his head. They'd reached the entrance of the mine. Sun heated his face, and shale rock slid under his feet.

The creak of leather and clatter of shale told him the horses stood to his right. He moved that direction. The click of a cocked rifle exploded like a bullet shot from a gun. He flinched. Who held a gun on them? Why?

His head pounded. He needed to face the gunman. He refused to be shot in the back. The weight of Rachel in his arms reminded him he couldn't face the man. A bullet would strike her first. Fear for her and anger at his impotence raged making it hard to think. He was at a disadvantage with her in his arms. How could he shield her?

Chapter 35

"Turn around."

Heat surged from Clay's toes to his hair. He knew that voice. He'd grown up listening to it. Rage burned in his gut. He moved a foot to pivot toward the coward, and Rachel moaned. Rachel. She was innocent. He had to keep her out of this.

"Miles." He turned slowly to a man he'd known since grammar school. "Let me put Rachel down. This is between you and me."

"You took the woman I loved away, why should I let you keep your woman?"

The man's high pitched accusation seared fear across his heart. He had to think fast, keep her safe.

"Because she's not my woman. She's the new doctor in the area." He'd lie, his fists clenched as at his side, and kill if it kept Rachel alive.

Miles laughed. "I seen you two getting cozy."

The clatter of shale scattered about ten feet in front of Clay. "Put her on the ground and step away."

Clay clung to Rachel. His heart raced. Once he put her down he couldn't protect her. May not be able to find her. Fear gripped him as tight as a noose around his throat.

"Now!"

Miles's command jolted Clay into motion. He knelt, placed Rachel on the ground to his side, and rose to face his enemy.

He walked five paces toward the voice, keeping himself between Miles and Rachel.

"Why did you follow me?" He stopped, unsure of the distance between them.

"Why? Because of you seeing me in the mine I can't live here, where I grew up, where my family is. You ruined everything for me by goin' in that mine." Miles's voice rose excitedly.

"You threw the dynamite leaving me blind. You were trying to kill part of my family by blowing up that mine. I'll not have you blaming any of that on me. You were the one trying to kill Aileen and her son." His heart pounded, booming in his ears. Anger swift and blazing swept through him. No one hurt the people he loved.

Something scuffled to Clay's left, but he kept his face toward Miles.

"I didn't want Aileen to get hurt, but her boy just wouldn't stay out of the way, then your brother." Miles's voice vibrated, and he pulled in a deep breath. "All I wanted was to have her care for me."

Damn. If only he could see. He sensed Miles weakening. His body tensed. He listened, searching for a sound to give him a clue as to how close

Miles stood.

An object cracked, and Miles yelped. Clay shot forward, ramming into the man, and wrestled him to the ground. He straddled Miles and drove his wrists into the jagged shale underneath him.

"I have some rope," Jeremy said next to him.

Rough rope grazed Clay's knuckles where he held Miles's wrist. Clay let go when that arm was pulled over to the other one he held. He fingered the rope around the man's wrists.

"He's tied," Jeremy said, patting his shoulder. "Go take care of Rachel. She looks like she's coming around."

"That's him."

Relief surged through his veins at Rachel's whispered declaration. But who did she mean?

"What?" Clay stood and aimed his steps toward her voice.

"The man who's been following us. That's him." She shivered as he wrapped his arms around her.

"Jeremy has him tied up—"

"Oh!" She cried out and doubled over.

Clay scooped Rachel in his arms. "What's wrong?" Fear tore through his chest like a hot bullet.

Rachel clutched her cramping abdomen. "No!" Tears burned behind her eyes. The blow to her mid-section had started cramping. Her heart snapped. She couldn't lose this baby. She wanted it as much as she wanted to breathe and be Clay's wife No. Don't do this to me. She sucked in a breath and willed her body to cling to the miracle they made. For all her talk, she wanted a baby. This baby. Clay's.

Clay clasped her to him. "What's wrong?" His fear hung in the air like a dense, grim fog.

"I'm, oh heavens..." She gulped air as another spasm wracked her body.

"Here's your horse." Jeremy brought Clay's horse up next to him. "Take her back to Sumpter. We'll be along as soon as we get a travois made to bring Harvey down."

Clay clutched her to him as he climbed on the horse. Jeremy handed him the reins and led the horse to the trail.

Rachel clung to Clay as the horse started a sliding downward ascent off the mountain. How did she tell Clay she was losing their child? Guilt paced in her head as warmth seeped from her body. He'd learn when they dismounted that she was bleeding. He knew how she felt. No. How she thought she felt. Would he believe her that she didn't want to lose their baby? Loved it already?

Pain twisted in her abdomen and shivers prickled her skin, beading it with perspiration. Anguish gripped her heart. What would Clay think of her? Could he still care for her? Love her? She moaned and his arms squeezed her closer. Tears ran down her face. Hiding her scarred face was nothing compared to the failure eating at her heart.

The ride took nearly an hour. Clay kissed her forehead and held her close. She was grateful for his silence. How did she tell a man his child, one he didn't know about was lost? She shivered. One he believed she never wanted? The ache in her chest grew, rivaling the cramps in her abdomen. She wanted this baby. Wanted it more than she ever wanted anything. Even being a doctor.

Darcy jerked the front door open and ran down the steps when they approached the house.

"What's wrong? Where's the miner?"

"Rachel had an accident. Jeremy and the Tuppers are behind us." Clay dismounted, still cradling her to him.

Darcy's eyes widened at the blood soaking her riding skirt.

"Take me to the washroom."

Clay's arms stiffened. "You should be in a bed."

"I need to clean up."

"A little dirt can be cleaned off once you're in bed." He moved through the door.

"This isn't dirt. It's blood."

He stopped, and his face paled to the color of the white wash on the house. "You didn't tell me you were bleeding. We could have applied a bandage."

Darcy tugged on his arm. "Come on, Clay, she's the doctor and knows what she's doing."

Rachel sent her a silent thank you. Clay stood her in the small washroom. He hung inside the door.

"Clay, I'll explain things—" A pain doubled her over, and she sat on the chair in the corner.

He reached out to her. She wanted to settle into his strong arms and find the comfort she needed right now, but first she had to clean up and wait out the cramping.

"Clay, why don't you make some coffee and a

pot of tea? I'll help Rachel get cleaned up." Darcy turned him out the door.

Clay pivoted. "Tell me what's going on."

Rachel's heart ached for him. He couldn't see where the blood was coming from he didn't know what had happened. But she wasn't ready to go into the whole story.

"I'll tell you everything when I'm cleaned up." She pushed to her feet, walked the three steps to him and held his hand to her lips. "I promise."

He nodded and shuffled down the hall. Darcy pulled her back into the washroom and shut the door. Her small fingers went to work unfastening buttons and slipping Rachel's dirty clothes from her body.

Darcy pumped the water spout. "Did you know you were with child?"

Rachel nodded, clothed only in a waist length chemise, and stepped into the tub, scrubbing the red stains from her inner thighs with a cloth Darcy shoved into her hand. Tremors shook her hand.

"I figured it out this morning." She sighed. That seemed like such a long time ago.

"You couldn't be that far along. What caused this?" Darcy stood by the tub, her eyes full of the misery Rachel felt.

"A board hit me in the mid-section." The tears she'd hidden from Clay slid down her cheeks in a torrent. "I wanted this baby. At first I didn't. All I could think about was how it would interfere with being a doctor." A cramp doubled her over. She clutched the side of the tub with one hand, avoiding Darcy's gaze.

Salty tears ran along her lips. She licked them and slowly straightened as the pain subsided. "Now, I'd give up doctoring to be able to save this baby."

Darcy rubbed her back. "I'll get some cloth for between your legs and your bed clothes."

She nodded and sat in the tub, watching the trickle of blood flow to the drain. A sob tore at her throat. She couldn't stop the anger, humiliation, and sorrow twisting her heart and scolding her conscience.

Would Clay forgive her for her first thoughts? Could she forgive herself?

A light tap on the door stopped her sobs. She sucked in a deep breath and sniffed back her tears.

"Who's there?" she asked in a shaky voice.

Clay opened the door and stuck his head in. "I can't stand not knowing what's wrong." His voice was laced with anxiety. "And I brought some warm water." He held out a bucket.

"Come here." She held out her hand, grasping his when he came near. "Pull up the chair." She waited as he found the chair and pulled it up next to the tub.

Holding hands, she stared into his face, thankful he couldn't see the tears and her guilt.

Rachel took a big breath, let it out, and squeezed his hand.

"A board hit me in the stomach in the mine."

He leaned toward her, and she put a hand on his chest.

"It was my fault. I was thinking we needed to put the boy on something to reduce further injury to his ribs and didn't think about what was behind the boards." She licked her lips. The hard part.

"Did the board cause damage inside you?" He held her hand so tight her knuckles ached.

"Yes, but not the kind you're thinking. I-I, oh I wish this was under different circumstances." Tears ran down her cheeks. She stared at his handsome face and wished she could tell him he would be a father instead...

"I discovered this morning, but had an inkling yesterday, that I am"—she took another deep breath—"was pregnant."

A sob burst out at the joy on his face. Heavens, how she wished that look would be able to stay.

She knew when her words sank in. The joy vanished, and his brow furrowed.

"You mean...the blood..." He slid from the chair and wrapped his arms around her, drawing her chemise clad body against him. "I'm sorry. I didn't know. I-I..." He burrowed his face into her neck and cried. His arms wrapped around her in a strong embrace, and she joined her tears with his.

Spent and realizing the cramps had subsided, Rachel drew out of his arms. She had to tell him or she'd go crazy. She held his face in her hands, gulped air and started, "When I first discovered I was with child, I didn't want it." Anger at her first reaction and remorse weighed her heart.

Clay nodded, still taking in the fact she was— had been—pregnant. A boulder landed in his gut. Damn! Pain sparked in his chest for the life he'd never see. He placed his hands over Rachel's to still their quivering. Her acknowledgement would have infuriated him if he hadn't just witnessed firsthand her sorrow and loss. She was devastated to have lost this child. Her tender words, broken sobs, and clutching arms shattered his heart.

"But as the day lengthened and the idea settled, I couldn't wait for you to get back so I could tell you. Then Mr. Tupper arrived and I had to go help." Her hands tightened on his cheeks. "I thought I could do both, be a mother and a doctor, but after today... I don't want to put you or me or our child through this again. I would give up my career to keep our family safe."

Clay placed their hands against his chest. He leaned in and kissed her lips tasting the saltiness of tears.

"This didn't happen because you're a doctor. This happened because the timing was wrong. I would have loved to start a family now, with you, but it wasn't meant to be."

Banging sounded through the house. "I think Jeremy and Mr. Tupper have brought you a patient. Are you up to it, or should I send Jeremy to Baker City for someone else?"

The door opened. "Rachel, Jeremy's here with that miner." Darcy said, stepping into the room and closing the door.

Clay squeezed Rachel's hands. He felt her strength waning.

"I'm too weak. The boy needs tending. Darcy, can you clean him up and stop anything that's bleeding. After I've..." Rachel drew a deep breath. After I've rested, I'll take a look at him."

"I'll get them settled," Darcy said, exiting the

room.

Clay handed her the bucket of hot water. "You're shivering. Use this to warm up. After a good night's sleep we'll discuss our future and wedding plans."

Epilogue

Rachel fussed with the midnight blue satin dress Clay insisted she wear for their wedding. She thought it highly impractical, and that's why he insisted she wear it. Of course, her mother and sister swooned over it, proclaiming it the perfect dress.

It didn't matter to her what she wore. Clay wouldn't see her walking down the stairs and up to his side. But he'd insisted on this dress because the stiff material rustled when she walked, and he'd know the soft inside would be caressing her skin. The thought warmed her to her toes. She also wore a beautiful silver bracelet made of small bells. He'd given it to her the night of the miscarriage and asked her to always wear it so he could find her in any crowd. She ran a finger over the colorful wildflower blossoms Darcy picked for her to carry.

Myrle poked her head in the door of the bedroom she and Clay would share the rest of their lives. "You ready? That man of yours is getting antsy."

Rachel nodded. She couldn't speak for the happiness squeezing her chest. She would be a doctor, a wife, and a mother, when the time came. Clay had insisted she couldn't give up what she'd worked hard to attain. And deep down, she knew she could do all three successfully.

Myrle stepped into the room and picked up the hat with a veil she and Darcy had made. Rachel had stopped wearing makeup once word went around the small community that the doctor had a scar. No one looked twice at her. Rachel fingered the veil.

She shook her head. "I'm not wearing that." She took a deep breath. It was time to stop hiding her scar and prove to herself and others that the mark didn't change who she was inside. She'd changed, grown more independent and resilient since she'd met Clay.

Myrle set the bonnet down and smiled. "You're the most beautiful bride I've ever laid eyes on." Her fading eyes glistened with unshed tears.

Rachel hugged her. "Thank you for everything. You're a wonderful friend."

"Posh. Go on. That man is going to come storming in here if you don't show soon."

Rachel took a deep breath, tightened her grip on the flowers, and followed Myrle down the hall. At the top of the stairs, Darcy and little Sadie waited.

Her soon-to-be sister-in-law gave her a one-armed hug and started down the stairs, leading Sadie, who tossed flower petals out of a basket.

Rachel waited until they reached the bottom before she took hold of the front of her skirt and descended. She drew a fortifying breath and stepped into the parlor. The surgical table and other doctor accoutrements were stashed in a spare bedroom for the day.

A collective "ohhh" from the guests stalled her next step. Had she made a mistake not wearing the bonnet and veil? She scanned the crowd. No one stared at her in horror; smiles welcomed her. She smiled back and held her head high. Her scar would no longer rule her life.

She smiled at Mr. Tupper and Harvey sitting in the back row. The young man had proved to be an excellent patient and would soon be healed.

Her gaze sought Clay. He faced the door, his dimple and wide grin brightening his whole face. If Jeremy hadn't thrown a rock at Miles, knocking the rifle from his hands, Clay might not be standing by a preacher waiting for her.

Rachel sent up a prayer for Jeremy's fast thinking and smiled at Clay. She would never tire of gazing upon his face or feeling the strength of his embrace. She nodded to the locals she'd come to know, and she smiled at her new family—Hank, Gil, Darcy, Sadie, Jeremy, and Clay's Pinkerton brother and his wife, Zeke and Maeve, who had arrived the night before.

She looked to the other side of the aisle. Her mother dabbed her eyes with a lacey handkerchief. Her father's eyes glistened, but she couldn't tell if it was from happiness or sorrow. He'd yet to talk to her about her choice.

Her family stayed with Myrle at her boarding

house/restaurant, allowing Rachel more time to work on the house and prepare for the wedding. Celeste and her fiancé had helped decorate for the wedding. Rachel smiled at Celeste, clinging to Oregon Representative Jeremiah Folsum's arm. She and Clay would soon be attending her sister's wedding in Salem.

Clay reached out to her when she passed the last row of benches. She slipped her hand in his and smiled. This man's strength and love would get her through anything. He pulled her close and ran his hand over her face, across her shoulder, and over a puffy sleeve of her dress.

"You're beautiful," he whispered before they faced the preacher.

Clay held onto Rachel's hand drawing in her love and reveling in the concept she would be his forever after today.

He didn't have to see Rachel to know she glowed. Her breathy vows, fingers clinging to his, and loving presence proved it.

"You may now kiss your bride."

The preacher's announcement couldn't have come too soon for Clay. He held Rachel's head in his hands. "I will always be here for you."

She nodded slightly.

He lowered his head and tenderly kissed her lips.

The veil didn't tickle. His hands traveled up her head. It was bare.

"Where's your bonnet?" he whispered against her lips.

"I'm not hiding anymore."

The proclamation rang loud and clear. She'd no longer allow anyone to make her feel inferior, and she wouldn't cling to her career.

He wanted to drag her against him, kiss her passionately, and then carry her up to their room and show her the power of her strength and convictions.

Clapping and hoots invaded what he would have liked to keep intimate.

Rachel drew out of the kiss, molded to his side, and wrapped an arm around his waist.

He hugged her shoulders and smiled at their guests. A room full, he'd been told.

Hank's voice quieted the murmur. "Before we start eating and visiting, I have a telegram from Ethan he'd like me to read."

A paper rustled, and Hank cleared his throat "'Clay and Rachel, Aileen, Colin, Shayla, and I are sorry to miss this special occasion. We're happy you found each other and may your love bind your hearts.'"

"That's beautiful," Rachel said and sniffed. "I can't wait to meet them."

Clay captured her tear on his fingertip. "No tears today unless they're full of happiness."

"That's all they will ever be with you in my life."

"I love you, and I never want to be without you," Clay said.

Rachel lunged into his arms and kissed him boldly in front of their full parlor. "I thought you'd never say those words. I love you, too."

About the Author

All my work whether it's my romance or my mysteries have Western or Native American elements in them along with hints of humor and engaging characters. My husband and I raise alfalfa hay in rural eastern Oregon. Riding horses and battling rattlesnakes, I not only write the western lifestyle, I live it.

I love to hear from fans. You can find or contact me at:
patyjag@gmail.com
or my website:
www.patyjager.net

Continue to the next page to find a listing of my historical western books or visit my website:
https://www.patyjager.net

Historical Western Romance
Gambling on an Angel
Improper Pinkerton
For a Sister's Love
Christmas Redemption

Halsey Brother Series
Marshal in Petticoats – Gil's story
Outlaw in Petticoats – Zeke's story
Miner in Petticoats – Ethan's story
Doctor in Petticoats – Clay's story
Logger in Petticoats – Hank's story

Halsey Homecoming Trilogy
Laying Claim – Jeremy's Story
Staking Claim – Colin's Story
Claiming a Heart – Donny's Story
A Husband for Christmas - Shayla's Story

Letters of Fate Trilogy
Davis
Brody
Isaac

Silver Dollar Saloon
Savannah
Lottie Mae
Freedom

Contemporary Western Romance
Perfectly Good Nanny
Bridled Heart

Historical Paranormal Romance
Spirit of the Mountain
Spirit of the Lake
Spirit of the Sky

Thank you for purchasing this Windtree Press publication. For other books of the heart, please visit our website at www.windtreepress.com.

For questions or more information contact us at info@windtreepress.com.

Windtree Press
Hillsboro, OR